SHADOW

OF THE

PHOENIX

By the Author

The Iron Phoenix

Phoenix Rising

Shadow of the Phoenix

Visit us at www.boldstrokesbooks.com

SHADOW
OF THE
PHOENIX

by

Rebecca Harwell

2018

SHADOW OF THE PHOENIX
© 2018 BY REBECCA HARWELL. ALL RIGHTS RESERVED.

ISBN 13: 978-1-63555-181-5

THIS TRADE PAPERBACK ORIGINAL IS PUBLISHED BY
BOLD STROKES BOOKS, INC.
P.O. BOX 249
VALLEY FALLS, NY 12185

FIRST EDITION: JULY 2018

CREDITS
EDITOR: RUTH STERNGLANTZ
PRODUCTION DESIGN: STACIA SEAMAN
COVER DESIGN BY JEANINE HENNING

Acknowledgments

The Storm's Quarry series would never have been completed if not for the support of many wonderful people. Many thanks to Ruth, my amazing editor, and the rest of the team at Bold Strokes Books; to Amanda, my fabulous critique partner and dear friend; to Mandy, who has been here for Nadya's story from the very beginning; and to my parents, who never stopped believing in me. Thank you.

For Karli and Laura:
your friendship and support made this book a reality.

CHAPTER ONE

It was said by traveling minstrels and merchants alike that the beauty of Storm's Quarry had no equal. The citystate rose up like a statue, its walls carved from ancient white marble. Its five tiers gave way to one another as if each was an ascending guardian of the rare gemstone mines the city was built upon. At its feet, the Kyanite Sea, a great inland body of salt water, filled the crater which had once felt the impact of a fallen star. The waters of the Kyanite would grow restless and dangerous during the frequent violent storms the city weathered, but tonight, they lay subdued. Storm's Quarry, however, had not yielded to the arrows and battering rams that besieged it.

Even surrounded by the First Legion of His Majesty's Army, the pride of the Kingdom of Wintercress, Storm's Quarry stood defiant. Or so Lode imagined as she approached the city gate.

The torches held by Cressian soldiers gave their light to the still, black waters of the Kyanite Sea, which in turn gave the marble walls standing before them an ethereal glow. Lode raised her hand in the flickering torchlight, marveling at the white sheen her already pale skin took on in the shadow of the mountainous city. Storm's Quarry was, she thought, the most breathtaking sight she had ever seen.

Of course, she could not remember if that was really true.

Overhead, arrows alight with explosive oils flew above the

walls, smoldering as they met their deaths on cold, unfeeling marble. The steady boom of the Cressian battering ram echoed across the bridge, though it left no mark upon the great gate of Storm's Quarry. In between strikes, a steady tinny sound filled the air as musket fire from upon the walls struck the kite shields carried by the first rows of the Cressian army.

It was a standstill.

"Hurry up, girl!"

Lode slowly looked away from the wall and to the soldier who had been tasked with bringing her to the front lines. He gestured at her with annoyance, as if she was some misbehaving hound. She stared at him for a moment longer before following once more.

"Ignorant wench," he muttered under his breath as he waited for her. Lode considered the insult as she walked, but it brought no clench of anger to her chest. Frustratingly, though, she was certain it used to. Before.

They wove between disciplined camps of soldiers, all standing at the ready, their eyes focused upon the great wall before them. Finally, she and her guide came through to the foremost part of the bridge.

Behind the first regiment, whose shields kept any retaliation from the wall at bay, a lieutenant, by his olive-colored cloak, was speaking with a tall man in white-gold armor. Surrounding them, a host of the royal guard, their plumed helms marking their import, stood at the ready.

"Months ago, the Erevans managed to blow a hole in their own wall, and they've done nothing but stuffed it with rubble in the meantime. Can we not simply walk over it?" the taller man asked, his voice betraying the barest edge of impatience.

The lieutenant's fingers twitched at his sides. "I'm afraid not, Your Highness."

"This is war," he snapped. "Soldiers of the High King do not fear."

"Of course." The lieutenant straightened. "We cannot scale the damaged wall, Your Highness. Storm's Quarry's forces have shored it up, and they have stationed a regiment of musket men just inside it. None of our soldiers have made it over the top."

"And our battering ram is just as useless. So be it. I did not wager upon a war with such common tools." The taller man turned away from the lieutenant he had been speaking to and looked to Lode and the soldier who led her.

The soldier bowed deeply, and then announced, "His Highness, Trillium, Crown Prince of Wintercress, favored son of the King."

Lode stared at the Prince. Trillium stood with ease in his ceremonial armor, its white-gold plating nearly glowing in the torchlight. Figurehead he might be, but his armor carried the scars of battle—small dents, silver scratches—that not even the greatest smiths could mend. His saber bore a well-worn hilt, and his left hand rested casually upon it. Fair hair, so blond as to be nearly white, was cropped short in military style, and his eyes, a shining blue, looked over Lode with great interest.

It had been only weeks…*months?*…since she had awoken to those same glacial eyes, edges soft in a gleeful smile. A stranger had hovered just above her as she awoke. His breath smelled sweet, of something familiar, but the memory was out of her reach and she couldn't identify the scent.

She would come to learn that this man was the Crown Prince of Wintercress.

"You are strong, stronger than the others. You survived where they did not," the Prince had said, eyes roving over her naked body, not with lust but excitement. "If you are as powerful as they say, then we will crush those *braka* beneath our armies. And you will be the lodestone of our plans."

Lode did not remember her name, and the chemists who wore elaborate masks and cut her arms for blood never remembered to give her one. So she took *Lode* for herself.

She blinked and the chilly salt-tinged air brought her back to the bridge before Storm's Quarry. "Yes?" she said without a bow or even a gracious nod.

"You speak to the Crown Prince, girl," the soldier barked. Inside, she felt his footsteps upon the bridge, felt his weight shift as he moved to strike her. "Show some res—"

The Prince raised his hand and his personal guard moved to intercept the soldier's progress.

Lode retreated internally as well, without moving, as she released the grip she had on the power. The Prince's icy blue eyes, bright even in the predawn darkness, rested on the man. "Show some respect to our victory, soldier. Know to whom you speak." His tone a dismissal, he turned from the suddenly sweating soldier and looked to Lode. "I have received positive reports of your progress."

"Yes, Your Highness."

"War is far different, you know."

"Yes, Your Highness," she said, for there was nothing more to say.

Prince Trillium gave a swift nod. "Then we should not keep our gracious hosts waiting another moment." He turned and walked through the regiment of royal guards, who parted for him like wheat. Lode followed him.

The bulk of the Cressian army still waited on the far shore of the Kyanite Sea. The narrow stone bridge that connected Storm's Quarry to the rest of the world did not allow a large force to pass, a natural defense the city had long employed against enemies. Coupled with its immense walls, which while cracked, had been impressively shored up, Storm's Quarry stood nearly impenetrable. A fact the guardsmen who defended its ramparts knew well.

A Cressian soldier advanced, carrying the red flag of negotiation. On the wall, a sharp order was barked out, and the muskets withdrew, no doubt still within easy reach of their masters.

When the ceasefire was complete, the regiment of royal guards remained behind Prince Trillium as he approached the gate, his soldiers falling in line behind him. Lode followed him. Two steps back, one to the left.

One of the city defenders stepped forward up on the ramparts. This guardsman wore a brilliant red uniform, a rapier belted at his side. He stood with practiced military posture, though he crossed his arms in front of him as if daring the Prince to speak.

Prince Trillium took the dare. "Guardmaster, have you come to hand over the keys to your city?" he said in near flawless Erevo, the language of Storm's Quarry. Lode understood the Prince as he spoke, knowing the foreign words nearly as well as her own Cressian. She could not remember having learned them, and the lack of memory itched at the base of her skull.

"We let your people into our city once, and you poisoned our water." The Guardmaster spoke in accented Erevo, revealing his nomadic Nomori heritage. "Your councillor betrayed the good faith of our Duke and conspired against Storm's Quarry. Wintercress will find no friends here."

"So send out your masked heroes," the Prince said, spreading his arms wide. "The Iron Phoenix and the Shadow Dragon, you call them? The ones who breathe fire and break stone? Where are they to defend their city?"

"The Guard of Duke Isyanov need none to fight for them," the Guardmaster said curtly.

Prince Trillium shook his head. "It was not your Guard that drove out the small regiment of Cressian soldiers under the command of my ambitious cousin, Guardmaster. It was those two Nomori. *Nivasi*, your people call them? They swore to watch over your city, so where are they now?"

Lode did not hear the Guardmaster's reply as she furrowed her brow, straining to remember. The word meant something, but her memory was a void before the moment she awoke to meet the Crown Prince of Wintercress. If it meant something once, it was long lost to her.

Prince Trillium was speaking. "Pity your Duke chose so poorly, placing only a Nomori in defense of the city."

"My Duke has my full confidence, and I his," the Guardmaster said, his tone ignoring the insult. "Return to your men. You will find no surrender here. Continue your pointless barrage against our walls. Not even a Great Storm can overcome them, and your army, Prince, has nowhere near the power of those winds."

A hushed silence fell over the Cressian regiment as soldiers peered forward, waiting to see if their leader would rise to the Nomori's baiting.

Prince Trillium laughed. A swift chuckle of personal amusement, unexpected of the general of an invading force. He looked to Lode, speaking loudly for the Guardmaster to hear while never breaking eye contact with her. "The skies are a force to contend with, no doubt. But only a fool thinks the wind the only power in this world." Then he lowered his voice and said for Lode's ears alone, "Bring them down."

Lode nodded. She stepped forward, while the Prince and his guard backed off, leaving her alone before the great gate of Storm's Quarry.

She studied the walls, the weathered marble that still stood unmarred, the sharp cracks that had been hastily patched in the wake of the Blood Sun Solstice and the damage it had wrought upon the city. Lode then turned inward and reached down. Far down to where the well of power sprung from her core, where the steadying pulse, still new to her and yet part of her, pulled at her mind.

In the moment before her grip tightened, it occurred to Lode that someone starting a war should feel something, anything. But her chest was calm and empty, and her Prince was waiting, so she brushed the annoying thought off and pulled back.

And the great wall of Storm's Quarry came crashing down.

❖

Standing in the center trade pavilion of the town of Kipperwell amidst the early bustle of the northern caravans making their annual stop, Nadezhda Gabori had only one thought running through her mind: a pride of sabercats was far less frightening than an angry forgemaster.

Nadya might be *nivasi*, with all the unnatural power that came with that rare Nomori blood. She might have saved the city of Storm's Quarry from a mad *nivasi* bent on civil war and then again from a convincing councillor from the Kingdom of Wintercress who threatened to take the city by poisoning its water. She might be known as the feared vigilante, the Iron Phoenix.

All of that paled in comparison to what she faced now.

The forgemaster in question was bent over the town's central forge, methodically working away at an order of delicate piping for the town's new water system. The forge, built out of red clay in the traditional South Marches style, sat under the pavilion's central awning. It was a workplace for visiting masters and teachers. Now clad in a simple cotton tunic, the powerful woman stoked the forge, working it as if she owned the market forge in the same way Nadya had seen her at every forge in the ten months she had been traveling with the caravan.

Jeta Forgemaster carried her title with ease, earned from decades of mastery of her craft. She was heavyset and stood two heads taller than Nadya. A lifetime of smithing had given her muscles any guardsman would be jealous of. Intricate black tattoos, a pattern sacred to the Blood Hawk tribe, spiraled down her arms, fading into the forge's soot that coated her hands. Nadya knew next to nothing about the woman's origin, as she never spoke of her past. She only knew that other than her erstwhile apprentice, Shay, the forgemaster valued nothing above her craft.

Which was why the last place Nadya wished to be was standing in front of the forge, holding the damaged breastplate that Jeta had forged for the Iron Phoenix, her infamous vigilante identity, out of star metal just ten months beforehand.

"I was clearing out that den of sabercats," Nadya was saying, her voice barely above a whisper. "The ones that have been harassing the farms? You suggested I take the bounty." Truthfully, she knew that Jeta had only handed her the Kipperwell bounty in order to rid her apprentice of distractions.

Nadya sent a silent prayer to the Protectress, something she found herself doing far more often since leaving Storm's Quarry. "My armor got a bit roughed up. Thought you might be able to take a look." She cringed as she said it and offered the breastplate to Jeta.

The forgemaster slowly put down her tools and came over. She took the breastplate from Nadya, who immediately stepped back. Jeta's callused fingers traced the shale-colored scratches in the otherwise flawless piece. "Cats did not damage my work."

"Er, no," Nadya said. She tried to focus on the details in the forge's smoldering coals and not the way its glow made its master look like Death itself. "I…um…fell down."

"Fell down."

Nadya winced. Even if Jeta believed Nadya was capable of such clumsiness, which, admittedly, she was, Jeta was sure in her own craftsmanship. In the past months, Nadya had become so as well, as the star-cut armor, a deep gray nearly black, stood against blades and bullets alike. It fit her body like a second skin, and with its dark hood and cloak, it concealed her identity.

"Down into a ravine," Nadya admitted. She rubbed the back of her neck, where the forge's heat broke her skin into a sweat. "The cats weren't too strong, but they were clever. A couple snuck up behind me. Tripped me back over the cliff." She held up her arms, where the purplish bruises were already fading to yellow. "Hurt a lot, actually."

Jeta's face showed no pity. Whether it was because she knew of Nadya's *nivasi* gift, her unnatural strength that made her fairly unbreakable, or because she actually couldn't care less for Nadya's well-being, only the Protectress herself knew. The forgemaster had certainly never displayed anything but annoyance toward Nadya.

"A warrior should respect their armor," Jeta said finally. She ran her fingers along the curves in the breastplate, no doubt feeling and noting each imperfection. "I can fix this, provided you treat it better in the future."

"Of course," Nadya said quickly.

"Do not make promises you have no intention of keeping. You need no armor. I am aware of that," Jeta said. Nadya flinched. She rarely heard the forgemaster allude so bluntly to her *nivasi* blood. "Armor makes little difference to the damage you take. But that is not what this is about."

She paused, and Nadya held her breath. She couldn't remember the last time Jeta had spoken this much to her.

Jeta held up the breastplate. "Respect it, not because it keeps a blade from slicing your skin, but because of what it is. What it symbolizes. What it protects. Remember who you are when you wear the armor, and respect that."

"The Iron Phoenix," Nadya said quietly.

"Good. Because if you don't, no one will. And it will be your own doing."

Nadya swallowed hard, but her throat remained stubbornly dry. She had chosen this, accepted herself as both Nadezhda Gabori of the Nomori and the Iron Phoenix. The thought of losing it all when she had struggled to make up for the bloodshed her carelessness had caused...

"Aww, don't scare her like that. You know how fragile Nadya can be." Familiar footsteps echoed softly against the cut stone floor of the pavilion. Shay walked up to the two of them, smelling of sweetened smoke as she always did. She slung an arm around Nadya, who leaned into the familiar embrace. "Shoot her with a musket and she barely flinches, but raise your voice, and she bawls like a newborn lamb."

Nadya relaxed. Shay's teasing was as constant and as comforting as the rattle of the old steam pumps that kept Storm's Quarry free of floodwaters. "Thanks," she whispered with a wry smile. "I'd almost swooned before you galloped in to save me."

"Much as I try, I can't help but be your knight in shining armor," Shay said, planting a kiss right below Nadya's earlobe. Shay's touch was warm, hot even, as the fire that burned within the other *nivasi* roiled just beneath her skin.

A loud clang broke the moment, as the forgemaster struck the edge of a newly formed pipe with her shaping mallet. "Anything else?" Jeta asked, her tone curt enough to convey that the answer had better be no.

"Um…" Nadya held up the torn hood.

Shay grabbed her arm. "Don't try your luck, love. Get it mended in the market."

Jeta's intense stare lingered on Nadya for a moment longer before she turned her back on both of them. "And where have you been?" the forgemaster asked Shay gruffly. She struck the glowing metal of the new pipe with practiced movements.

"Making charcoal, or did you forget that wonderful assignment?" Shay grimaced. "Your charcoal is waiting outside, and I'm going to smell like charred logs for days."

Shay was the only person Nadya had ever heard speak to Jeta like that. She figured anyone else who had dared to found their remains feeding her forge.

"You weren't seen?" The edge of concern in Jeta's voice made Nadya's chest tighten. She was so happy that Shay had a mentor like Jeta in her life, a mother, really, who had taken the young *nivasi* child to spare her from the death to which Nomori tradition doomed all her kind. Nadya couldn't imagine the patience, and the ability to dodge angry firebolts, it had taken to raise Shay, but watching them work together, conversing casually in the way only made possible by a decade of bonding, Nadya's heart ached with jealousy. Her father, Shadar Gabori of the Duke's Guard, might have accepted her *nivasi* nature, but it had come years late.

"Of course not," Shay was saying. "Kipperwell's tiny enough. Plenty of places to burn wood without being spotted." She snapped her fingers, ignoring Jeta's disapproving glare. The ghost of a flame sprouted from them and disappeared. "Easy as sweetpie."

"As sweetpie?" Nadya asked with a giggle. Shay made it all too easy to forget the things that troubled her, seemingly without trying at all.

Shay shrugged. "It's a thing they say here. And we would not be subjected to such unrefined colloquialisms if we moved on from this tiny town and headed out to one of the big cities in the South Marches," she said with a suggestive look to Jeta.

The forgemaster didn't even look up. "If you do not want to be given a task to make more charcoal, I suggest you both leave me in peace."

"Yes, ma'am." Shay grinned at Nadya as they left the forge area and made their way into the market proper. "You know, she likes you a lot," Shay said when they had left the heat of the forge behind.

Nadya snorted. "Hardly. She rarely says more than two words to me. And did you see her? I thought she was going to eat me alive."

"If she didn't like you, she most certainly would have. I've seen her tear people apart who showed far less idiocy," Shay said, cuffing Nadya lightly in the arm.

"Thanks." Nadya caught her hand, threading her fingers between Shay's. Soot stained, as well, she thought with a small smile. One day, they would be as callused as the forgemaster's own. As much as Shay grumbled about her work with Jeta, Nadya knew she harbored fierce loyalty to the older woman and cherished her position by her side.

"She thinks you're good for me," Shay said, suddenly.

"Oh?" Nadya frowned. "I thought she wanted you to focus on your work, not go off every night with another *nivasi*."

Shay dodged out of the way of a string of children chasing a stray dog. Their shrieking laughter filled the nearby market stalls, and more than one shopkeeper sent them a disapproving glare as the bunch sprinted past. "Little cretins," Shay said, but she was smiling. "Hard to believe that was once us, running through the streets of Storm's Quarry."

Nadya nodded. It seemed like a lifetime ago, the two of them as children, making mischief in the damp alleys of the Nomori tier. Hiding colored pebbles, digging for treasures in the dust, dodging the chores their mothers hounded them about. Such memories were bittersweet, as Nadya knew what came after: Shay disappearing without a trace, her kin denying her existence. Only years later did the two reunite. Nadya, disguised as the Iron Phoenix, had confronted a *nivasi* in the streets of Storm's Quarry. Unbelievably, that *nivasi* revealed herself as Nadya's childhood friend.

A turn of fate Nadya could not be more grateful for.

"She doesn't necessarily approve of all the vigilante work, and she thinks the names are ridiculous." Shay turned to Nadya. "Which you know I agree with. The names are a bit much."

Nadya gave her a playful tap on the nose. "The names were given to us by Storm's Quarry. You were talking about Jeta."

"Yes, right. Well, she doesn't like the whole Dragon and Phoenix thing, but she likes you. She thinks you're good for me. You're...steady. And I need that." Shay squeezed her forearm, entwining their arms to walk side by side through the market.

"I didn't know that." Of the two of them, Shay had always been the fiery one, her *nivasi* nature—her ability to conjure fire and focus it into blades of light—and her quick personality feeding off one another. Nadya did not know if that made her the steady one. She could be, had been, just as quick and careless. And she had blood on her hands for it.

"Don't think too hard on it, Nadya." Shay gave her cheek a brief peck. "Try to have a little fun this morning, all right?"

"I think I can manage," Nadya said as they wandered through the crowds of Kipperwell's market square.

Nadya marveled at just how unremarkable they were here. Nomori—the once nomadic psychic people who traversed the world's waterways, now the newest inhabitants of the city of

Storm's Quarry—were uncommon here, true, and their golden-brown skin and dark braids earned the two women a curious glance or two as they threaded their way through market stalls, dodging eager sellers brandishing their dried meats and wool skeins. But their clasped hands, the way Shay rested her chin on Nadya's shoulder when they stopped to examine some embroidery, the small touches that had become all too easy over the past months—those did not draw a second look from any of the merchants or Marchers alike. In the Nomori tier of Storm's Quarry, such intimate familiarity would be the subject of gossip and ostracism. In the Nomori tradition, women married men, bearing children and carrying on the leadership of their families. They did not wear capes and hunt crime after nightfall; certainly, they did not share kisses with another woman.

Only Nadya's mother, Mirela Gabori, knew of her preference, knowing even before Nadya had confessed her feelings for Kesali Stormspeaker, her childhood friend and now wife of the city's heir, during the last Great Storm. Mirela had accepted her daughter without question then. That changed, of course, when she learned of Nadya's *nivasi* blood.

Nivasi were the bane of Nomori society, children born with unnatural powers outside the traditional psychic gifts of their women and preternatural fighting ability of their men. Once discovered, *nivasi* children were taken away and disposed of for the protection of all.

Given the past destruction caused by *nivasi*, Nadya could not blame her people. Even if she and Shay found themselves branded as the same dangerous menace as the others.

"Oi, stop dwelling," Shay said, cuffing Nadya's shoulder and drawing her out of her dark thoughts.

"I'm not," she tried to argue, but Shay shook her head.

"Don't lie, Nadya. I can see it in your eyes, when you start thinking of it all. You've left it behind. Let it stay there." She put a hand on either side of Nadya's face. Her skin radiated warmth, fueled by her natural *nivasi* fire.

Nadya closed her eyes, letting Shay's warmth soothe her tightened throat, calm her restless hands. It had become so familiar that her body's reaction was instinctive. She took a deep breath. "I know."

Shay gave her a quick kiss, tasting ever of smoke and metal. "You don't, but you will one day. Let's get your hood mended before it gives Jeta chest pains."

Letting herself be led off by Shay, who seemed determined to distract her, Nadya couldn't help the wandering nature of her thoughts. Back to Storm's Quarry, to the only home, the only *Natsia*—her Nomori *long road home*—she had known before Shay. To its ancient walls and the salty scent of the Nomori tier, to the old Gabori house and her loft, to the Nomori fountain where she and Kesali had shared their first kiss and danced under the stars.

To the bloodstained courtyard of the Duke where she, under the influence of a mad and powerful *nivasi*, slaughtered dozens with her bare hands. Her heart pounded from within her chest as it always did when the memories surfaced. But now, Nadya had something to defend against them.

"Nadya, love," Shay said, touching her arm. Grounding her in the present.

Nadya gave a weak smile. "I'm fine." She should be. She should be more than fine, happy even, Nadya knew. She had love, adventure, freedom all at her fingertips. No longer did she live under the threat of those who hunted *nivasi*, or wished to see the Iron Phoenix hang. No longer could the ghosts of Storm's Quarry haunt her every step.

As the midmorning sun warmed the edges of the pavilion, the market hit its peak, with nearly all of Kipperwell's one thousand citizens in the central square. Languages, from the dozen tongues of the South Marches to Erevo and even Cressian, echoed against each other as patrons conducted heated barters. The oversweet scent of sugar dough wafted through the line of market stalls; it overpowered the softer smells of the native fruits and vegetables of the March lands on display. Despite all the activity around her, Nadya was an island unto herself. A deep ache rattled her bones as the differentness of this place squeezed down upon her.

Natsia...

"Nadya?" Nadya looked up to see the worry in Shay's black eyes before the other woman hid it with a smile. "Come, I know a tailor from the last time our caravan came through here. And maybe we can get one of your favorite pastries on the way?"

She should be happy, Nadya knew, so she put on a smile of her own and nodded and followed Shay.

Chapter Two

S hay was no fool.

Perhaps—most assuredly—Jeta would disagree with her assessment, but Shay trusted her instincts, about Nadya most of all. And she was hurting terribly and doing an equally terrible job of hiding it.

Shay bit her lip as Nadya's half-hearted smile faded the instant Shay made to look away. She kept walking alongside Shay through the market. Every once in a while, the sight of a juggler or a beautiful dress would bring out a little smile, but those moments quickly faded. Even speaking to the tailor, whom Shay had contracted before, elicited nearly nothing from Nadya. Shay backed away as the tailor drilled Nadya with questions about the mending job, keeping her partner in the edge of her sight as she headed to a nearby stall.

Shay could have found the place by scent alone. Spiced pumpkin flooded her senses as she gazed over the display of delicate pastries and hearty breads. Two men watched over the stall, both wearing easy smiles.

"Can we tempt you today, ma'am?" one asked in the thick language of the South Marches, of which Shay had some basic knowledge.

"Easily," she replied. "Two rolls, please."

She paid a silver for both and turned away from the stall,

nearly running into Nadya. "Stars, you need to make some noise. Give me an early death of fright."

"I see you left me for the food," Nadya said, raising an eyebrow at the bundle of rice paper in Shay's hands.

"I was keeping an eye on you, never worry. Here, it's worth it." Shay handed her one of the wrapped rolls.

Nadya sniffed it. "I can't place the fruit." She took a bite of the steaming orange bread. "It's good, but what is it?"

"Pumpkin. Large orange fruit. Grows in winter down here. It's the best damn thing about this part of the Marches." Shay ate her roll in three bites, hardly savoring the cinnamon-tinged pumpkin bread. "I used to spend all the pocket money that Jeta gave me on pumpkin pastries when we traveled in this part of the world."

Nadya snorted. "I can believe that."

They wandered the market, pointing out bits and pieces to each other, passing the time as the tailor mended Nadya's cloak. It was easy and comfortable, and Shay knew that it was all too much a facade.

Sadness still hung around the edges of their conversation, in the way Nadya hesitated before speaking, her faraway stares.

It wasn't the first time in the months since they left Storm's Quarry that Nadya had succumbed to the stupor that came with thoughts of the city. It seemed to always float just above her, ready to swoop in and overtake her at any moment.

Shay had never quite figured out how to pull Nadya back out from it.

The first time it happened, Shay did not handle it well.

"Do you even want to be here?" she had yelled, throwing her arm out. Poor choice of phrase, since at the time they had been arguing in a cow field of a cluster of farms on the far northern border of the Marches, a place no one *really* wanted to be.

"Of course I do!"

"Then why does a single mention of that cursed city have you gazing longingly north, like a lovestruck courtier? Why can't you just leave it in the past? Move forward in your life? Move forward with me?" Shay added, her voice rising in pitch and breaking.

Nadya reached out to her. "There's good there as well as bad, on both sides, and I need time to untangle it all. You got a clean break from Storm's Quarry, from our people. I didn't, Shay." She must have realized the error of her words, and quickly added, "It was horrible, what happened to you. I'm not saying—"

"Yes, you are." Shay drew a ragged breath. The air around her burned with heat. Tufts of grass, worn down by roaming herds, burst into flames at her feet. Shay knew she should clamp down on the fire, but at the moment, she didn't want to be in control. She wanted the anger. "You still seem surprised that I hate them. Well, I do. And I always will. I didn't save the whole stars-cursed city for the sake of it. I did it for you. If that's not enough…"

"It is, Shay, it is, I just—"

"You just wish you were back there. Wish it would have all worked out differently." Her words dripped with a poison that fueled the unruly fire within her. "Wish you could have stopped her wedding."

Nadya stepped toward her, taking her hand despite the flames that danced around Shay. "I chose you, Shay. I chose you, and I have not regretted it once. I wish you would believe me," she whispered.

Later that evening, Jeta had cuffed Shay upside the head. "Do not be foolish."

"Why do you care about my love life?" Shay had replied, keeping her temper under control. Jeta brooked no mistakes when it came to her *nivasi* gift.

The forgemaster was silent for a long time. "Because she steadies you. And now you need to do the same for her."

"This was supposed to be her happy ending, don't you get it? She's supposed to put all that behind her and live her life. With me, without me"—those words had hurt, but she meant them—"it doesn't matter. What matters is that she finally gets to be at peace."

"Maybe she does not believe that she deserves peace."

"Oh," was all Shay could say at the time.

Now, months later, Shay kept returning to that conversation every time she needed to understand why Nadya could not sever whatever tied her to Storm's Quarry. Knowing that Nadya did not regret her choice to travel south with Shay was not the same thing as knowing how to comfort her partner when the past overcame her.

"Just give it enough time," she muttered. Another few months away from that cursed city, and maybe Nadya would finally accept that her life was now good.

And that she deserved it. It and a damned sight more.

"Time for what?" Nadya asked, breaking Shay out of her thoughts.

Cursing the other *nivasi*'s supernatural hearing, Shay shook her head. "Time to get that cloak mended. Can't let your secret identity get out. What would the neighbors say," she teased gently.

"Nothing worse than what's already said of us." Nadya paused. "Or has been said."

Shay bit back a sigh. It was not Nadya's fault that she twisted every word to feed her dark thoughts. "Try not to dwell too much on that." She paused. The middle of a crowded market in a godsforsaken town in the South Marches was not perhaps the best place to bring up Nadya's melancholic tendencies, but Shay clasped the tendril of courage and began, "There's something I've been meaning to speak to you about. I know how hard—"

"Nadezhda? Nadezhda Gabori?"

An unfamiliar voice, male and carrying the strong tones of Erevo, broke through the noise of the market square, cutting Shay off. She swallowed back a curse word and looked up from the spot of dirt she had been intently staring at.

Instantly, her feet shifted into a ready stance. She held her hands loosely at her sides, but the air shimmered ever so slightly with heat. Her blades lay just below the surface of her skin, tingling with power.

A young man, brown haired and wearing the bright white sash of a messenger, slipped through the crowds. "Miss Gabori?" he asked again.

At her side, Shay felt Nadya shift. While she still stood with casual ease, Shay knew she could lunge forward and snap a neck faster than anyone else could take a breath.

"And you are?" Nadya asked.

He looked between the two women, before his eyes settled on Nadya. "No one, miss. Only a messenger, here with a delivery from your father."

"My father?" Nadya whispered, as if she didn't dare believe it.

Shay felt her insides tighten with anger, and she hated herself for it. *It's not Nadya's fault that she's got a family, or at least part of one, that still cares for her.* She did not drop her guard. It could still be a trap of some sort, and a not-very-small part of her wanted it to be.

"He sends this message to you, Miss Gabori." The young man reached into the satchel belted around his chest and pulled out a tightly rolled parchment. A single seal adorned it, the wax depicting a sun. "The seal of the Guard," Nadya muttered as she took the message. "Thank you."

"Just doing my job, miss."

"I bet," Shay said, unable to keep her annoyance from flooding her words. "Waiting on this, are you? Well, take it and be off." She tossed a single copper to the suddenly frowning messenger, and turned to Nadya. "You don't need to read it, you know."

Instantly, she regretted her words as Nadya's posture turned defensive, and she cradled the parchment against her chest as if she feared Shay might burn it.

Truth be told, the thought had crossed Shay's mind.

"Why wouldn't I? Papa understood why I left. He knew it before I did, to be honest. He would not send me a missive if it wasn't important."

Shay took a deep breath. If she stuck her tongue in it now, Nadya might be furious at her for days. "All I meant was…you're getting away from all that. You're building a life." *With me.* "You don't have to go running just because Storm's Quarry thinks it needs the Phoenix to solve all its problems. Not to mention, half that city wants you dead. They want me dead, too, by the way. There's no way of knowing that this isn't a trap to lure you back now that the Guard has regained its strength."

"He wouldn't do that," Nadya whispered fiercely, clutching the parchment. Her other hand curled into a fist, white-knuckled fingers charged with enough strength to crush stone. "He's Guardmaster now. He wouldn't let them…"

"You don't know that, Nadya," Shay said softly, touching her shoulder.

Nadya jerked away. "I do." But the waver in her voice betrayed her. With trembling fingers, she opened the parchment. She did not move when Shay stood over her shoulder to read the note.

Nadya,

I write in hopes that this will find you wherever you are traveling. Unfortunately, it is not a message of good tidings.

Your mother has entered the final stage of her illness. The medicine no longer soothes her cough, and her lungs struggle for every breath. It won't be long now before she joins the Protectress for her journey to the next realm.

She calls for you, Nadezhda. She wishes to make it right before she passes.

I cannot expect you to come, not after how she threw you from our home, and I, to my great shame, let *her. I can only hope you one day find it in your heart to forgive us. To forgive your people.*

In case you wonder about the city, it is quiet, though I do not expect it will stay that way for long. Our people dance in the fountain square on clear nights, honoring the stars as they always do. Kesali asks after you. I know she worries for you and wishes to hear your voice.

I do not know when we will see each other again.

Until then, you have my love.

Your Papa

Shay let out the breath she had been holding. "He's not asking for the Phoenix. No impending crises, I guess." No reason to go running back. "I am sorry about your mother, Nadya. She made her choice, and well…at least she regrets it." *More than my family.*

Nadya acted like she hadn't heard. "Nomori don't dance," she muttered, staring at the parchment.

"What?

"We don't dance." Nadya looked up at Shay, her eyes shining wide with worry. "Papa knows that. Kesali and I scandalized the Elders when we danced together at the last Arane Sveltura festival."

Shay ignored the old flare of jealousy that rose in her chest at the mention of Kesali. "What does that have to do with your mother?"

"Nothing. Everything. Don't you see? It's a message."

Shay raised an eyebrow. "Um, yes, it is."

"Don't act like a fool. It's a secret message, coded in case it fell into the wrong hands."

"And whose hands would those be?"

"I don't know." Nadya shook her head. "I don't know what's happening in Storm's Quarry, but something is wrong. Perhaps my father and Kesali really are requesting our help."

She can fix her own damn city. But Shay swallowed the words back. Nadya had made a promise to protect Storm's Quarry when its need was great, and if she thought that time was now, Shay wasn't going to be able to convince her otherwise.

And stars take her if she wasn't going to end up following Nadya back to that cursed place.

"So your mother isn't really dying?" Shay winced as the words came out far blunter than she had wanted.

Nadya shook her head. "I don't know. Maybe. She has been fighting against the damp for years now. The damp of the city always wins, in the end. But it might just serve as a cover to write the letter."

"In case some unknown enemy gets ahold of it."

"Stop it."

"Stop what?"

Nadya threw her hands out into the air. "Talking to me like I'm a foolish child who believes in fairies. This is real, Shay. I know it. My father wouldn't send this message if Kesali—if the city didn't need me."

Kesali. The name burned hotter than Shay's own fire. The Nomori girl she once played with as a child turned Stormspeaker of their people turned Duchess-to-be of Storm's Quarry. The woman who had captured Nadya's heart for a long time, with whom, Nadya had admitted, she'd shared her first kiss. The Stormspeaker's name should not have bothered Shay as much as it did, slipping under her skin like a swarm of stinging gnats; after all, Kesali was married to the Duke's son, and Nadya had left the city before the wedding, choosing to come with Shay and the caravan.

Choosing Shay.

But it did hurt, a dull ache that expanded from her chest out to her fingertips. Because, within the darkest parts of Shay's mind, she had always known that the instant Kesali called, Nadya would go running. And damn anyone who got in her way.

I guess I was right. Bitter gall rose up in her throat. "You're going, then."

"Yes, I have to. They need me," Nadya said matter-of-factly. She tucked the parchment in her belt.

"*She* needs you."

"What?"

"Kesali calls for you, so you run back to her. Like a puppy begging for scraps." She knew her words were cruel, that Nadya needed support from her now, that she had been dealing with the messy knot of feelings that Storm's Quarry left her, but Shay couldn't hold her own bitterness back. "Never mind who you leave behind."

Nadya's eyes widened. Her mouth opened slightly, as if she had been struck. Apparently, unlike a physical blow, Shay's words had the power to stagger her. In the midst of the bustling market, they stood facing one another in a world apart.

Shay hated herself for the surprised hurt her words had brought upon Nadya's face. *You've never been a good enough person for her. This just proves it.*

"I'm not—Shay, I chose you," Nadya said softly. "I'm not going back because of anything that might have happened between us." She reached out to her, but Shay, as the voices rose in her mind—*You've always been a terrible person. She deserves someone who trusts her, who stands by her side no matter what—* batted the hand away, and Nadya let her.

"You keep saying you don't regret your choice, but you have a poor way of showing it, you know." Shay kicked at the ground. "I sure never asked for you to leave her, and I am not going to stand in your way. True love and all that, right?" Tears stung the edges of her eyes and burned away. "I have work to do. Travel safe, Nadya."

She turned around and left Nadya standing in the middle of the market, gaping.

❖

The forgemaster said nothing as Shay stormed into the smithy. Silently, she threw on one of the heavy aprons that hung on the crooked hooks fastened to wooden beams above them. She took up a pair of tongs, for show. She could reach into the white embers and pull out the melted ore with her bare heads. As strong as the anger and self-loathing that fought inside of her, she'd probably char the ore with her fire if she touched it.

If Jeta noticed that she'd been crying, or the slight jerkiness in her movements, she said nothing and got back to work.

They found their rhythm quickly, moving to the steady hiss of the bellows. Shay pulled each pipe out of the forge; Jeta took each one to the anvil, her hammer shaping the soft metal with expert swings. The pipe switched hands again, as Shay put it back to the heat for further shaping. Round and round they went until Jeta silently proclaimed a piece fit, sinking it into a vat of water, calling forth a storm of steam that filled the silence for a few seconds.

Hours passed. Shay fell into the familiar patterns of the smithy. Despite all her complaints, she had always loved Jeta's work. It allowed her to pull back from the world, to discard her thoughts, to lose herself in the intricate movements of the forge.

As she worked, her mind quieted, her inner flame slowly patterning itself after the consistent embers of the forge. Shay breathed in iron-tinged smoke, and the knot in her stomach loosened a bit.

Nadya would go to Storm's Quarry, she knew. To reunite with her mother, who had turned her out after learning of her *nivasi* blood, if nothing else. But Nadya was sure of the note's hidden meaning, and nothing Shay could say would dissuade her of it. Shay's choice, therefore, lay in whether or not she chose to follow.

But was it worth risking her heart for someone who might run after another?

Damn it all, Nadya was worth it. Shay shook her head at her own foolishness. There had never been a choice, had there?

Stormspeaker or not, Shay would follow Nadya past the edge of the world.

"I'm being an idiot again, aren't I?"

The forgemaster remained silent, only the slight shrug as she bent over the anvil indicating she had heard her apprentice speak.

Shay knew from long experience this was an invitation to keep talking. "Maybe my worst fears are true. Maybe she'll finally see me for what I am. Maybe she'll run back into the Stormspeaker's arms, and I will be left standing outside the gates of that damned city alone. Forced to come back to you and slave away at a forge for the rest of my life," she joked, but her raw tone made the forced levity fall flat.

"So do not go."

Shay wiped her sleeve against her eyes. "That's the end of it, isn't it? Only thing that would hurt more than seeing her fall into Kesali's arms is letting her go, knowing I was the one who chose to give her up. I saved Storm's Quarry for her. Faced my old family for her. The least I can do is trust her now. Try to be the person she thinks I am." Shay shrugged off the apron. "I've got to go."

Jeta's hand closed in around her wrist, her callused hand a familiar comfort. The forgemaster's dark, unreadable eyes softened as they met hers. "You are that person, Shay. Never doubt it." She released her grip and turned back to forge. "Be sure to say farewell this time."

Shay swallowed the lump in her throat and nodded. "Of course."

❖

Nadya was alone in the canvas tent the three of them had been given in the caravan line, a spacious dwelling with room for a fire pit and several bedrolls. Of course, their tent currently only had one bed, as Jeta preferred to sleep in the forge and Nadya and Shay preferred each other's warmth.

Here in this tent, as they traveled south with the caravan, they'd first made love. Slowly, in the beginning, they learned one another as they fumbled through the awkwardness and hesitation. Time passed and Shay soon memorized Nadya's every curve and freckle. She'd learned that Nadya's hesitance to touch her came not from indecision, but the fear of hurting her. *I trust you*, Shay had whispered over and over again, *I trust you, Nadya*. Eventually, Nadya began to believe her. As the sun finished setting, the small fire within their tent illuminated Nadya's silhouette as she moved through the space, throwing her few belongings into a knapsack. Shay stood outside, watching her. The words she needed kept falling away as she tried to compose an apology.

I am sorry I was such an oaf. I am sorry I thought you would leave me for Kesali. I am sorry for not trusting you after promising that I did. Every line felt inauthentic, and Shay swore aloud.

Nadya's silhouette stiffened and turned toward the tent flap, and Shay silently cursed her *nivasi* hearing.

"Shay?" Nadya called, and Shay's heart broke at the hope in her voice. Instead of hating her, as Shay's behavior warranted, Nadya seemed hopeful that she might get to see her.

Screwing up what remained of her courage, Shay pushed the flap aside and walked in. The flames of the small fire pit rose and flickered, feeding off her far-flung emotions. Shay took several breaths and tried to calm herself. Setting the entire caravan camp ablaze might be a welcome distraction, but it would not solve anything.

"Nadya, I—"

"You have soot on your face," Nadya cut her off gently, her eyes saying, *It's okay, I forgive you*, in a way that words never could.

Shay smiled in spite of herself. "Too embarrassed to be seen with me, then?"

"Never." Nadya caught her arm in the nearly too strong grip

that Shay had grown to love. "Not now, not at Storm's Quarry. I am not doing this for Kesali."

Shay wanted to say, *I know, I know you would never leave me*, but the words stuck in her throat. She was spared having to answer as Jeta entered their tent. In her hands, she held Nadya's armor, as perfect as it had been the day she forged it.

"Thank you," Nadya said quietly, taking it carefully. She placed it upon her pack, where her newly mended cloak lay.

"I guess it's farewell, then." Shay cleared her throat. She'd spent plenty of time away from Jeta in the years since the older woman took her in. But this...this felt more permanent somehow. She had a terrible feeling curling around the base of her spine, that whatever had transpired in Storm's Quarry, whatever the message from the Guardmaster meant, she'd lose this.

"For now," Jeta said, as if she sensed Shay's churning thoughts. She wrapped a single arm around her apprentice. Shay breathed in the scent of ash and iron, of safety, as she had come to know in the years since Jeta rescued her from Storm's Quarry.

"For now," Shay agreed, releasing her. She hoped her words were true.

"Nadya."

Beside her, Nadya stiffened. Shay didn't blame her. She was pretty sure this was the first time Jeta had spoken to her partner by name.

"Yes, Forgemaster?" Nadya said, eyes flitting to Shay for a brief moment.

"Protect her."

"I don't need protection," Shay argued, indignant at the suggestion. She had saved Nadya plenty of times; not to mention, when they'd fought at first meeting, Shay had been winning before they recognized each other. She could take care of herself.

But Jeta ignored her, staring intently at Nadya, her black eyes unreadable. The soft flames of the fire pit illuminated the deep lines of Jeta's face, giving her an age that she rarely seemed.

"Please, protect her. In this life, she matters most to me, and I am entrusting her to you. Do not take that lightly." The forgemaster's gaze never wavered from Nadya as she spoke.

Shay's protests died on her lips as Jeta's words sank in. "Oh." Heat rushed to her face. She knew that Jeta cared for her; it certainly was not her work ethic or talent at the forge that made Jeta put up with her for the past years. To hear it so clearly articulated, in a way so unlike the stoic forgemaster—Shay swallowed back the lump that had formed in her throat.

Beside her, Nadya solemnly nodded, as if accepting a responsibility from the Duke of Storm's Quarry himself. "I understand."

Shay glanced from one to the other as the two most important people in her life, the two only important people, shared a look that she hoped to one day understand as well.

Chapter Three

The road north to Storm's Quarry held little traffic outside of Kipperwell, and even less scenery. The scrubby brushlands of the South Marches soon gave way to the softer meadows that sprawled from the northernmost point of the Marches up until the mountains of Wintercress. Groves of pines trees dotted the landscape, and from within, Nadya heard the sounds of woodpeckers and squirrels. She listened to them as they went about their business, and it brought some measure of calm to her racing heart.

Several hours into their trek, a lone figure appeared on the road ahead. Shay nudged her. "Don't like the look of that. But we can handle it if anything goes poorly."

Nadya was about to remind her that they wanted to keep a low profile, when the figure turned into a man. Erevan, by his freckled skin and reddish hair, with a scraggly beard and a thick aura of liquor. He wore patched cotton clothes and held out a rusted pistol. His grip shook, and the barrel wobbled between Nadya and Shay.

"Stars, we have all the luck," Shay muttered, stepping slightly in front of Nadya.

"Shut up! Give me your coin. All of it," he barked in slightly slurred Erevo.

"Believe me," Shay said, not bothering to conceal her grin, "you do not want to rob us."

"That so?" He returned her smile, showing missing teeth. "It's me and a couple o' girls on a big scary road. No one else. Maybe you'd be able to convince me, darling, but with the trouble up north, the war and all, it gets hard for a man to make an honest living. Sorry 'bout that." He shrugged.

"What's happening up north?" Nadya asked quickly, ignoring Shay's sigh.

The Erevan snickered and leveled his pistol. "Coin, if you want news."

Before she thought better of it, Nadya snatched the pistol away with a speed that drew a gasp from the would-be thief. In the same movement, she grabbed his collar with her other hand and lifted until only the tips of his boots trailed the ground.

"Tell me," she said quietly.

Heat hit her skin. Beside her, Shay had drawn a small flame into her hand. "I'd answer her if I were you."

"What—what are you?" he sputtered. Nadya heard his heartbeat race, and the fear that oozed off him twisted her stomach. "I don't know anythin', I swear. Just saw the smoke rising from Storm's Quarry, you know? Soldiers marching across the bridge. Got out of there real fast. Swear it."

Her fingers turned numb, and she dropped the man. He scrambled away on all fours. Nadya didn't make a move to pursue; neither did Shay.

"I'm sure it's all right," Shay said, grasping Nadya's arm. "The word of a drunken thief is hardly anything to take seriously. He could have been seeing his own vapors, not smoke."

Nadya desperately wanted to believe Shay's lighthearted words, but she could not stop the weight that crept over her. "Let's keep moving. The sooner we arrive, the sooner we know what happened."

They passed many groups of travelers on the road north as the day grew longer: merchant carts pulled by donkeys with jingling bridles, families with young wide-eyed children sitting on the shoulders of their parents, single men with their faces concealed by scarves and their footsteps quick. Few other travelers made notice of them as they trekked slowly north. Those who did catch their eyes gave them a wide berth. Something in their demeanor, the stubborn determination in Nadya's set jaw, or the dangerous gleam in Shay's eyes, told everyone that they were not to be trifled with.

When the final rays of sun descended behind the blurry mountains, hundreds of leagues in the distance, Shay nudged Nadya. "There's an inn ahead, maybe half an hour's walk. Nothing fancy, but decent enough when Jeta and I have stopped there on our way north. We should rest there tonight."

Nadya glanced ahead. For the first time in months, the fog around her thoughts had lifted. Returning to Storm's Quarry brought a purpose that she hadn't realized she lacked, and she was desperate to hold on to it. "I think we should keep moving. We don't know what's going on in Storm's Quarry, and if it is urgent..." Her voice trailed off, as a thousand possibilities tore through her mind, each more harrowing than the last.

"Neither of us will be in any position to help if we arrive exhausted," Shay said. She spat onto the ground. "I need a hot meal. You need to sleep. I don't care about your superhuman stamina—you are worrying yourself half to death."

Nadya thought to argue, but Shay's mouth was a thin, unyielding line, and Nadya knew any debate was moot. "All right," she relented, but her chest still squirmed with nerves. "But we leave before first light."

"You have never been awake before first light," Shay teased, but her eyes didn't carry any amusement. "Storm's Quarry will still be standing, Nadya. We need to be at our best if we're to do anything."

Nadya swallowed hard and nodded. They resumed their walk, Shay's strong hand on her back.

The Old Crow inn sat nestled between the road and a huge

forest of evergreens. A few buildings, no doubt the homes of its workers, stood on the opposite side of the road, all built from stained pine. The inn itself was two stories, with a simple garden of flowers out front and a stone birdbath that rose up from a bush of lilacs. A wooden sign bearing *The Old Crow* in faded script creaked on its hinges, welcoming them to the simple establishment.

The cider tasted sour, but the stew, made with thick cubes of boar from an old family recipe, according to the beaming cook who served them, warmed Nadya through. After finishing the hearty meal, she waited while Shay paid a few coins for a room, then followed her up the rickety stairs to a small room with a single bed and a bowl full of water for washing.

One of Shay's many gifts was the ability to brood in silence. She went through the motions of washing her face and stretching out with a scowl that dimmed the entire room. In fact, Nadya was certain her partner's mood reduced the glow of the bedside candle. Finally, she couldn't stand it any longer.

"You're angry that we're going back, aren't you?" She sat on the bed, and its coils squeaked under her weight.

"Not at all."

"Shay, be honest with me," Nadya pleaded.

The other woman sighed. She finished her final stretch, wrapping each arm around her body, and then sank onto the mattress next to Nadya. "I'm not angry—I promise. I'm just... worried."

"About what?" Nadya asked. Shay was no coward; it couldn't be the prospect of danger that had her on edge.

"About you. About what this might do to you, after you've just gotten away from it all. And..." Shay's voice faded. "Just—just promise me something, all right?"

Nadya tried to reach out to Shay, but she looked away from her. "What is it?"

"Promise me you won't seek her out."

"What?" Nadya couldn't help the hurt that seeped into her tone. Did Shay really think she could be unfaithful?

"You are going to Storm's Quarry to see your mother before she dies. Fine. I may disagree, but I'll support you in that. And if you turn out to be right about your father sending a hidden missive of danger in that message, and Storm's Quarry is actually in peril, I will help, just as I did last time. Stars, the Guard and the Nomori Elders may run us out the gate with rapiers and pitchforks. I can handle all of that." Shay took a deep breath, and Nadya felt her lungs tremble in the still air. "But what I cannot handle is seeing the woman I love run off after someone else. So promise me. Promise me you will not seek her out."

Nadya reached out. Shay did not pull away as she took her hand, threading their fingers together. Holding on to her as if this connection would bring the understanding Nadya desperately needed Shay to have. She tried to find the words. "Kesali is my best friend. I've known her as long as I have known myself."

Shay's pulse quickened against Nadya's hand. "Promise me," she whispered.

"Kesali might need me," Nadya said, moving closer until her knee pressed up against Shay's. The familiar warmth of her partner raised goose bumps down her calf. "As the future leader of Storm's Quarry, she might need the Phoenix."

The Iron Phoenix. Not Nadya Gabori.

"Promise me," Shay said again. A moment later, she silenced Nadya's next breath as she half turned and then crushed her lips against Nadya's. The sheer heat behind the kiss overwhelmed any explanation that Nadya had ready. On the bedside table, the candle flared bright, its wax sizzling and popping.

Nadya closed her eyes. "I promise," she whispered to Shay's neck. "I promise." She kissed down to where neck met shoulder and lingered there. "I promise that I love you, Shay." The burning oil scent of her partner filled the air around her as Nadya acquainted herself with the stretch of skin along Shay's shoulder.

"I promise that when I chose you, I did it for real. I promise that my duty to Kesali means nothing more than my duty to Storm's Quarry. I promise that Storm's Quarry will not break me."

Under her touch, Shay stiffened. Nadya raised her eyes to meet the unreadable dark gaze that fixated on her. "Trust me, Shay," she pleaded.

Shay grabbed the back of her head, and Nadya let herself be yanked upward to crash against Shay's lips once more. It was not an acknowledgment nor a pledge of trust. Both of them knew it, and neither of them cared as Nadya fell backward upon the thin mattress. The bed's coils squeaked again as Shay maneuvered atop her, straddling her hips. Her quick fingers undid the ties on Nadya's tunic, before pausing. "We can just go to sleep, you know. Probably should, with the day that's ahead of us tomorrow. We don't need to do this," Shay added, her eyes soft and gentle, despite their arguments over the past day.

"No," Nadya said, running a hand up the muscled skin underneath Shay's shirt. "I want this. Want you." *If not to trust me, then at least beside me.*

Before Shay, Nadya's only experience had been one unfinished night with Kesali, when the fear of her strength and the guilt of Kesali's betrothed being in the next room had caused Nadya to flee out the window. That night had been all hurried touches and soft kisses. With Shay, Nadya learned it could be different.

With Shay, it was everything.

There was no fear as Nadya laid a practiced trail of kisses down Shay's spine. No hesitation that she might hurt her partner. She would always have to be careful of her strength, in the same way that Shay had to restrain the fire that churned just beneath her skin. But the bruises and the burns seemed such a small price to pay when Shay's touches brought stars across Nadya's vision.

Then there was heat and fire, and smoke made Nadya's nose twitch as the mattress smoldered. She couldn't help but laugh at

Shay's muffled curse. "Hope they don't notice," she muttered, yawning. "We do need to sleep, love."

Nadya found herself too tired to disagree. Shay draped an arm around her, pulling her close, and she fell into the familiar embrace. Would it be the last time, she wondered with a stab of worry. Would Storm's Quarry be enough to break apart what they had built?

"Trust me," Nadya whispered into Shay's shoulder before sleep overtook her.

❖

The early morning saw Nadya and Shay on the road before dawn. No words passed between them, not even the usual morning greetings. The weight of what they would find in Storm's Quarry hung over their travels, and Nadya found no beauty in the grasslands that they passed. Only when a stone tower came into view did she jerk to attention. The tower of Eagle's Reach, a Cressian stronghold built just on the border of their lands as a challenge, looked abandoned, but neither of them wished to take any chances. The poisons and chemicals of that place had nearly killed them when they broke in to steal what they thought had been the cure to the sickness in the well water of Storm's Quarry. Nadya was not keen to repeat the experience, so they gave the stronghold a wide berth as they descended the ridge that rimmed the Kyanite Sea and headed for the marble bridge.

Nadya stopped at the first hint of smoke in the air. For a moment, she wondered if Shay really was angry, that her emotions were seeping out through her *nivasi* gift. But while Shay's fires smelled sweet, with a metallic tinge, this smoke burned Nadya's nostrils, acrid and stale.

Protectress, she begged silently, quickening her pace, *please tell me you looked after them. After the people in your care. Please…*

Her prayer disappeared into silence as the city before her came into focus.

Behind her, Shay swore, but Nadya barely heard. The world around her retreated until the only sound she heard was the harsh thump of her heartbeat. An age passed between each beat as she gazed upon the island in the middle of the Kyanite Sea.

The great gate of Storm's Quarry stood no more.

CHAPTER FOUR

Just as the great gate of Storm's Quarry had fallen, Nadya's knees gave out and she crashed to the ground. Bits of jagged-edged marble littered the bridge amidst cracks in its own stonework. The cracks ran down past them like veins, reaching far away from the heart that used to be Storm's Quarry.

Beyond the fallen gate and the rubble strewn in its wake, Storm's Quarry lay in ruins. The smoke of smoldering fires lazily twisted among charred piles of what had once been the homes and shops of the Nomori tier. Some of the sturdier buildings, those made of the same stone as the city walls, still stood, though shakily, missing large pieces of rooftops and windowpanes.

"We left," she whispered, the words barely gaining enough traction to get through her rapidly closing throat. "We left them."

When night falls here, you and your armies will not be safe, Kesali had told the ambassador of Wintercress. *If you choose war, then you will face the guardians of Storm's Quarry: The Iron Phoenix and the Shadow Dragon.* Guilt curdled in her stomach. She had vowed after Gedeon took over her mind, making her slaughter dozens of innocents the eve before the Blood Sun Solstice, that she would repay the city for that massacre. That she would use her *nivasi* strength to do good, to protect the people of Storm's Quarry.

She had failed.

"Do not put this on yourself, Nadya." Shay knelt beside her.

"Then is it yours? Do you take responsibility for this?" Nadya's eyes burned as the smoky air mixed with her tears.

"I never asked you to come away with me." Shay said it so quietly that had Nadya not possessed supernatural hearing, she would never have caught it.

"Shay, I—"

But what was there to say?

"Never mind it. You were right. About the note, I mean." Shay stood up. "Sitting here crying won't solve anything. We don't even know what happened, let alone how the walls came down. We need a plan."

Nadya found her footing and rose. The world swam around her for a moment before it settled. She wiped her eyes. "Whatever happened, they need us."

"Cannot believe I'm saying this, but they don't need us." Shay bent down and dragged her fingers across the stone. She straightened, drawing a dark mask around her eyes with the bridge's dark silt. Nadya understood, pulling her hood up and fastening her mask. "They need the Iron Phoenix and the Shadow Dragon."

Nadya and Shay ran. Past the crumbled remains of the once-great gate of Storm's Quarry. Into the Nomori tier, barely recognizable as the place she had grown up, its streets torn up and burned with gunpowder. Through empty streets, past emptier dwellings. Each step increased the weight on Nadya's chest. *Where is everyone?* Her thoughts ran frantically, faster than even her feet could carry her through the city.

A gathering was being held in the Duke's courtyard on the fourth tier. The wide open space was normally reserved for speeches given by Duke, but it was not only Duke Isyanov atop the ornate dais at the head of the crowd of forlorn faces. Nadya's heart lurched as she saw the chains that bound the Duke. And her heart fell completely as she recognized the two figures that stood at the back of the dais, guarded by Cressian soldiers.

Marko Isyanov and Kesali Stormspeaker.

"My father, where is he?" Nadya scanned the dais frantically. "Papa would not let the Duke be captured, not without…" Her words died in her throat. *Not without giving his life to try to save him.*

Shay gripped her shoulder. "Don't dwell on what you don't know now. We need to get up there. A better vantage point at least."

Dodging civilians and the gazes of Cressian soldiers, they made their way through the crowds and onto the rooftop of a neighboring building. Nadya had to suppress a shudder. It was here that she had fought Gedeon over a year ago, and here that he took over her mind and turned her into a murderer.

"Stay with me," Shay muttered, squeezing her hand. Nadya gave her a grateful smile and refocused upon the dais.

Her enhanced senses included uncanny eyesight, and so the scene down upon the dais was as clear to her as if she stood next to the Cressian royal guard.

A lone figure stepped out to the center of the raised platform. Nadya's skin crawled as she recognized the haughty smile.

"Aster!" Nadya hissed. "She's come back." The serpent of a woman wore her customary floor-length white gown, which fluttered about her in the slight breeze. Even from a distance, Nadya saw the twinkle of jewels at her ears and throat, the sparkle of a tiara nestled into her blond hair.

The councillor stood with such perfect poise that Nadya wanted to throttle her right there.

Shay swore. "That woman will get hers." A lash of heat flared around her. "I will make sure of it."

"Why did she come back?" Nadya wondered. "Why risk it?"

"Doesn't seem like much of a risk from here." Shay nudged her. "What's she saying?"

Down below, Councillor Aster spread her arms wide before the crowds of stone-faced Erevans and Nomori.

"People of Storm's Quarry, we have returned to fulfill the promise that I left with."

Her voice echoed down the grand stairs. Those too far away from the palace tier heard through Cressian heralds, stationed along the staircase and into the lower tiers, who repeated her words.

"To do just that, I introduce His Highness, the Crown Prince Trillium of Wintercress, favored son of the High King." She raised her hand in a flourish, and a man stepped forward.

Next to him, Aster looked like a pauper.

The white-gold armor of the Prince shone in the midday sun. Delicate gold leafing edged the carved chestplate, gauntlets, and plumed helm. The shield on his back was edged in gold filigree, its crest of a three-edged leaf encrusted with sapphires. It was so unlike the simple crimson-dyed leather of the Duke's Guard that Nadya wondered how a person could even fight in that armor.

"People of Storm's Quarry," the Prince began, speaking in rumbling, near-flawless Erevo, "your salvation is upon you. In the name of my father, High King Aton of Wintercress, may the old gods bless his line, I claim this city of Storm's Quarry for the Kingdom of Wintercress."

The finality in his words washed over Nadya, chilling her to her core. Not even Shay's natural heat beside her could warm the biting cold that settled within her. It had come to pass, just as they had been warned. Storm's Quarry was no longer free.

She glanced to Shay, who surveyed the crowds with calculated precision. *Not if we have anything to say about that. This Prince Trillium might have soldiers enough to defeat the Duke's Guard, but he cannot overcome the power of two* nivasi.

"Your Duke and his heir brought this upon you." The Prince's voice rang out as he swept his hands toward the ruins of the great gate below. "This war. Your kin have died, your homes brought down because of this man's selfishness."

"How can he say that?" Nadya asked. Her fingers gripped the stone, cracking it. "Wintercress, Councillor Aster, they—they violated us! With their poison, the sickness it brought. That damned treaty they drew up was a noose around this city's neck."

Her blood pounded in her ears. Nadya felt helpless. There were too many crowds between them and the dais. Not to mention the scores of Cressian soldiers, sabers drawn, ready to cut down civilians at the first sign of trouble. *Your city. Your city and you failed to protect it. Left it alone like the selfish little girl you are.* Her thoughts took on Gedeon's voice, and his black eyes rose in her vision, clouding out the proceedings below.

"*Nadya.*" Shay's voice cut through Gedeon's, and her burning hot hands wrapped themselves around Nadya's.

She exhaled.

"I know. We know," Shay said, tracing circles around Nadya's whitened knuckles. "Everyone here knows what you said to be true. Doesn't help. Wintercress is building its own story, something they'll tell their grandchildren. About the great battle of freedom against the tyrannical duke of Storm's Quarry or some nonsense. We can change that."

"You're right."

"'Course I am," Shay said, returning her attention to the scene below.

Nadya allowed herself a small smile before doing the same.

The Prince pushed Duke Isyanov to his knees. Marko cried out, struggling against the grip of the two Cressian soldiers who held him. Beside him, Kesali stood stoically, watching the scene unfold with the same iron will that she had faced Gedeon with.

Beside her, Shay whispered, "This is not good, Nadya."

The Duke of Storm's Quarry, dressed in the torn remains of once-fine clothing, knelt before his entire city. The gathering had been quiet before; now, it had gone completely silent as the people, both Erevan and Nomori, beheld their ruler so helpless before them.

"Do as you will to me, Trillium. But spare my people. Swear to it. It was my choice to forfeit the treaty. They are innocent," Duke Isyanov pleaded. He stared up at the Prince without flinching.

Perhaps, Nadya thought as her chest swelled with emotion

as the Duke's words, the highest compliment that could be paid him was that his words were utterly unsurprising. No matter what the Erevans of the run-down second tier or the Nomori still stubbornly clinging to the old ways said, Duke Isyanov lived and breathed this city; he was devoted to it in the way that Kesali was devoted to the Nomori people, and Shadar to the Guard. Absolutely and without reserve.

The Duke's plea, however, fell upon unhearing ears.

"The High King of Wintercress will brook no disobedience. Not from the vigilantes of Storm's Quarry, nor its citizens." He leaned down until his face was a mere hand's length from the Duke's. "Nor its leader."

Trillium straightened. He drew the saber at his side. Its ornamental golden hilt shimmered in the sunlight. Nadya stiffened. She glanced down to the crowds below her.

"Don't be a fool!" Shay hissed. "They'll start slaughtering civilians if you interfere now."

"People of Storm's Quarry," Trillium said, sweeping his blade aloft, "welcome your new governance, and see what becomes of those who cross us." With practiced movement, he spun on his heel and brought his saber streaking downward.

The head of Duke Aleksandr Isyanov, ruler of Storm's Quarry for these past twenty-six years, hit the stone of his beloved city with an empty thump.

"Father!"

Marko's scream reverberated against the stone, searing itself into Nadya's heart. In that moment, she left caution behind and acted.

The gray cloak of the Iron Phoenix billowed in the air as Nadya launched herself over the rooftop's edge.

"Damn it, Nadya!" Shay shouted behind her.

Wind thundered around Nadya as she fell. The ground rose up to meet her, and she landed on one knee. Underneath her boots, stone cracked.

The Iron Phoenix rose.

Instantly, the crowd erupted. Erevans and Nomori stumbled away from her, some with wide-eyed fear, others triumphant smiles. From up on the dais, Trillium's gaze hit her like a pail of ice water. He shouted in Cressian, and the soldiers mobilized.

Nadya dodged the first wave of the Cressian regiment. They tried to surround her, sabers flashing in the midday sun, but she was faster. She wrenched blades out of their owners' hands and snapped them. Her kicks smashed rib cages and broke arms. Blood pounded in her ears and her vision began to turn hazy. Her mind went back to the last time she had fought in this place, to the darkness and the blood that drenched her hands...

"Kesali!" Marko's voice again, grief stricken and frantic.

Nadya snapped out of her memories. Duke Isyanov was dead, but his heirs were not, not yet. Nadya's boots slammed into the ground as she surged through the crowds, desperate to reach the dais where Marko and Kesali were held. She caught a glimpse of Marko's fiery locks before a sea of Cressian white swallowed her again.

"Marko!" she shouted, rushing forward.

A pillar of stone appeared out of nowhere. As wide as a man, stretching up from the shattered cobblestones as if it had stood there since the city's founding. Nadya registered its existence only an instant before she slammed into it, shattering the stone and falling limply to the ground.

The world rumbled and fell silent as if the rest of the battle had suddenly disappeared.

What in the Protectress's name...? Nadya winced. She lay on her back amidst broken shards of stone. Her vision swam with grays and reds, and when she coughed, she tasted copper.

"Nadya! Nadya!"

"Kesali?" she croaked. She heaved herself up on her elbows, and then slowly sat up. A blurry figure stood in front of her, and Nadya vaguely registered a warm touch on each of her shoulders.

"Sorry to disappoint, but it's me. Come on, let's get you up."

She was being pulled upward, despite her protesting legs.

One of the hands on hers suddenly disappeared, and flashes of fire erupted from it, slamming into a squadron of Cressian soldiers who had begun to approach them.

"Shay," Nadya whispered.

Her partner's lips quirked up in a grin, though it did not soften the venom in her eyes. "Glad to see you didn't get hit too hard. What happened?" She looked around them. "And why has everyone retreated?"

Nadya glanced around. An uneasy feeling rooted itself in the pit of her stomach. The Cressian soldiers stood back along the perimeter of the destruction. Most of the civilians had escaped the area, but too many bodies lay buried in the rubble. It looked like a keg of gunpowder had exploded, tearing up the ground and raining stone down upon the city. She smelled no trace of smoke, however.

"I'm not sure." Nadya's thoughts still spun from the impact. "Where is Kesali?"

"Don't know." Shay faced away from her as she said it, and the part of Nadya that wasn't fuzzy groaned. They would need to talk again, but not now. Not in the middle of a battle against… What? The city itself?

The remains of the stone pillar that Nadya had crashed into stood rooted in the ground in the middle of the great staircase of Storm's Quarry. Nadya studied it with puzzlement as she shifted her feet to remain balanced, scrutinizing the scene. "How—"

The stone in front of her feet erupted. Nadya cried as the ground vanished. Her boots scrambled for purchase against a waterfall of tumbling stone. Only her supernatural reflexes saved her from falling into the black abyss that now cut its way across the staircase. Pieces of marble bent and broke from the edges, streaming down into its hungry maw. Nadya found her footing for a moment and leapt away. Her knees hit the stairs going up, and her arms flailed as she fought to keep from tumbling backward into the canyon.

Shay!

Nadya lurched forward, struggling for purchase. She couldn't see Shay anywhere, and her chest grew tight. *No, Protectress, please let her be safe.* She gazed down into the depths of the canyon but saw no one.

The stairs she stood upon suddenly crumbled. Nadya sank into the ground up to her knees. The marble constricted her legs, and for all her strength, she could not free herself. Sweating, fingers scrambling frantically at the stone that had latched on to her, Nadya realized that this might be it.

This might be the end of the Iron Phoenix.

Above her, the regiment of Cressian soldiers parted. Nadya expected the Crown Prince to appear, but it was a woman who stepped forward. She wore chain mail under the white jerkin of the Cressian army. Her blond hair was done up in a smart bun, and her eyes surveyed the carnage of the battlefield, unfeeling. Around her, the soldiers stumbled backward to give her a wide berth, as if she carried a plague upon her breath.

The ground rumbled once more as the strange woman raised her hand. Chunks of earth broke away from the cobblestone at her feet and rose into the air, suspended as if held upon invisible string.

Her stone prison temporarily forgotten, Nadya gaped at the woman. This was impossible. A scene from a nightmare, where her city stood at the mercy of a creature with the power to control the very ground it was built upon...

Without a flicker of emotion, the Cressian woman's hands moved, and a mountain of rock hurtled straight for Nadya. The earth released her legs as the sky pummeled her, knocking her down and cutting off any means of escape.

Stone rained down upon her, concealing the midday sun and burying her in darkness. Beyond the crushing weight of stone, Nadya thought she heard shouts and the clashing of blade upon blade, but that too faded. Nadya had only time for a single panic-stricken thought before the darkness consumed her: *They have a Cressian nivasi. Protectress save us all.*

Chapter Five

Shay was sure she had died.

Darkness surrounded her, a comfortable suffocating black that weighed down her limbs. Shay groaned and tried to remember something, anything. A searing pain threatened to split her skull in two, so she stopped trying to think. Instead, she floated through the haze.

Death wasn't the worst fate. Acceptance brought some form of relief, and any regrets she might have had fell back. Plenty of time in the eternity of darkness to linger over what might have been. She imagined the home she might have built with Nadya, after the itch to adventure left both of them. It would have been built of stone, she decided, with a flat roof to lie upon and watch the stars.

Her eyes flickered open. An orange glow scorched her eyes. She shut them again, moaning.

A soft groan reached her ears. Not her own. Shay frowned. Who else was struck down in this dark after-death with her? Another groan. Familiar, this time, and Shay forced her aching eyes open again.

Nadya's fuzzy form came into view. She lay prone, head lolling to her side. Her chest moved up and down with a constant rhythm, and her eyes fluttered. The background remained indistinct, but Nadya came into sharper and sharper focus.

This wasn't right, Shay thought, ignoring the splitting pain in her head.

Shay knew little about the afterlife, only that Nomori and Marchers and Cressians and Erevans all disagreed about where a person went. Good places, bad places, the stars, the earth, the nothingness of the vast universe—she did not know what was true, and she'd never cared enough to dwell on it.

I'm dead, but Nadya...Nadya shouldn't be here. Shay knew that for sure. If any bit of morality was taken into account for a final afterlife destination, there was no possibility that she and Nadya would end up in the same place.

Damn it, she was still alive.

Drawing a ragged breath, Shay began taking stock of herself. She was being carried, strong arms gripping her shoulders and legs; beside her, Nadya was similarly trussed up, her hood and breastplate gone in favor of a simple tunic and trousers. Numerous aches spotted Shay's body, and she knew she'd have a mosaic of bruises in the coming days. Her jaw cracked as she tried to move it, and her skull spiked with pain. Something was sprained, but she'd deal with it later. She was in bad shape, she knew, but the heat of her flame still flickered within her, and she was fit enough to put up a fight with her captors.

Which is exactly what she did.

Fire ignited in her hands, and her captors dropped her with a yelp. Shay slammed into the ground—rough stone and dirt—and bit back another groan. Lurching to her feet, she willed her flames hotter and hotter until their white light formed into thin blades, illuminating the walls of the tunnel.

Tunnel? Shay inwardly swore. She did not know where she was, but she was going to get out of here, Nadya in tow.

Her captors did not remain idle as Shay struggled to regain her balance. They surrounded her with rapiers and bayonets and shouts that she could not make out through the thudding behind her ears.

Nadya. She whirled around, desperately trying to find her.

"Where is she?" Shay demanded.

"Calm down. We are on your side." One of the figures, a man wearing a nondescript tunic, stepped forward. Within reach of her blades of light.

Shay frowned. "You expect me to believe that? After you take me, take us, down to who knows where, trussed up like pigs for the slaughter?"

"Come with us, and everything will be made clear."

"Not likely." Shay snorted.

"I have orders to bring you two in," the leader said as, around Shay, his soldiers gripped their weapons more tightly.

"I do not give a rat's ass about your orders. Where is—?"

"Shay?"

"Nadya?" Shay lashed out with a whip of flame. The soldiers jumped aside, giving her a clear path to where Nadya lay on the tunnel floor. She rushed to her side, leaving her back vulnerable. "Are you all right?"

"Am I dead?"

Shay chuckled. "I thought so too. Guess we aren't that lucky." Her throat tightened. Flashes of their fight with the mysterious Cressian woman came back to her. Shay swallowed and stroked Nadya's hair. She had come so close to losing her.

Behind her, the soldiers' leader said to one of his men, "Go and get them. We don't need a fight here if we can help it."

Nadya sat up, grunting. "Where are we?"

"That's what I'd like to know." Shay gave her a hand as Nadya got to her feet.

Four men stood at their backs, six in front. A strange mix of Nomori and Erevan, armed with rusted rapiers and ill-fitting bayonets. Shay's blades flickered with hungry light. Her head throbbed, and she knew she could not keep up any sort of fight for long. Nadya looked just as bad, swaying a bit on her feet as she moved into a defensive crouch.

"Hold on, we aren't the enemy here," the leader said. "Just come with us. We're nearly there, and your questions will be answered." He made a show of sheathing his weapon. Around them, his men did the same.

"Shay," Nadya whispered.

Her meaning was clear, but Shay wasn't about to extinguish her blades. "Not until we get some answers. What happened and where are we?"

"I was told you were attending the speech," the solder said. "You were nearly killed by what appears to be a Cressian *nivasi*, as impossible as that sounds. And you're in Storm's Quarry. Or, rather, underneath it."

Nadya and Shay exchanged unbelieving glances as more footsteps echoed in the tunnel. The soldiers in front of them soon parted for two figures.

The Duke and Duchess of Storm's Quarry: Marko Isyanov and Kesali Stormspeaker.

Shay remained rooted to the spot. "What the—"

Beside her, Nadya whispered, "Kesali?"

"Nadya. Shay. Apologies for the means of transport. We don't have a lot of other options at the moment," Marko said.

"What is this?" Shay asked sharply. She had not yet let her blades vanish.

"This is what is left of Storm's Quarry. The true Storm's Quarry." Kesali spread her arms wide. "Welcome to the resistance."

❖

Storm's Quarry was named centuries ago for both the frequent and unrelenting storms that ravaged the island and for the precious gemstone mines that lay beneath it. On the Blood Sun Solstice, when the magistrate-backed zealot blew up the outer wall, releasing the floodwaters into the city, most of the waters found their way into the mines. Tunnels and walkways were flooded completely, and the mines shut down by the late Duke, as the city had more pressing needs to attend to.

Now, it seemed like new life had come into the old mines.

"We have been making preparations since Councillor Aster's retreat months ago," Marko was saying. "War was inevitable, with the greed of Wintercress and the weakened state of the city from the Blood Sun Solstice and the poisoned waters. My father"— his voice hitched slightly—"my father had been siphoning off provisions to safe houses in the lower tiers for months. After Wintercress destroyed the main gate and entered the city, we began moving people as well. Members of the Guard. Craftsmen and Nomori psychics. This became our base almost by accident, but it has served us well."

Marko and Kesali had led them through the tunnels to an innocuous pile of boulders, a routine collapse in the tunnel's roof. What seemed like an impenetrable barrier, however, was soon shown to be a carefully concealed entrance. After sliding through an all-too-small gap in the rocks, Shay nearly fell at the sight before her.

Lanterns lit up the sides of the…well, it could no longer be called a tunnel. Cavern, perhaps. The ceiling, sharp with stalactites, rose far above Shay, and the cavern's edge stretched out nearly the length of the great staircase. It sloped downward toward a central lake that glimmered in the low light, clear enough to see the blind mine-fish that scurried along its bottom. A few children splashed in the shallows under the watchful eye of an older Nomori woman who sat sharpening bayonets. Shanties sprouted up around the lake. The cavern housed a veritable town of misshapen dwellings, built of aging wood planks and primitive bricks.

Erevan and Nomori men, lacking uniforms but carrying themselves with the immaculate posture of the Duke's Guard, patrolled the outer walls, some stationed around the tunnel entrances that led into the cavern. Others sparred in a makeshift ring beside what appeared to be a smithy. A repurposed smelter had been poorly reconstructed, with its smoke being pumped upward through precariously fastened pipes of differing sizes.

Shay's head hurt just looking at it. The forgemaster would find someone to smack upside the head and then get to work fixing it up if she was there.

"How many people are here?" Nadya asked as they paused in the middle of a rough-hewn path that wound around the various buildings. Nomori and Erevans bustled around them, most pausing to greet their leaders with a bow and to cast a curious eye to Shay and Nadya.

"Several hundred. More every day," Kesali said. As soon as they had left the others behind, the uncomfortable courtesy and formality had ceased in their words. "It started out with those wanted by Wintercress for various crimes, mostly members of the Guard. Then their families. Whispers started to travel, and many who have lost someone to the Cressian invasion have joined up, willing to do anything for a bit of vengeance."

Marko nodded. "This isn't our only refuge, either, just the largest. We have a few more camps deeper into the mines, and we've taken over several safe houses in the Nomori tier. When the time comes, we'll have enough of a foothold throughout the city to turn it to our advantage."

No one spoke for several moments. Shay glanced at her three companions. Each wore a grim expression, Nadya's tinged with worry. That was all there was to it, Shay thought. She watched a young girl help buckle a leather breastplate onto her father, before he kissed her and left, no doubt to relieve a guardsman of his watch. *They are all going to have to wage war to get their city back. No more negotiations or daring plans to thwart the enemy. Wonder if they know that.*

"Cressian forces can't find this place," Marko said suddenly. "They know the mines exist, and they've scouted them out, but our spies report that they have concluded the mines are flooded. Useless, for now. They'll want the gemstones, of course, but not until the city is under control."

"But you have no plans to let that happen," Shay said flatly.

Marko flashed her a tired smile. "Not in the least."

Do you know what that means, little Duke? Do you know what you'll have to sacrifice to bring your city any kind of future? She swallowed back any further comments. This was not her city. She had no stake in the outcome of the war.

Well, she thought, brushing her fingers against Nadya's arm, almost no stake.

"This is…" Nadya shook her head. "Incredible."

"It's something. Enough to give us hope that the city might be ours one day again," Kesali said.

Marko led them into the most stable looking of the buildings. It was a simple structure with one room and four walls that barely rose above Shay's head. Jeta would have had to duck in two in order to get into the room. A table without chairs stood in the middle, covered in parchments and pens.

"Not much of a headquarters," he remarked. "I've only been here a few days. Already made a mess. It does the job, though. The people here have already taken to calling this place the Bulwark."

"A few days?" Nadya frowned. "But you were there during the Prince's speech. You were there when…How long has it been?" she asked. "How long since…"

Shay saw her swallow the words *your father died.* The young Isyanov, to his credit, did not flinch.

"A week. Several of our operatives staged a distraction. Smoke bombs, modeled from Cressian recipes. Kesali and I got you two out of there. Dragged you to one of our safe houses. Once a physician deemed it safe to move you, we brought you here."

Shay tried to process his words. "You two rescued us."

Kesali nodded. "You'd been buried beneath rubble. The Cressians must've thought you were dead, but we assumed they would try to verify. With the distraction, we were able to get ourselves and you two out."

"Thank you," Nadya said. She touched Kesali's arm, who gripped her hand for a moment.

Damn it all, even in the midst of the demise of Storm's

Quarry, Nadya and Kesali really did look perfect together, Shay thought bitterly. She couldn't help the awful thought that it was only the young Duke who stood next to the Stormspeaker, a marriage of politics, that kept the two of them apart.

The temperature of the surrounding air rose a bit, enough that Nadya must have noticed. She withdrew her hand quickly and cast Shay an apologetic look. Shay glanced away. She hated herself for the jealousy. *Nadya chose you. Act like it.*

She was saved from having to explain herself to Nadya by the appearance of a guardsman. Former guardsman, she supposed, now that Wintercress had dismantled the Duke's Guard and its uniform painted a large bullseye on any who wore it. The older man, salted hair slick with sweat, bowed to Marko and Kesali.

"Apologies for the interruption, but I have an urgent message for you, my lor—Your Grace."

Marko waved a hand. "Thank you, Sergeant. Come, we can discuss it outside." He nodded to Kesali and left without looking at Nadya or Shay.

When he had disappeared around the makeshift wall, Kesali sighed. "The past week has been hard on him. On all of us, but him especially."

"Duke Isyanov was a good man," Nadya agreed. "He did not deserve that death."

"He will be avenged. He and every other death that Wintercress played a part in. We will not stop until we have taken back our city. Every person here, from the elders to the children, is dedicated to regaining our city. But to do that, we need you." Kesali cleared her throat, looking away from Nadya to Shay. "Both of you."

There it was. Shay's inner fire rose with each word Kesali uttered. It raged and crawled at her insides, shouting with the anger that she did not dare show. She clung to the anger, because it was easier to deal with than what lay beneath: hollow sadness. An emptiness that had simmered inside her since the messenger first approached them in Kipperwell. From that moment, she knew their life on the road together approached its end. Storm's Quarry was insistent on swallowing her lover up in its madness.

"Of course," Nadya said.

Shay spat out at the same time, "Well, that's unfortunate."

Shay felt the heat rise to her face as both Nomori women looked at her, Nadya in surprise and Kesali in resignation.

"What do you mean? We have to help. Storm's Quarry..." Nadya's voice trailed off, as she must have realized that appealing to Shay's loyalty to her birth city would do no good. "Shay, we promised. We swore an oath to protect this city."

"*You* swore an oath." Shay's words came out before she had even considered them, and instantly she wished to take them back. Not because she had lied, but because of the sudden pain in Nadya's eyes, the flash of disgust and anger. Aimed at her.

"You came back. You saved the city, Shay." Nadya reached out to her. "You overcame your past and the hatred you harbored for Storm's Quarry. We swore an oath together, the moment we put on our masks. We pledged to protect the city. You were part of it, Shay."

"For you!" Shay grabbed Nadya's hands. She ignored the audible breath that Kesali drew, stealing the air from the already stifling room. "I did it for you. Not for them. It is your oath, not mine."

"So what does that mean?" Nadya whispered, voice shaking.

Shay opened her mouth but hesitated. What did it mean? she wondered. Since arriving in this war torn place, the sadness that had plagued Nadya's step seemed to have lifted, and purpose sparked in her eyes. How could Shay deny her that? She cursed all the gods, living and dead, as her mind froze and no words came out.

"Nadya." Marko's voice cut through the moment, breaking any chance that Shay might explain.

If she found the words, that was. *How can you reassure her when you do not even know yourself?* The voice took on the tone of Jeta, and Shay tried to push it back to focus on whatever new crisis Marko surely brought.

The instant she hard Marko's voice, Nadya dropped Shay's hands like they burned her. Maybe they had.

The new Duke stood in the doorway, face grim. Shay could not tell if the message had borne terrible news, or if this was the new countenance of the heir to Storm's Quarry. She had barely known him before but admired the fire he had. Nadya had always spoken well of him too, and she would not wish the loss of a loved one in such a violent way upon someone with his courage and heart.

"I need to speak with you. The message I received concerns you," Marko continued, oblivious to the strained emotions in the small room.

Nadya frowned slightly. "What is it?"

"Not here."

"I trust Shay. We both trust Kesali." Nadya crossed her arms. "Any message for me can be said in front of them."

"Not here," Marko repeated, and his words now carried a slight edge.

Shay did not want Nadya provoking a fight on her behalf. At least, not over this. "Go on. If it's as exciting as the princeling is making it out to be, you can tell me of it later." She nudged Nadya forward.

Nadya glanced between her and Kesali, obviously not wanting to leave them alone together.

I'm not about to set her ablaze, Shay wanted to say but thought better of it. The royals, or their loyal subjects, might take her jest seriously. She did not, as Nadya no doubt did, hold on to the hope that no one knew of her being *nivasi*. Caution, however, would be prudent. Jeta would like that, so she settled for, "I will behave. Promise."

Nadya nodded, gave her a strained smile, and followed Marko out. Suddenly, it was just Shay and Kesali in the all-too-small Bulwark.

Kesali stared at her, making no attempt to hide the way her iron gaze fixed upon Shay's face. Shay tried looking elsewhere. The floor was worn down, hundreds of paces having packed the earth tightly. The room's two lanterns flickered nearly in tandem. Shay felt each movement of their flames as her own fire hummed along.

Finally, when she could not take the intense silence anymore, she remarked, "Even deep underground, Storm's Quarry still finds a way to be hot and humid. Don't know how you do it."

"I know the truth," Kesali said, ignoring her attempt at flippancy.

Shay nodded. She, unlike Nadya, did not expect that her abilities nor her vigilante identity would stay a secret. It did not take a scholar to guess that the Nomori child exiled for her *nivasi* blood and the Shadow Dragon were one and the same. Even so, she did not intend to give Kesali the satisfaction of confession.

"Nadya and I haven't been hiding it. We've shared a tent on the road for some time."

The queasy look on Kesali's face gave her no small sense of victory. "Not that—I knew that. I—that's not what I meant." The Stormspeaker did not often trip over her words, and it took some time for her to get righted. "Your powers. Your blood. *Nivasi* blood. You are the Shadow Dragon."

"Genius," Shay said. "Of all the fire-caller *nivasi* to choose from, you realized it was me."

"This is no joke. I hid the armor you two wear away in your bunk for Nadya's sake. To keep her secret. Not yours."

"I am not laughing, Duchess."

Kesali shook her head. "You take nothing seriously, do you? Not your forbidden powers, not your city's fate, not the pain you cause her—"

Shay's grin disappeared. She held back the fire that roared up at the jabs from the Stormspeaker. "I do not cause her pain, Your Royal Highness," she said, letting the title roll off her tongue as insultingly as possible. "I'm not the one who wanted to lock her up in a closet, to keep her as a pet one brings out when you get tired of your noble husband or when your city needs saving."

"I would never—"

"But you did." Shay enunciated each word with a sharp hiss. She knew she did not deserve Nadya, that her angry past and violent tendencies only ever pulled down the good-hearted Nomori woman. She knew she was given to flares of jealousy. Despite all that, Shay had never abandoned Nadya. Had never forced her to make such a choice. Kesali could not claim the same. "You asked it of her, and she nearly gave it to you. You might be surprised to learn this, oh, wise Stormspeaker, but you cannot always have everything in life. You tried, and you lost."

Kesali's hands shook ever so slightly at her sides, the only outward sign of her anger that she let on. Shay had to admire her control.

"You think Nadya's affections are a prize to be won?" Kesali threw back at her. "Just like everything with you, isn't it? We have to buy the help of the great Shadow Dragon to save her own city. Is nothing sacred to you?"

Shay clamped down the cold fury that threatened to overfill her chest and spill out in waves and waves of white fire. Even so, translucent flames raced up and down her arms. Kesali took a step back. Her mouth opened slightly, and the blood left her face. Shay bit her lip. The pain focused her. She stalked toward the makeshift door. Resting her hand on the door frame, she half turned. "Let us make one thing clear. I do not care about this city. I do not care what happens to its people. All I care about is Nadya. I am here for her, nothing else, and I will fight for her, and nothing else."

Shay withdrew her hand, leaving a smoking print on the wood, and left the Bulwark of Storm's Quarry's final resistance.

Chapter Six

Nadya let herself be led away from Kesali and Shay, muttering a prayer that they would not kill each other, and into the wider cavern. In the midst of the shanties, makeshift barracks, and smithy, she felt as if she was in a town. If not for the spiked ceiling above, this could have been one of the small, destitute March villages she had traveled through in the past months.

"It really is amazing," she found herself saying.

Marko looked at her, eyes heavy. "It is. A miracle, even. A bit of hope, like she said," he added of his wife.

Wife. Nadya rolled the odd thought around in her mind. That would take some getting used to. *You made a choice*, she reminded herself sternly. *Do not give any credence to Shay's notion that you still love Kesali.*

Even if Shay refused to stay and fight for the city they had pledged themselves to. Bitterness curdled in her stomach. That *she* had pledged herself to.

"Your Grace!" A young Nomori girl ran up to the two of them. She gave Nadya a curious look before bowing to Marko. "Your Grace, the smithy's piping is acting up again. Alla said to come see you."

Marko sighed. "Again? Tell her I will assign one of the craftspeople to it as soon as they are able."

She bowed again and ran off.

"I'm not used to it yet," he remarked suddenly. "The title. It was only ever my father's. Theoretically, I knew I would inherit it one day, but I never pictured any but he upon the throne." He shook his head, the edges of his eyes shining. "Still don't."

"Your father would be proud. Of you. Of this." Nadya reached out to give him a comforting touch on the arm, but Marko flinched away.

She recoiled instantly. Beneath the echoes of the cavern, she heard his heartbeat speed up. Nausea rose in her stomach. How much had the new Duke of Storm's Quarry seen at his father's execution? How much did he know? She had awoken without her armor or cloak, any indication that she might be more than just Nadya Gabori, truthseer of the Nomori.

Nadya cleared her throat. "You said you had a message for me?" she asked in an attempt to get both of them focused on the present.

"From your father."

Her breath froze. "Is he…" Did Marko have her father's final words for her? Nadya felt the dirt floor shift beneath her feet. It took all her strength to remain standing as the walls suddenly began closing in around her.

Marko watched her, his expression oddly detached. "He's alive."

"Oh." She found her breath. "Alive? You're sure?"

"Hard to be sure of anything now, but the message he sent is not yet a day old."

"Where is he?" she asked quickly. "Has he seen fighting? Was he attending the Duke's speech?"

Marko raised a hand. "He is safe for the moment. He's commanding the resistance in the lower tiers. My father ordered him there, and I doubt Shadar will ever forgive him for it. He wanted to be there, during the speech, to protect my father."

"Of course," Nadya whispered. Her father's blood ran thick with loyalty, to family, to his people, to his city and his Duke. She had feared the worst when he did not appear when the Crown

Prince of Wintercress forced Duke Isyanov upon his knees; only a direct order or death would have kept him from fighting at his Duke's side in that moment.

"For all his loyalty, he lied to us. To the man he pledged his service to." Marko's voice took on uncharacteristic distress. "Over and over again, he spat lie after lie at us."

Her breath left her as if several bullets had struck her chest, knocking the air from her lungs. Nadya tried to make sense of his words as a coiling feeling of dread rose in her chest.

He knows.

"I don't—" Nadya tried to say in a feeble attempt to dissuade him, but Marko cut her off.

"Do not keep lying to my face, Nadya. You know exactly what I speak of."

Her cheeks burned. She looked at the dirt, at the scuff marks her boots made as she shifted her weight. Anywhere but at the accusatory stare that Marko now leveled at her. "Marko, I..." The words died in her throat. She swallowed. "You know?"

"I know."

"*How?*" she choked out.

"Your appearance before Councillor Aster when the false treaty was to be signed. You spoke, and though you tried to disguise it, I knew your voice. After that, it did not take long to piece everything together." Marko laughed, but it was hollow. "You must think me an idiot. Poor Marko, the fool. Running in circles around me, having the confidence of my fiancée, of the captain of my Guard. Everyone in on it but me. Wearing that thrice-damned cloak right in front of me."

Marko's words went on and on, each one a new barb. A curious onlooker or two stopped for a moment to witness the scene, but the unusual emotion with which their new Duke spoke soon had them scurrying off. In the midst of the resistance's headquarters, he and Nadya might as well have been totally alone.

"I never thought that, Marko," she tried to say, but the words sounded disingenuous. "I hated lying to you, believe me."

"How can I believe anything of you?" Marko stared at her as if she was a stranger, and it struck right at her core, twisting sharply.

He hadn't deserved the deception, Nadya knew, because Marko was a good person. Marko, who despite her Nomori heritage and his royal lineage, never thought less of her. Never spoke down to her. Looked up to her father, paid deference to her grandmother. Marko, the Duke's son, who invited an unknown Nomori girl to be his adviser, who took serious note of whenever she spoke. Kesali's husband, who embraced the Nomori as his own and fought for them against Wintercress.

Marko, her friend. Her friend whom she had lied to, whom she had nearly betrayed with Kesali, and whom she had stood before as the Iron Phoenix without saying a word.

Marko's voice barely rose above a whisper as he said, "You owed me the truth, Nadya. A long time ago."

She said nothing, for what could she have said? He was right.

"Nadya Gabori, say something," he commanded. Not as her friend, but as the new leader of what remained of Storm's Quarry.

"I—I do owe you the truth. Always have."

"That's it?" He stared at her with shining eyes. Around them, the work of the resistance faded into the background, no more than a gentle thrum. It was just the two of them, and Nadya had nowhere to escape.

"What else is there? I am sorry. I wanted—no, that's another lie, isn't it?" She sighed. "I did not want to tell you. I owed it to you, I know, to tell you of my blood." Even here, she did not dare utter the word *nivasi*. "But I never wanted to."

"Why not?" Marko's voice cracked with unshed tears. "Why didn't you trust me?"

"I do trust you, I just—"

"You were my friend," he whispered. "We were on the same side. I trusted you, but you never could trust me. Neither could your father or Kesali, apparently."

"Leave them out of this." Nadya put a hand to her chest. "Be angry at me all you want, Marko, but they lied in order to protect me. Not out of any malice toward you."

"I am angry at you." Marko sighed. His shoulder slumped forward as he drew a deep breath. "Gods help me, I am furious, and I wish that were the worst of it."

"You and Kesali?" she ventured as his silence stretched out.

"Haven't spoken on it. She treads lightly around discussions of you. Now I know why."

No, Nadya thought, nausea spreading across her tongue, he really didn't.

"Fate has a terrible sense of humor, I think. We have moved forward, neither of us daring to bring it up, because of the Cressian invasion. Because of our duty. That's what has always bound us, hasn't it?"

Nadya stared at him. The bitterness in his tone was so unlike the Marko she had known. Could one secret truly have done this to him?

"Imagine it, Nadya. Your wife, the commander of your Guard, and your trusted adviser and friend. All liars. I had only my father—" His voice hitched. "Now, I have only my city. And even that slips through my grasp."

She wanted to embrace him, to attempt to mend what her secret had broken, but such an act wouldn't be welcome, she knew. He looked at her with the skittishness of a March deer, as if she was the hungry sabercat. The wariness in his gaze hurt, and she realized, with a sour feeling, it was unlikely to go away.

"So what will you do now?" she asked quietly. She noted the guardsmen that patrolled the cavern. Twenty, maybe more. She and Marko stood two hundred paces from the nearest tunnel exit, with a dozen buildings and even more innocents in the way. And Shay was still in the Bulwark with Kesali.

Protectress, if this goes badly, do not let Shay do anything we will both regret, Nadya prayed.

"I will fight for my city. I will protect its people." Marko straightened. His right hand reflexively went to the rapier belted at his waist. "Kesali and I will lead the resistance against Wintercress, and we will win."

"Does that include protecting it against me?"

"What?" Marko voice carried genuine surprise.

Nadya held her ground even as bits of her world began slipping away beneath her. "Your duty is to protect Storm's Quarry. Some would say I'm one of its greatest enemies. So what will you do? Will you order your Guard to hunt me down? Do you wish to strike the killing blow yourself?"

"I…" Marko hesitated. His hands fell limp against his sides. "I don't want to kill you, Nadya."

"Then what do you want?" Her brusqueness surprised even her. "I cannot go back in time and make this right, so what would you have me do?"

"The Iron Phoenix is dangerous." He spoke as if reciting from a book.

She held out her hands, throwing away any regard to the activity that surrounded them. "I am the Iron Phoenix, Marko." Her seal of the Protectress burned hot with those words. Once, Nadya would never have been able to utter them, not without overwhelming revulsion and guilt. She had spent over a year coming to terms with her powers, her past. The death her hands had wrought and the lives her hands had saved.

Nadya could not blame Marko for being tongue-tied. He had had far less time to accept that his friend and the infamous vigilante of Storm's Quarry were one and the same, and much of that time had been spent leading his city through a war.

"I know." He sighed. "My father deemed it necessarily to work with your…alter ego…once. In doing so, he saved Storm's Quarry from Aster's plotting. I can do no less now that Wintercress has overtaken us."

"You will have me in your war?" Marko nodded, and Nadya continued on, despite a sharp voice inside her pleading to not press her luck. "And afterward?"

The new Duke of Storm's Quarry squared his shoulders.

"There will be a reckoning, Nadya. I cannot let the crimes of the Phoenix stand. Once this is over, you will need to answer to the city."

She swallowed. *Did you expect any different?* she chided herself. A temporary truce was the best she could hope for. If they managed to win, she and Shay could leave Storm's Quarry for good and make a new life away from memories of the Iron Phoenix and the Shadow Dragon.

That is, if Shay decided to stay on to fight. Nadya curled and uncurled her fists, feeling the sharpness of her fingernails sinking in her palms. Too many uncertainties hounded at her, but she needed to rise above it for the sake of her city.

"You said you had a message for me. Or was that a ruse to get me to come out here so you could shout at me?"

"I gained no satisfaction from this, Nadya. You should know me better. Better than I know you." Marko looked at the ground, unwilling or unable to meet her gaze. "Your father sent word that your mother is…the damp is taking her. She doesn't have much time left. He suggests that if you want to see her before she passes, go now."

The world stopped.

Nadya breathed, but her lungs got no air. The cacophony of sounds of the cavern, from the chattering of old men to the clanging of rapiers to the low crackle of the smithy, faded out until Nadya heard only her own heartbeat.

Then that too dwindled away, and a great nothing washed over her.

It was suffocating, bringing back the worst memories of Gedeon's control.

My mother is dying. The words were so detached that they came from outside her, echoing around in the nothingness. *My mother is dying.* Again, as if repetition would make it more real.

"Where is she?" Nadya asked, the only words she could get out of her rapidly closing throat.

My mother is dying.

❖

Shay hated this place.

The cavern felt suffocating, its air thick with the smell of oil and sweat. The heat was nearly unbearable, even for her. Shay had stripped off her tunic and tied it around her waist. Even in just the thin fabric of her undershirt, she sweated like a cold forge.

The worst, however, were the people.

After the third *Oh, who might you be?* and the fifth *Anything you might need?*, Shay had had enough. She nearly sprinted through the settled part of the cavern until she reached the scarred, arching walls that glittered with the remains of gem dust.

To escape the curious eyes of the resistance, Shay walked the perimeter of the cavern, dodging between makeshift buildings whenever she heard someone approach. With only four hundred currently living and working in the cavern, a new face brought out questions and pestering that Shay did not want to deal with any longer. Word must have spread about how she and Nadya were recovered, and the last thing she needed was their pity or their friendship. As far as Shay was concerned, accepting kindness meant owing a debt, and she'd rather slice off her right hand than owe Storm's Quarry anything. No, it was best for her to remain out of sight until Nadya finished her business with the young Duke.

She found an unusual formation on the cavern wall, an indentation wide enough for a seat and hidden from the eyes below. Only the cave rats, eyes white and glassy from generations of living in the dark, skulked about, and Shay thought they were fine company.

The only disadvantage to tucking herself away from the racket of the cavern was she had no company but her thoughts, and she really did not wish to dwell on her current predicament.

Her conversation with the Stormspeaker rattled around inside her head. She tried to push Kesali's words about the pain she'd caused Nadya away, but they continued to come back, stubborn as ever. *She knows nothing about us,* Shay told herself sternly. *She is the one who betrayed Nadya, not me. I have only ever been there for her because I care about her.*

So you're going to stay and fight for the city?

Annoyingly enough, the question came in Kesali's voice, all precise enunciation and commanding tone.

Shay still did not have a good answer. Nadya would want to, of course. Despite her months on the road with Shay, this was her home, and she felt like she owed it to the people to defend them. Shay understood that, even if she did not have close to the same sense of loyalty to Storm's Quarry.

If she was honest with herself, it wasn't the city that had Shay so on edge. Neither was it the bloodthirsty Cressians or their impossible *nivasi.*

It was just how perfectly Nadya fit in. To Storm's Quarry. With the resistance and its leadership. With Kesali.

She knew Nadya would never betray her like that, but Shay couldn't help but think that their ten months on the road together were a fluke, and that this was where Nadya belonged. If that was true, who was she to stand in the way? Traveling away from Storm's Quarry had brought a terrible despair upon Nadya, one that Shay had not been able to fix, no matter how hard she had tried. A week in this city, however, most of it unconscious, and Nadya had found herself again.

How could Shay deny her this?

"Damn it all," Shay muttered. She threw a fragment of rock at the cavern floor, causing the nearby rats to freeze. "Damn it all to the stars."

If Shay went one hundred years without seeing the Stormspeaker or hearing her talk again, it would still be too soon.

"Shay!"

Unfortunately, the fates seemed to have an awful sense of humor.

She turned to see Kesali striding toward her hiding place.

"Damn the stars," she muttered again. How in the known world did the Stormspeaker find her here? She glanced suspiciously at one of the blind rats that scuffled in the dirt near her seat, wondering if the rats themselves had betrayed her location.

Sighing, she stretched her sore muscles and looked down at Kesali. "Did you come to berate me again?" Shay asked. "Must we rehash everything we just went through?"

"I am here to give you information, nothing more."

Shay frowned. "Couldn't a messenger have sufficed? Be honest, you want to yell at me again."

Kesali sighed audibly. "I didn't trust this to a messenger, for Nadya's sake."

"What's happened?" Shay jumped down from her perch, wincing as her ribs twinged in pain. "What did the princeling tell her?"

Kesali ignored her jab at Marko. "Her mother is dying. She has been for a while—damp in her lungs—but she has little time left. Nadya left to go see her."

"Ah." Shay kicked at the ground uncomfortably. She and Nadya had never seen eye to eye on family. Between Shay's bad experiences with her own and her anger at Mirela Gabori's treatment of her daughter, she and Nadya had mutually decided it was best not to discuss such things.

Better for Nadya, she thought, and only a tiny part of her was ashamed at the thought. That woman didn't deserve to have her there.

"Well?" Kesali demanded, cutting through Shay's thoughts.

"Well?" Shay repeated, but she knew she had to say more.

Before she could put together the words, Kesali said, "She and her family are in the city. Where she first learned control. Mean anything to you?"

It did. Nadya had told her of the abandoned storefront she and her father sparred in during the months after the Blood Sun Solstice. "Yeah, I know where it is."

"Good." Kesali waited expectantly.

"All right," Shay said. "Is there anything else, or…"

Kesali frowned. "You aren't going to stay here, are you?"

"What I do is none of your business." Shay gestured into the air. "Why are you telling me this? You've made it pretty clear how you feel about me, clearer still how you feel about me and Nadya. What are you trying to do?"

"I'm trying to help Nadya, if only you'd take a moment to see that." Kesali's face softened, and the stoic veneer of the leader of the resistance faded, replaced with a very tired woman. "You need to go to her. She should not be alone in this."

Shay's stomach turned at the thought. Nadya would not be alone; her very traditional Nomori family would be there as well. Revealing herself as Nadya's lover would bring more complications than support. "I think…I think I will stay here," she said finally, avoiding Kesali's gaze. "Nadya does not need the difficulty that I bring, not now."

To her surprise, Kesali let out a harsh laugh, causing the cave rats to scramble away in fear. "Well, I guess I was right about you."

"Which part?" Shay shot back. "Me being a danger or me being bad for Nadya? Or was it something else? Hard to keep track."

"You are selfish," Kesali said, crossing her arms. "Nadya would do anything for someone, and you hide up here, like a scared bat, too wrapped up in yourself to care about the pain of others."

"I'm here, aren't I? I saved the city once for her, and I am following her into it again."

Kesali shook her head. "It's not the same."

"What is that supposed to mean? You have no idea what I've done for her. I faced—" Shay swallowed the words. *I faced my sister, who betrayed me to my family and nearly got me killed.* She drew a deep breath. "I do not need your approval, Stormspeaker."

She turned back to her perch amid the ragged walls of the cavern, hoping Kesali would take the hint and leave.

She did not. "Maybe I don't know all you have sacrificed, but I do know this. You are more than happy to follow Nadya, to be the soldier who has her back in a fight. But when you are needed to comfort her, to support her through pain that isn't physical, you vanish."

Shay's chest throbbed with each word. Kesali's voice seemed to echo about the entire cavern, ringing into her rib cage. "You don't know me," she threw back, but it was half-hearted at best. "If you are so concerned, maybe you should go and be with her." The words tasted sour even as she spoke.

"I know enough about you. I know—" Kesali paused, and Shay turned to see her wipe at the corner of her eye. She stared at Shay defiantly, as if challenging her to remark on it. "I know that Nadya needs someone with her right now." Her gaze softened, and for the first time, Shay heard a thick note of regret in her tone. "And I know that the person she needs is not me."

Chapter Seven

Your father didn't risk writing their location plainly," Marko told her. "He only said to go to where you were first taught control."

Nadya nodded, understanding, and turned to leave.

"I am sorry about your mother." It was, perhaps, a peace offering.

"Me too," she whispered.

Now, an hour past midnight, Nadya stood in the near-deserted streets of the city's second tier. Rats ran along the gutters, being chased by stray cats and hounds alike. A drunken pair of Erevan men lay slouched together against a charred brick wall. Nadya's nose twitched at the scent of their seaweed ale. In the distance, the smart clacking of a Cressian military unit echoed off the cobblestones of one of the tier's main thoroughfares. She had dodged her fair share of patrols on the way here; the mining tunnel had dumped out into the Nomori tier, not far from the city's prison. It had taken the better part of an hour for her to sneak up here to the place where she was taught control.

The dilapidated building was unassuming, just one of dozens that leaned over the streets of the second tier. Rotting boards covered the door and the second-floor windows. Bits of foggy glass littered the abandoned storefront. It looked like no one had set foot here since the Blood Sun Solstice.

Nadya stood before it. She and her father had spent countless mornings here sparring as he taught her to control her strength, maintaining contact with his daughter against the will of the family matriarch.

Against the will of her mother.

Her chest ached with a veritable Great Storm of emotions, and Nadya couldn't parse out any singular thought or feeling. It numbed her, the cacophony of sentiments that welled up inside her, and Nadya clung to that numbness. It was the only thing keeping her on her feet.

Taking a deep breath of the tier's piss-scented air, Nadya pulled open the door's hidden latch and stepped inside.

She had scarcely crossed the threshold into the safe house when she was enveloped in a strong embrace. She breathed in the familiar scent of sea air and leather that she knew so well.

"Papa," she whispered.

Shadar Gabori released his grip and looked down at her. In the ten months since she had seen her father, age had taken him. More gray dusted his temples, but the lines that now creased his forehead and around his eyes did little to impede his sad smile.

"Nadya," he said, running his hand along her cheek. "I have missed you."

"I missed you too, Papa."

It was strange to see her father out of the crimson uniform of the Duke's Guard. In his plain brown tunic and black trousers, he could have been mistaken for any of the Nomori laborers who worked the mines, save for the familiar rapier hanging from his belt.

"There is so much I want to ask you, so much to tell you, but there will be time for that later. I am glad you came." He looked toward the stairs, and reluctantly, Nadya's gaze followed. The distance stretched out before her, dizzying.

"What does she want?"

She had not realized she said it aloud until Shadar answered, "To see you. Anything else is between your mother, you, and the

Protectress." He put a hand on her shoulder. "This is your choice, Nadya. I sent the message so that you would be able to make it."

Her feet didn't move.

"What do you want to do?"

She didn't know, and it froze her limbs, numbed her thoughts. *I want things to be like they once were, before Mama found out about my* nivasi *blood, before Gedeon and the Blood Sun Solstice.*

But such a fantasy meant going back to a time she did not have Shay by her side, and that thought turned her stomach.

"Come with me?" she finally said, unable to hide the uncertainty in her voice.

Shadar squeezed her shoulder. "Of course. I'll be right behind you."

The creaking stars that led to the second story, once the living quarters of its long-missing proprietor, suddenly seemed all too short as Nadya ascended to the top before she had gathered her thoughts.

It was much like she remembered: a large open space ideal for sparring. She noted dents in the plastered walls she had slammed into after taking a particularly bad hit. If she closed her eyes, she could almost picture the row of practice rapiers hanging on rusted hooks and the bark of her father, "Do it again, Nadya!"

"Go ahead." Behind her, Shadar's voice was now soft.

Nadya took a deep breath that failed to calm that storm in her chest and did so.

Mirela Gabori lay on a pallet in the center of the room. Above her, the stars shone down through a rough-edged hole. A single candle burned in the corner, illuminating the left side of Mirela's face. Her cheeks were sunken, her lips dry and cracked. Nadya's eyes traced down her bony shoulder to where her chest struggled to rise and fall. Each breath echoed throughout the silent room, a battle for her diseased lungs to take in enough air to put off the inevitable for one more moment.

Bile rose in Nadya's throat, and if it hadn't been for the solid presence of her father at her back, she would have turned tail and run.

Mirela was not alone. Drina Gabori, former matriarch of the Gabori family, knelt beside her daughter. Strands of hair escaped her silver braid, and her simple plum tunic bore the wrinkles of several sleepless nights. She dabbed a damp cloth against Mirela's brow, muttering a prayer in ancient Nomori.

"Nadya?" Mirela's voice grated as if pulled through metal teeth. "Nadya, is that you?"

Drina stood. "Yes, your daughter is here." Even in the dim light, her eyes shone sharply. Nadya had never seen warmth in them before, and she didn't now. She had also never seen tears, but Drina's red-rimmed eyes glimmered at the edges with moisture.

Nadya took one small step forward. "Hello, Mama."

"Nadya." Mirela tried to sit up, triggering a coughing fit. Her shoulders heaved as she hacked into a handkerchief that Drina held out. Nadya smelled blood before her mother's cough subsided.

"Do not strain yourself," Drina chastised. "You need your strength."

"I have no strength left. The stars are calling to me. It will be soon."

"Nonsense," her grandmother said, but Nadya heard the lie in her quickened heartbeat.

"Mama," Mirela said to Drina. She raised her arm with what looked like an enormous effort and brushed her fingers along Drina's cheek. "I am not afraid." She coughed again. "But I would like to speak to Nadezhda alone."

Nadya's heart lurched. She hoped her grandmother would object, but Drina only bowed her head in acceptance.

"Very well. Come, Shadar, help me downstairs."

Her father gave Nadya an encouraging smile before offering his arm to Drina and then guiding her down to the first floor.

Except for the rats that skittered inside the walls, Nadya and her mother were alone.

"You asked for me?" Nadya said, proud of the steadiness in her voice.

Her mother nodded weakly. "I did. I wished to see you once more."

"Even though..." Nadya's voice caught. "Even though I'm *nivasi*?"

Mirela glanced away. Her gaze lingered upon the gap in the roof where the stars of the witching hour glimmered. "With each breath, I move closer to our Protectress, and she has shown me how foolish I was to let fear rule my heart. She has forgiven me, I know, but I would like to ask for your forgiveness as well, Nadya."

Nadya's mouth opened, but no sound escaped. Her mother lay upon her deathbed, begging her for forgiveness. Instead of peace, however, Nadya felt as though a great weight pressed against her chest. "Mama, why?" The words tumbled out of her in a rush of emotion that she had been avoiding these past ten months. "Why did you do it? Why did you cast me away?"

Mirela looked up at her, shame etched across her gaunt features. "You will not like the answer, Nadya."

"I need it."

"Very well." She sighed. "I feared what you might become."

Nadya's breath caught in her throat. *Did you expect anything different?* she told herself, even as the first tear slid down her face.

"The *nivasi* and the zealot had unleashed chaos upon the city. Rumors of a slaughter during the Duke's speech, perpetrated by another *nivasi* with incredible strength, had made its way down to the Nomori tier. I fled the house for my life in the midst of this, and I grabbed ahold of your seal..."

Nadya touched her upper arm, where the metal band sat underneath her clothes. It wrapped around her arm, and its surface held the imprint of a five-petaled flower. The seal of the Protectress.

"I felt your power, Nadya. I felt the lives that Gedeon had

crushed through you. Not of your own volition. I understood that. Even when you came to the house several months after, at the behest of your father." Mirela shook her head. "I never did deserve him, but at least you had the father you deserved. He tried to reconcile us, but I resisted. When you came to the house—"

"You said it was because of Gedeon. Because of what he made me do. Because of how I killed him."

"I lied." Her mother coughed again, and the shallow cough soon turned into a deep hack that wracked her entire body.

Nadya acted automatically. She fell to her knees and braced her mother's shoulders as she had done so many times before. Mirela did not flinch away from her touch, despite knowing what her hands were capable of. They rode out the coughing fit together.

Her mother grasped her hands when she moved to pull away after the coughs had faded to deep, ragged breaths. Nadya hated how cold and thin Mirela's fingers felt against her own.

"I lied because it was easier to blame what you had been made to do by Gedeon. What you had been made to do to him."

Nadya looked down at their entwined hands. She vividly remembered the sensation of tearing Gedeon's head from his body after she had fought her way out of his control. It wasn't that she regretted her choice to kill him; he had needed to be stopped before he could get ahold of her or anyone else again. But it marked the first time she had purposefully killed someone, and that choice took something away from her that she would never be able to get back.

"In truth, I saw you overcome Gedeon. For all his power, you defeated him. You tore his head from his body."

Those blunt words stabbed Nadya in the chest, and she wished that she had Shay's steady presence at her back. She made to withdraw her hand, but Mirela held tightly, her strength surprising given the shallow breaths she took.

"It frightened me, that the woman I once swaddled as a babe

had that kind of power, that kind of cold-bloodedness in her." Nadya looked away, her face burning, but Mirela continued, "I was so wrong. What my own fear, my cowardice, took for ruthlessness, was actually loyalty. A drive to protect your home. Though this city has never been deserving of such devotion from you.

"Despite everything our people—everything I—had done to you, you risked your life and your freedom to save us." Mirela blinked as slow tears escaped her. "My shame knows no bounds, Nadya. For not believing in your goodness. In this." She raised shaking fingers to brush over Nadya's chest. "And now we need you once more. Whether the Cressian weapon is *nivasi* or not, we need you to protect our city. And you came back."

Nadya could barely speak through the emotion that choked her throat, but she needed to hear one more answer. "How can you trust me?"

Mirela's eyes gleamed with tears as she ran her thumb across Nadya's knuckles. "Because I choose to. Because you are my daughter. Because your father and I raised you, and I lost sight of that. Your blood may be *nivasi*, but it is also Gabori."

"I—" Nadya's voice caught in her throat. Carefully, she covered her mother's hands in her own. "I forgive you, Mama. I always did."

Silence stretched between, but it was a comforting, warm stillness that draped over them like a woven blanket. Only Mirela's harsh coughs and the reality of the life that struggled for breath within her mother's body broke the moment.

"She needs me, damn it! Let me pass."

Nadya did not dare believe her ears as she and her mother looked toward the stairwell. After a bit more familiar cursing, a tall figure sprinted up the dark steps. Nadya's heart leapt in her chest, lifting a weight she hadn't realized was there.

Shay slowed to a stop before Mirela's pallet, shyly saying, "Nadya, Mistress Gabori. I—I am here."

Nadya rose. She walked over to where Shay lingered awkwardly and wrapped her in a tight embrace. "Thank you, *Natsia*," she whispered.

"Who is this?" Mirela asked, eyes suddenly mischievous as she looked Shay over.

Shay edged backward, but Nadya reached out and took her hand. Shay's strong pulse underneath her fingertips grounded her. "This is Shay."

"Shay…" If Mirela remembered the young girl from the Rissalo family who was supposedly killed for her *nivasi* gift of fire, she did not let on.

"Yes, Mistress Gabori."

Nadya could not help her smile. She had never heard such formality from Shay before, but the woman beside her trembled with nerves.

Mirela's small laugh led to a deep, hacking cough. She wiped her chin. "I carry no title, Shay. You are a good friend to Nadya to come for this."

A friend. That word bit deep, and before she had thought better of it, Nadya shook her head.

"She's more than a friend, Mama. She is—" Nadya hesitated. Her heart drummed against her rib cage. She recalled an afternoon over a year ago, curling up against her mother on the pallet, confessing her affection for Kesali. Mirela's acceptance had been a surprise then, but now Nadya grabbed ahold of the memory and plunged forward. "She is my partner, my…" There was no good word in Nomori or Erevo to describe their union. So Nadya simply settled on, "I love her."

Shay's hand went rigid in her grip.

A slow smile grew across Mirela's face. "I am happy for you," she said hoarsely. "Both of you." She reached out a trembling hand to Shay.

Shay glanced at Nadya, eyes wide, before cautiously taking the outstretched hand.

"I am grateful I had a chance to meet you, Shay. Take care of my Nadya."

"Of—of course."

❖

Overhead, the clouds drifted between stars, casting faint shadows upon the near-dark room. Hours passed, and Mirela's breath grew more and more labored. Nadya knelt next to her. She heard the faint rattle of her mother's chest, and if Shay had not been kneeling beside her, a firm hand on her shoulder, Nadya was sure she would have collapsed. Her family had joined them in the vigil soon after Shay's arrival. Shadar knelt on Mirela's other side, clutching her hand, and Drina sat at her feet. Ancient Nomori prayers poured from her mouth. They created a strange melody that masked the harshness of Mirela's breath.

If Drina or Shadar noticed the way Shay held Nadya's shoulders, absentmindedly running her fingers through Nadya's braid, neither gave any indication.

An hour before dawn, Mirela took her final breath. It was soft and easy, and with a comforting smile, she slipped away from the world.

Nadya felt her heart tear itself in two as the tears that she had held back flowed silently from her eyes. A hand clasped hers, and she looked up to see her father, his eyes shining in grief. "In you, she will carry on," he whispered.

A proper send off for a Nomori matriarch would have included a somber ceremony with steady drums and the chanting of the Elders. Mirela was no matriarch, not after passing over the title, and the invasion of Wintercress had sent the Elders into hiding. Perhaps one day, she might get the death rites she deserved.

Nadya stood. Suddenly, she couldn't be in the room any longer with the ghost of her mother so close at hand. She stalked out without a word to anyone, even Shay. Behind her, she heard her grandmother whisper, "Let her go, Shadar."

Down the stairs, out the door, and running into the night. Nadya sprinted past the rundown buildings of the once-vibrant tier. She did not care if a Cressian patrol saw her as she scrambled up the face of a boarded-up bakery and ascended its rooftop. With a running leap, she flew through the air and landed on the next rooftop over. Again and again, Nadya soared across the rooftops of the second tier like the Phoenix whose name she had taken. The wind dried her tears and carried her mind back to a simpler time when she had run like this every night.

Finally, her legs buckled beneath her and she crashed into a pile of rubble that littered a roof. Nadya ignored the ripe smells that came from the refuse. She drew her knees up to her chest and rocked back and forth, unable to cry any more tears.

Time passed. She wasn't sure how much; she only knew that after a while, she was no longer alone.

Shay stood behind her. Her breath came heavily, but instead of berating Nadya for taking off and leaving her behind, Shay said nothing and knelt beside her, wrapping her arms around Nadya's shivering shoulders.

An hour passed without a word between them. Nadya's frantic heart was lulled into peace by the steady presence of her partner. Finally, when the first rays of morning sun had fully crested the remains of the great wall, Nadya spoke. "You stayed," she said simply.

Shay pressed her face against Nadya's neck, winding her arms around Nadya's chest. "Of course I did."

Nadya felt the steady rhythm of Shay's heart against her back. It drove off the darkness that threatened to consume her, as it always had. "We should go."

"Sure you can stand to leave the view?"

She cuffed Shay's arm lightly, and she returned it with a peck on Nadya's cheek. Together, they found their way down off the roof. Before they could leave the alleyway, however, they were met with a familiar sharp gaze.

Drina stood at the mouth of the alley. Her eyes shone with tears, but her voice was strong and steady. "Nadezhda, I need to speak with you."

"Can't it wait?"

It was Shay who spoke with unconcealed anger. Nadya felt the air grow slightly warmer as her partner spoke, but she was too surprised by Shay's vehemence to say anything.

"You're always appearing out of nowhere, giving awful advice, and expecting Nadya to bend to your whims." Shay crossed her arms. "Have a damned heart and give her a bit of peace. She just lost her mother."

Nadya grabbed Shay's hand, the heat behind her skin near scorching; to Nadya, it was a welcome anchor. Shay's pulse relaxed under her fingertips as Nadya ran a thumb over Shay's knuckles.

"And I just lost my daughter."

The quaver in Drina's voice as she uttered the final word broke through the walls that Nadya had managed to erect, and tears burned at the corner of her eyes. Every child expected to send their parents off to the stars; such knowledge rarely made the passing of a mother or father any easier. A parent, however, should never have to send their child to the Protectress, and Nadya's already broken heart cracked a little further at the thought of the pain her grandmother now bore.

Drina said, "I wish I could have given her all the rites due a Nomori woman, but we find ourselves in a chaotic time, and so we must have faith that the Protectress cares for those who leave this world." Her bony fingers stroked the seal at her throat. "We will mourn properly when the time comes, but there is much to attend to now."

Nadya swallowed the lump that had hardened in her throat. "What do you want of me, Grandmother?"

"The creature that brought the walls down. Until it is overcome, our city will never be reclaimed." Drina spoke in the commanding tone Nadya had heard her use to cow the Duke and his son at their council meetings. "You must do this."

"That woman nearly killed her. Nearly killed both of us," Shay said. "How do you expect us to go up against a Cressian *nivasi* when we don't even know how she exists?"

"I suggest you start by finding out just that," Drina said dryly.

Nadya knew her grandmother did not trust Shay; she had warned Nadya away from the other *nivasi* woman. She wasn't sure if she trusted her grandmother, but her words rang with the wisdom of an Elder, and Nadya listened. "What do you mean?"

"There is someone you know whose knowledge of the Nomori and the *nivasi* that come from us surpasses even that of the Elders." Her upper lip twisted in disgust even as she admitted it. "Someone who might have valuable knowledge that could defeat the Cressian *nivasi*."

Nadya's eyes widened. "You cannot mean—"

"In times of war," Drina said, "sometimes we must put aside our own prejudices for a greater good."

"It's hardly a prejudice, not after what he did," Nadya argued, but with a sinking feeling in her stomach, she realized her grandmother was right.

"I do not disagree with you, child, but we cannot be particular when it comes to our allies, not now." She cast a glance toward Shay. "Not even I can afford that pleasure."

"What are you talking about? Nadya, who is this person?" Shay asked, ignoring the irritated look that Drina leveled at her.

Nadya swallowed. She turned, angling her chin up to meet her partner's gaze. "You really don't want to know, Shay. Believe me. You do not want to know."

Chapter Eight

Waking up next to Shay in the cramped cot they had been assigned in the rough-hewn bunkhouse brought a sense of peace to Nadya she was surprised she was still capable of feeling. If not for the invaders above who had stolen away her home, Nadya thought she might be able to stay like this forever, watching the soft rise and fall of Shay's chest as she slumbered. It was impossible, of course; she had a mission, as much as she might dread it.

Shay argued vehemently against Nadya going alone when she awoke. "You are being an idiot, Nadya. You aren't invulnerable, and they have who knows how many traps and weapons lying in wait. Do you remember the last time you broke into a Cressian stronghold?"

Nadya winced. She did. Her throat tickled from the memory of the suffocating poisonous gas she had triggered. If not for Shay, she would have died in that room. "This is different. I know the prison. I've broken in to it before. Two of us will draw more attention than is wise."

After another few minutes of arguing, Shay let out an overly dramatic sigh and agreed. Nadya knew the theatrics hid actual worry, so she kissed Shay and whispered, "I'll be fine."

"You had better," was the answer.

❖

Seeking out Marko—she could not bring herself to think of him as Duke Isyanov quite yet—was not something Nadya wished to be doing, but she found herself nonetheless wandering through the makeshift shanties of the cavern and listening for the familiar Erevan accent. She did not want to force her presence upon him, not when he was still so uncertain about her identity as the Phoenix. But she did not trust anyone else here enough to ask, and after the argument between her and Shay, she couldn't quite face Kesali.

Fate seemed to have a cruel sense of humor that morning, as the Stormspeaker was the sole occupant of the Bulwark. Nadya stood in the doorway and tried to sort out her thoughts.

"Are you going to stand there all day frozen like a hunted hare?" Kesali looked up at her and smiled. "Come in, Nadya. Want do you need?"

Straight to business it was, then. It certainly made it easier to get her thoughts in order as Nadya walked up to the table that Kesali leaned over. She couldn't make heads or tails of the myriad of charts and sketches that littered it, but Kesali's intense concentration reminded her of a general directing battle movements.

Perhaps the comparison wasn't that far off.

"I was looking for Marko, actually. I have a favor to ask of him," Nadya said.

Kesali drew in a breath. "I—I do not think he will be up for granting you favors for a while, Nadya."

"You knew? That he found out about me being…" Nadya pitched her voice lower. "About the Phoenix?"

"I suspected for a while, but there was too much to do. Too much at stake for us both to be distracted by it," Kesali said without looking up. "We never really discussed it, not until you two showed up at the…execution."

"He's avoiding me, isn't he?" Nadya asked, but she already knew the answer.

Kesali sighed. "He is taking time to come to terms with it. Don't try to hurry him."

"Wasn't planning to. I just—" She hesitated. She deserved any anger or fear Marko harbored toward her. Knowing that did not stop the empty ache in her chest. "I just want to stop losing people."

Kesali put a hand on her arm, and Nadya drew in a slow breath, separating the sweetness of Kesali's scent from the sweat and metallic tinge of the cavern air. It lifted old memories to the surface of her mind: she and Kesali dancing in the Nomori square, standing upon the great wall and surveying the damage of the Blood Sun Solstice, falling into Kesali's bed together in the palace...

And other memories. Shay's blades of light twirling through the air the first night they fought. Shay burning the poison gas out of her lungs in the tower of Eagle's Reach. Shay appearing in the palace throne room, saving the city. Shay holding her shoulders at her mother's deathbed as she wept...

"I can't," Nadya whispered. She pulled her arm back.

Kesali looked like she had been struck. "I—I am sorry, Nadya. I intended nothing. I just, with your mother's death...I am sorry."

"I know." Nadya cleared her throat. "It was never meant to be. Us, I mean."

"Are you saddened or relieved?" Kesali asked. Her fingers found the tip of her braid, and she fiddled with it as she looked at Nadya for an answer.

Nadya considered the question. For so long, she had thought her impossible happily ever after would be with Kesali, owning a tiny house in one of the cramped streets of the Nomori tier, and waking up to her best friend by her side each morning.

She had truly loved Kesali, and she still did. But that love had turned from fiery romantic passion to the softer affection of friendship.

"I am happy for us," she said finally, and Kesali's brow rose in confusion. Nadya shook her head. "Not in that way. I just mean, we are where we are supposed to be." She swept a hand over the Bulwark. "This is where you belong, Kesali. You have the strength to bring these people out of the darkness, to resist Wintercress and win."

"You are far stronger than I."

"Not like that. I cannot lead anyone, not the way you and Marko can." Nadya smiled, and it was genuine. "I see the way you are with these people, with this cause. No one cares more than you. I am happy you found your calling, and I am grateful to call you friend."

Kesali flipped her braid over her shoulder. "I am as well. And I'm happy that you have found someone, even if she isn't what I expected."

Nadya laughed. "Shay does take a bit of getting used to, but I am happy with her."

"Do you think you will remain together? Even with..." Kesali's voice trailed off, but Nadya nodded.

Even with you choosing to stay and fight for your city? Even with all that separates the two of you?

"I hope so," she said honestly.

Kesali nodded, and after a moment, she too smiled. "I don't think either of us could have ever pictured this—me married to Marko, leading a resistance to retake Storm's Quarry from invaders, and you, you wearing the mantle of the Phoenix alongside another *nivasi*."

"No, I don't think so either." So much had happened in the past two years, so many horrible things intertwined with a few precious moments of light. Nadya sobered, dropping her grin. There was much darkness ahead of them. Wintercress had power they could not have ever imagined, and she had no idea how to combat it.

"I need to access the prison," she said abruptly.

"I figured you were not here for idle chatter." Kesali led the way out of the Bulwark and pointed to the northern edge of the cavern, where a slim, dark opening could be seen. "That tunnel takes you to the entrance of Miner's Tunnel. The prison isn't far, but it will be heavily patrolled. Do I want to know why you're going there?"

Nadya shook her head. "No, you don't, believe me. I'll be careful," she promised.

Kesali grasped her hand then let go, a gesture of friendship and nothing more. "I will hold you to that. The last thing I want to do is explain to Shay how you came to be captured by Cressian forces."

She imagined Shay's fiery reaction and winced. "Noted. You won't have to worry about me."

❖

Nadya practically sprinted through the narrow mining tunnel. Traveling at such speed meant occasionally bashing into a wall when the tunnel curved sharply, but bruises that instantly faded and a faceful of rock dust were far preferable to spending an extra moment in the claustrophobic passage. The air twisted in her lungs, choking her, as she recited the mantras her father had taught her in an effort to remain focused. After what seemed an eternity, she smelled fresh sea air and slowed.

Two shadows moved against the faint light of the tunnel's exit. Their soft voices, too low at this distance for even Nadya to make out the words, carried the unmistakable purr of Cressian.

Stepping back, she secured her cloak and pulled the hood of the Iron Phoenix over her head. Her breastplate shone like new in the small stream of moonlight that reached her. Nadya had only taken a few moments after speaking with Kesali to prepare before entering the tunnel, having retrieved the guise of the Phoenix from the secure trunk Kesali had left in her bunk.

Time to get to work, she thought and sprinted forward.

Neither soldier had time to loose a cry before Nadya was

upon them. Her fist connected with the iron breastplate of the first, denting it and throwing him to the ground. In the same movement, she swept her foot into the other soldier, slamming him into the rocky face of the carved tunnel.

Nothing but unconscious groans marred the quiet of the night. Nadya surveyed the area. The squat marble prison stood silent in the shadow of the upper tiers. Its high iron fence had been torn down, and she saw several white uniforms patrolling its perimeter.

She bit her lip. Killing in cold blood had never been something she did. Had Shay been there, the other *nivasi* would have had no trouble permanently silencing the soldiers. *They're the enemy, Nadya,* she imagined Shay saying. *They will show you no mercy, so show none in return. Kindness on the battlefield is weakness, and we are at war.*

She lifted her foot. Her boot hovered over the chest of the taller of the soldiers. It would be painless; she could snap his neck before he even awoke.

"No," she whispered, stepping back.

She imagined Shay rolling her eyes, but Nadya shook it off and ran off down the road.

The prison of Storm's Quarry stood alone, an odd sight for the crowded city, where buildings leaned into their neighbors until entire blocks became inseparable units. Built of the same glowing white marble as the outer wall, its thick facade challenged the world to stay out, and in Nadya's memory, no one had ever broken out of the prison.

Breaking in was another matter entirely.

It took her less than ten minutes, three more unconscious Cressian soldiers, and a few bars pried off one of the upper windows. Nadya padded silently along the dark corridors. Her skin prickled with the eerie silence that permeated the prison. Her unrest only grew as she turned down another cell block and heard a singular heartbeat coming from the last cell on the left. Slowly, she crept forward, stopping in front of the barred door.

Nadya's gaze fell on the figure on the cot, and she bit back a wave of revulsion that nearly sent her scurrying back down the hall. Lying perfectly straight, hands clasped on his chest, Levka Puyatin, former magistrate to the Duke, looked more like a statue than a man. More than a year behind bars had taken some of the smugness from his appearance. His cheeks carried a gauntness that Nadya didn't remember, and his hands were roped with scars, no doubt from the labor that long-term prisoners used to pay off their sentences.

Levka had been charged for every death on the Blood Sun Solstice, and knowing that he could work until his bones turned to dust before disbursing his sentence gave Nadya the small boost of satisfaction she needed to grab the cell door and wrench it open. Iron pins snapped in half, falling to the ground.

She paused, listening to tell if additional Cressian troops had entered the prison, but she heard nothing but the snores and mutters of other prisoners.

"Who?" Levka shot upward. His eyes widened when he saw the cloaked figure standing before him, wearing the unmistakable guise of the Iron Phoenix.

Nadya expected a scream. Or begging. The last time she saw him, Nadya had been holding Levka aloft by his throat, nearly strangling him before her father and the Duke's Guard had shown up.

But the former magistrate stared for a moment and then gave her a gesture of welcome as if she had knocked on the door of his manor and not torn down the bars of his prison cell. In near-flawless Nomori he said, "To what do I owe this pleasure, Nadezhda?"

"Levka," she managed finally. She leaned the broken door against a nearby wall and stepped into the cell. "You look horrible."

"On the contrary, I feel wonderful." Levka stretched. "Fresh air and exercise have done wonders for my physique. And I've had so much time to devote to my studies."

Nadya glanced around. The cell contained only a cot, a bucket for waste, and a tray that sat upon the ground holding only a dented tin cup. No books to speak of. She smiled.

"Prison suiting you well, then?"

"Better in here than out there, if our sudden change of guard is anything to judge by." Levka shrugged. "Storm's Quarry, Wintercress. Who carries the keys makes little difference here."

His heartbeat picked up as he uttered the final sentence, and Nadya wondered why he would lie about such a thing. To throw her off balance? So far, the former magistrate was doing an excellent job.

"So, what brings you here, and in the regalia of the Iron Phoenix, no less? I'm guessing this isn't a social call."

She started to speak, but Levka waved a hand. "Please, Nadezhda, take off that hood. Such machinations of secrecy are moot, are they not?"

She groaned but complied. He was right, after all. He was the first person, unknown to her at the time, to learn of her *nivasi* gift. She had been fifteen at the time, and his monstrous older brother had preyed upon who he thought was a defenseless Nomori girl. Instead, she had accidentally snapped his spine while defending herself, and Levka had witnessed the entire thing.

"That's far better, don't you think?" Levka said.

Nadya ignored him. "Tell me what you know of *nivasi*."

Levka laughed, and she silenced the urge to throw the dented cup at him. "So that's why you stole into the city prison in the dead of night. Why ask me? You have the personal experience. Not to mention, don't your people pride themselves on their histories? Ask one of the ancient women who sit by that disgusting fountain." He smiled and waited.

"You've done research," she said, hating the way he had taken charge of the conversation. "You were a magistrate. You had access to records and books the Elders never did."

"Maybe I did. That life is far beyond me now."

"It was your life's work," she said, remembering with a

slight shiver the way had he spoken about *nivasi*. The pure anger, the hatred in his words—*I always knew you were a killer*—still twisted her stomach. "Don't try to tell me that a year in this place has wiped it from your memory."

"Of course not," Levka said. "I'm telling you that I have no interest in aiding you. Now, run along before Cressian soldiers appear, and I get caught in whatever scuffle you're sure to incite."

She had not expected it to be easy to get the information from him. Nadya stepped forward. "You will tell me," she said in a low growl, "or—"

"Or what?" Levka laughed again, but this time, it sounded hollow. "You'll kill me?"

"You have no idea what I'm capable of."

"On the contrary, rumors of the Iron Phoenix's exploits have made it down here. I've heard the guardsmen gossiping about the daring escapades of the Phoenix and..." He paused, pretending thought. "The Shadow Dragon, was it? Tell me, how is Shay these days?"

In three steps she had crossed the cell and shoved a hand into Levka's chest, forcing his back against the wall. "What do you know of her?"

"As you said, I've done my research. *Nivasi* have been appearing with more frequency among the Nomori, but they are still extremely rare. More than a decade ago, a young girl was killed for being able to call flames into her hands. Years later, a grown woman appears who can conjure blades of fire. Too coincidental to be separate *nivasi*. Relax, I haven't spoken of her to anyone."

Her grip didn't lessen. "I do not believe you."

"If I had wished to divulge either of your identities, I would have. But doing so would have given the monstrous Phoenix and Dragon enough humanity to make *nivasi* seem safe, acceptable to trust. Not something I want."

Was he speaking the truth? Nadya hadn't been listening to his heartbeat, as her own thundered in her ears. She had considered over the past months that Levka could have revealed her identity, but when no regiment of the Duke's Guard had shown up at her doorstep in the weeks after the Blood Sun Solstice, the worry had faded.

"If you're trying to threaten me, or her, I swear—"

He coughed. "If you are going to kill me, then do it. If not, stop manhandling me like a common bull."

Surprised by his cavalier tone, Nadya released him. "You shouldn't taunt me like that, you know."

He smiled once again, but it was more of a grimace. "I do not fear you, Nadezhda. What can you do to me that hasn't already been done?" Levka threw his arms wide. "I am a prisoner in an occupied city. How long do you think it will be before Wintercress decides to cleanse this place? Death by your hand might be preferable to what they would do. Any threat you make is nothing against the reality I face. If you intended to pry answers out of me with pain, then you should just turn around and leave."

Nadya stepped back. The raw anger in Levka's voice surprised her. "I wasn't going to torture you, if that's what you thought."

"Then go. I have nothing to say to you, Nadezhda." He sat back upon the bed without looking at her.

She felt her own temper rise in her chest. "How can you say that?"

"Were you harboring the impression that I liked you in some way? I wanted to see you destroyed. Still do," Levka said, glancing at her, unfettered hatred gleaming in his eyes.

"I don't care about that." She walked up to him, standing right in front of his knees, but Levka did not flinch. "This is your fault. You egged Gedeon on. You delivered gunpowder to the zealot, who blew a hole in the wall. Wintercress wouldn't be here if not for your selfish schemes. Don't you feel even the least bit of shame?"

Levka stood suddenly. Nadya resisted the urge to fling

herself backward. They stood toe to toe. The former magistrate was over a head taller than her, and he glared down at her with venom in his eyes.

"Do you think I wanted this? I strove to cleanse Storm's Quarry of filth like you, of *nivasi*, and then Nomori, to prevent them from birthing more monsters within the city's walls." His voice faded to a hoarse whisper. "If you had asked me a year ago if any price was too high for the extermination of *nivasi*, I would have declared a resounding no."

"And now?" Nadya asked, matching his low tone.

Levka was silent for a long moment. His eyes roved over her face, as if searching for any crack that might give him an edge. Finally, he sighed. "Now I wish for my city to be free. I fought for Storm's Quarry when I allied with the zealot, and however reluctantly, the Chaos-maker. I never intended to incite war with another nation."

Regret poured out of his words, and Nadya fought back an urge to put a hand on his shoulder. This was Levka Puyatin, a man responsible for untold death and the current invasion of Storm's Quarry. She did not pity him—she did not.

"The Cressians have a *nivasi*," she said suddenly.

"What? One of your kind is helping them?"

"No, not like that. The woman is Cressian, but she has the power of a *nivasi*." Nadya's sides ached in memory of slamming into stone. "More power than me. Or Shay."

"How?" Levka collapsed back onto the cot. His brow wrinkled. "*Nivasi* are unique to the Nomori people. There has never been any record of another race producing a person with that kind of power."

After considering it for a moment, Nadya sat on the floor of the cell, cross-legged. She kept an ear out for any stir of Cressian soldiers, but for now, they were undetected.

"That would explain the quick takeover of the city…" Levka continued, as if speaking more to himself than her. "After all, our

Guard had the upper hand, and repairs had been made upon the wall. It would have taken countless lives to overwhelm the main gate, and there is no other entrance to the city."

"She can move the earth at will," Nadya supplied. "The main gate is gone, half the wall as well."

"Impossible," Levka whispered, but there was no disbelief in his tone. He looked at Nadya. "This is why you're here?"

She nodded. "I spoke with a Nomori Elder, and she had no knowledge of such a possibility. You have done extensive research into the *nivasi*, and I thought you might have come across something." She paused, considering. It might be foolhardy to reveal anything of the resistance; Levka could turn around and tell his Cressian captors. But without his help, she reminded herself, they might never see Storm's Quarry freed. "There is a resistance," she began.

Levka straightened. "The Duke's son?"

"Alive. And his wife," Nadya added, and disgust flashed across Levka's face. "Like it or not, the Nomori are part of this city, and they are dedicated to seeing Wintercress driven out."

He inclined his head, but his expression didn't change. "You said there was a resistance? How is it avoiding Cressian attention?"

Last hope or not, Nadya was not going to tell him of the cavern in the mines. "With careful planning. They are gathering forces, and with enough support, they will be able to strike in the coming weeks. But…"

Realization dawned upon the former magistrate. "If this so-called Cressian *nivasi* still lives, no resistance will be strong enough to take back the city. Not even with two *nivasi* on its side."

"Exactly." Nadya drew in a deep breath. "If you have any sense of loyalty to Storm's Quarry left, you will help us."

Levka rose. "My loyalty to the city was never in doubt. Only my methods in ensuring its safety." He gestured to the broken door. "Take me to the resistance, and I will aid you."

Nadya stared at him, uncertainty rising in her chest like a plume of smoke. "You will?"

"I see—you don't trust me. Hard to blame you, really. I can only offer my honesty when I say that I mean the resistance no harm, and I will do what I can to defeat Wintercress." He waited expectantly.

She had listened carefully to his heartbeat, and it remained strong and consistent as he spoke. Still, she hesitated. He knew of her ability to measure truth by listening to a person's heart, and Levka was devious enough to know of a way to manipulate it.

"Do you have another expert on the *nivasi?*" he asked, as if reading her thoughts.

"Tell me what you know now."

Levka shook his head. "That is not my offer, dear Nadezhda. I want to speak to the Duke's son and learn the machinations of the resistance. Only then will I share what I know."

Damn you, she thought, but nodded. "Fine. But I'm keeping an eye on you at all times."

"I expected no less. Now come, before the Cressians wake up from the naps you put them down to." Levka stepped forward, but Nadya held up a hand.

"Not so quickly. I have one provision of my own." Without waiting for him to reply, she walked to the cot and tore a strip of linen from its thin mattress. She held it up with a smile.

Levka looked from her to the cloth and back to her once more. "Really, Nadezhda, is that entirely necessary?"

"Oh yes, it is," Nadya said, a small smile touching her lips. "It is entirely necessary."

CHAPTER NINE

The commotion reached Shay's ears as she sat on her cot in the makeshift bunkhouse, finishing the final polish of her leather breastplate. Thinner and more supple than Nadya's, it fit her like a second skin, and she cared for it with a devotion imparted by Jeta. Oiling it had become a bit of a nightly ritual for her, done to calm her thoughts before she went to sleep.

When the shouting grew louder, unmistakably the voices of Marko, Kesali, and Nadya, she sighed and set her breastplate back in the trunk that Kesali had provided for their armor. She hadn't been the only person to notice the tumult, as several guardsmen and workers sent curious glances toward the Bulwark when she emerged from the barracks. She was, however, the only one foolish enough to approach the shouting royals within.

Five people stood in the Bulwark, their loud voices making the room seem a lot smaller than it was. Marko's face was nearly as red as his hair, and beside him Kesali's dark eyes flashed dangerously.

Nadya stood opposite them, in front of a blindfolded Erevan man Shay did not recognize. Whoever he was, he had certainly caused quite a fuss.

Nadya's father was also there, dark circles hugging his eyes. He had been weeping, but Shay could hardly begrudge him that. His wife, his partner, had died, and yet here he stood in the midst of headquarters, ready for orders. If something ever happened to

Nadya, she doubted she would be approachable for months, and they had only been together a year.

Shadar Gabori caught her eye, and he frowned. Shay swallowed thickly. *He might have had the respect to ignore the two of us on his wife's deathbed, but he won't let it go forever.* She found a very interesting crack in the floor to examine.

The Nomori discouraged relationships like theirs, to say the least. In the Nomori culture, women grew up to lead their families, choosing the best suited man to take his place as her husband. Other choices, other…preferences were simply unheard of. Shay was almost grateful for the war; it provided much needed distraction from Shay and Nadya's involvement.

"How could you even think of bringing him here?" Marko asked, his harsh tone cutting through Shay's thoughts and commanding her gaze. The young Duke held his rapier in a white-knuckled grip pointed at the blindfolded man.

"We need his help." Nadya stood in front of the stranger. "We need answers, and he's the only one who has them."

"At what risk? He is not one to be trusted, not after he betrayed us all."

"I know." Nadya's voice softened. "It is not your people whom he has attempted to destroy."

"What?" Shay asked, interrupting. "Who is this man?"

Kesali answered without looking at Shay, her glare fixed upon the mysterious Erevan. "This is Levka Puyatin. Former magistrate to the Duke and orchestrator of the Blood Sun Solstice."

Oh. Shay stared at the lanky man. He wore the spun clothes of a laborer but lacked the muscles of someone born into that life. Even bound and blindfolded as he was, his face carried a permanent smirk that oozed smugness.

"I do not like it at all." Marko hesitated for a moment. "Guardmaster?"

"I like it less than you, Your Grace. But in times of war, we must take any alliances, no matter how distasteful, offered to us."

"The risk to the Nomori," Kesali muttered. "I don't like it." Her eyes did not leave the former magistrate, and hatred burned behind her gaze.

Shay shrugged. "It will be all of us if we don't find a way to deal with the Cressian *nivasi*," she said.

Everyone turned to look at her. It was silent for a few moments, before Levka Puyatin laughed.

"I like her."

Shay rolled her eyes. "I couldn't care less if you liked running around the ramparts with your trousers down screaming about being a bird. You are going to help us defeat Wintercress, and so you can stay."

"That is not for you to decide," Shadar said, but Nadya reached out to her father.

"She's right, and she is the only one thinking clearly here. Shay and I cannot defeat the Cressian *nivasi*, not without help. Levka is a..." She paused, searching for the right words. "A murderous bastard who wants to see Storm's Quarry cleansed of Nomori, but he'll do anything to save it from outsiders. Including working with us." She turned back to the blindfolded man, the last statement a question to him.

Levka nodded. "Yes, yes, I'm a monster, none of you trust me. If I even so much as think about escaping or breathing in the general direction of the Prince, I will be drawn and quartered."

"More like burned to a crisp," Shay muttered.

"Whatever strikes your fancy. Now, get this horrid blindfold off me."

Marko sighed but gestured for Nadya to do so. Levka let out a few grunts of pain as she removed it.

"Good, thank you. It is nice to know that the royalty of Storm's Quarry hasn't lost all its civility," he said, rubbing the bridge of his nose. "Now, I believe I know where we might learn how a Cressian *nivasi* came to be."

Kesali gestured for him to continue. "We haven't got the time to bask in your genius. What do you know?"

"The High Cleric's scrolls mentioned ancient ruins off the coast of the western ocean, the Brine of Lazuli," Levka said. "They weren't identified as being ancient Nomori, but the doors bore an etching of a five-petaled flower."

"The Protectress," Nadya said quietly.

"Indeed. Physical temples are nearly unheard of for the Nomori, but it is in a place that would have been a waypoint for the ancient Nomori, who sailed the coasts and rivers. It is possible they built it for some purpose. Perhaps to house something of great import."

"So your entire plan rests on a perhaps," Marko said, frowning. "It's too risky."

"*Perhaps* there is nothing there, Your Grace." Levka shrugged. "Perhaps the Cressian who can move the earth with her mind is not *nivasi* after all. Perhaps Wintercress has devised an entirely different way of turning a person into a weapon."

Shay swallowed hard. The thought of a Cressian *nivasi* was hard to wrap her mind around, but the thought of that woman being something other than *nivasi*—that was worse. Far worse.

"You are suggesting sending our people into an enemy nation during a time of war in order to find a temple which may or may not be there, for answers that might not even exist." Marko shook his head. "It's a fool's errand. Unless you plan on offering yourself as a volunteer to take the journey, then we have nothing left to discuss."

Levka spread his hands. "Of course I am. You do not have anyone else with my training here. Do you, Your Grace? My expertise will be vital to the mission's success."

"Good. I'm sure you'll be quite able to survive the trip on your own," Kesali said. "It's one way to be rid of you."

"I doubt it, Stormspeaker," Levka said with his horribly smug leer, "as the Iron Phoenix will be coming with me."

❖

"Absolutely not."

Shay and Kesali objected at the same time, then glared at one another across the room. Nadya was too preoccupied with Levka's words to care. *Go with him?* She played through the possible scenarios. It was all too likely he'd try to get her killed somewhere along the way. Or that he was lying through his teeth about this entire thing.

The resistance could spare her, though. It had Shay if *nivasi* firepower was needed, and Nadya knew she would not survive another fight with the earthshaking Cressian woman who, despite all impossibilities, might carry the same blood as her.

Was there another choice? She instantly knew the answer. No, there wasn't. Not if Storm's Quarry was to be saved.

They could not defeat Wintercress without defeating this creature. And they could not do that without knowledge that Levka was convinced he knew how to obtain. Nadya did not trust him at all, but if he did try to double-cross her, Nadya could handle herself. *The enemy of my enemy...*

"I'll do it." Every eye turned to her. Nadya felt Shay's betrayed gaze more than any other. Her voice grew quieter, but she continued. "We need knowledge to defeat Wintercress's weapon. Without it, this resistance will fail. Storm's Quarry will fall."

"Then I am going with you," Shay said firmly. Her dark eyes glared around the room, daring argument.

"No," Levka said firmly. "One *nivasi* is more than enough trouble for me. I will not travel with two of you creatures."

Shay's hands flared orange, and the temperature in the Bulwark rose considerably. "You do not get a say, now do you? If Nadya goes, then I go."

"No, he's right." Shadar shook his head. "Two will slip into Wintercress more easily than three. Besides, we need you here, Shay. The resistance has much use for the Shadow Dragon."

"Please, Shay," Nadya whispered, praying that her partner

did not decide to set the entire building ablaze. "Please, it's the only way."

Shay's mouth opened and closed. Then she stormed out of the Bulwark without another word, leaving only the scent of burning iron in her wake.

"You'd better talk to her before she burns this entire place down," Marko said. "We can go over the details with him." He glared up at Levka, who only smirked in return.

Nadya agreed and left. It wasn't hard for her to find Shay. She had gone to the edge of the cavern, as if to escape as much of the resistance—and Storm's Quarry—as she could. When Nadya approached her, she didn't turn her gaze away from the stone wall.

"You're leaving me. With them." Shay's hand waved at the Bulwark. "I followed you this far. Why not to Wintercress?"

"Because you are needed here." Nadya took Shay's hands in hers. "Because in order to save this city, we have to be parted. At least, for a little while."

Shay shook her head. "I don't give a rat's ass about this city—you know that. I came here for you." In Nadya's grasp, Shay's hands began to burn hot. "I won't be left behind. Not again."

Nadya swallowed hard. "I'm not abandoning you, Shay. I'll be back, and we can then finish this fight for good." She pulled Shay closer, and the other woman did not resist. Their lips met. Soft. Hesitant. Tripping over the emotions that boiled over between them.

"Promise me, then," Shay whispered into her neck. "Promise me you will return. We'll save the day, again, and then we will be together. Promise me."

"I promise." Nadya did not know if it was a promise she could keep, but Shay's sudden fierce kiss stole the words from her mouth, and she swore to herself that she would keep it, no matter the cost.

"Ahem."

Drina Gabori stood only a few paces away, leaning against the wall of the cavern.

Nadya's instinct was to spring apart from Shay, but her partner held on to her tightly. "Grandmother," she said, clearing her throat. "What—what are you doing here?"

"The Stormspeaker told me what you plan to do," Drina said without looking at Shay. "I wished to say good-bye."

"Why?" It slipped out before Nadya could stop herself. Her grandmother had always disapproved of her. Before her *nivasi* blood had been discovered, Drina had thought her to be a poor truthseer who avoided marriage. Now, she was *nivasi* and in a relationship with another woman, another *nivasi* at that. She couldn't imagine her grandmother cared for her anymore.

"Because you are all of my blood that remains. I wish to see you safely home. Nadezhda," Drina added, after a long pause, "your mother was proud of you, in the end. And while I cannot approve of your alter ego or your companions"—Shay snorted, but Drina ignored her—"I am proud of you as well."

Nadya thought she had expended every tear left to her, but her eyes welled up at her grandmother's words. She stepped forward and wrapped her arms around her grandmother. Drina stiffened but did not recoil.

"Thank you," she said into Drina's shoulder, breathing in the familiar scent of spices and sea air. After a long moment, her grandmother pressed a hand into her back, returning the embrace.

"*Pani nevi lungo drum cher,*" she whispered in the ancient Nomori tongue. *Go fast with the current and follow the stars.*

CHAPTER TEN

It was amazing, Shay thought, what a difference one year could make. She had always believed herself to be a loner, her relationship with the forgemaster notwithstanding. She had her apprenticeship duties, her training in the martial ways, and her nightly forays into the darkest and most desolate places of the world. It had always been enough.

Then Nadya crashed back into her life, quite literally, and Shay had grown accustomed to her steady presence. To the light that Nadya had brought into her life, brighter than any fires Shay could summon. Now, with Nadya and Levka gone off to Wintercress, Shay was left alone in Storm's Quarry, fending off the shadows of her past. Her time spent in the city earlier that year, meeting Nadya and eventually confronting her sister, had healed some of her old wounds, but Shay would never enjoy Storm's Quarry. She certainly had never thought to be part of a resistance fighting to regain it.

Nadya's absence became a nauseous hunger that wormed its way into the pit of Shay's stomach, growing sharper by the day. Nighttime, marked only by the extinguishing of two-thirds of the cavern's lanterns, was the worst. Despite the heat of the mines, Shay could never get warm enough. Her body missed the solid presence of Nadya on the narrow cot beside her. Each artificial morning that she opened her eyes, she couldn't help the wave of disappointment that crashed over her.

Shay wasn't sure she believed in the Protectress, but still she found herself looking up, to where the stars hid beyond the cavern's peak. *If you're there in any form, keep her safe. Bring her back to me.*

At least there was plenty to distract her. The resistance swam with activity day and night, and each turn of the clock that hung above the headquarters brought more citizens of Storm's Quarry through the tunnels, guided by whispers and rumors, to join the cause.

More people for Shay to avoid, but the new royals seemed to be set on making that as difficult as possible.

"You'll be in charge of the forge," Marko told her when she half-heartedly reported for duty the morning after Nadya and Levka had left Storm's Quarry.

"What?" She wasn't sure she had heard correctly. "You want me on the smithy?" The smithy was located in the center of the cavern, paces from the lake, in case of accidents, she had been told. It was exactly where she did not wish to be to avoid attention, but she couldn't understand why the Duke would suggest such a thing.

He nodded. "We don't have anyone with your experience, and we will need weapons and armor. Good ones. If half the things that I've heard about Jeta Forgemaster are true, then as her apprentice, you'll be a welcome addition indeed."

Shay stared at him. "I'm *nivasi*."

Marko flinched and glanced around, but none of the guardsmen who whacked at crude dummies with bayonets and rapiers had taken notice of the two. "And?"

"And don't you want me out in the city, taking on Cressian forces?"

"Any kind of assault without more intelligence on the enemy would be foolhardy at best." Marko shrugged. "You're more than *nivasi*. You're a skilled smith, and we need that. Why do you think Kesali and I wanted you to stay here so badly?"

"Oh." Shay had not considered that the resistance might

have wanted her for more than her ability to set the enemy on fire. Her cheeks grew warm. "I will do my best. Your facilities leave much to be desired, you know," she added, giving the Duke a nod and walking away.

"And I expect to never hear the end of it," Marko said with tired resignation behind her.

❖

Just as Shay had anticipated, working the smithy brought her to the center of attention in the resistance. Gaggles of children stopped in front of the forge, and she had to shoo them off, lest they burn their fingers from touching its coals. She complained to one of the Erevan women who brought her new supplies. Alla, her name was.

"Why are there children here in the first place? Aren't we supposed to be in the middle of a war?"

Alla set down the basket of leather scraps with a thump. "The city isn't safe anymore, not even for children. Wintercress doesn't care your age, only if you share the blood with a traitor, guardsman, rioter, or anyone else they decide needs to be put down. This is one of the few places the children are safe." Her hand lingered at her midsection, and Shay swallowed back the question it drew.

"Well," she finally replied, "at least they're being put to work." It was true—six-year-olds washed the cooking pots while ten- and twelve-year-olds ran messages throughout the cavern. Older children worked alongside the adults at whatever task they had been assigned.

Of course, that couldn't be said for all of the refugees who found their way into the cavern. Filipp, an Erevan drunk from the second tier who had once apprenticed to a city blacksmith long ago, had forced himself into Shay's daily schedule. He liked to sit on a nearby rock and comment as she worked, incorrectly remarking upon everything from the coals she used to the angle of her hammer as she brought it ringing down upon the bayonet blade she forged. "Not like that, stir the coals with your left hand. Like you're twirling a daisy girl on the last day of summer," he'd say, and Shay never figured out what he was talking about. Or, "Breathe with the metal, see. That's what I been taught. *With* the metal, see."

The first day, Shay made the mistake of correcting him—that no, the flames of the forge shouldn't be so hot as to scorch the hair off the back of someone standing forty paces away—and he stood up, puffed his chest out, and lectured her for a solid quarter hour before wandering off to find something to drink. She had to restrain herself from setting his trousers on fire the entire time.

Her fourth morning found a muddy child waiting in front of the forge. He picked up her iron poker, and Shay barked out, "Oi, leave that be."

The child dropped it but kept his annoyingly large smile. He was missing two front teeth. "You're the forgemaster, ain't ya?"

"I'm the smith." She hadn't earned Jeta's title, not by a long shot.

"Lady Stormspeaker wants to see ya. She's in the Bulwark."

Shay rubbed her eyes. The thought of speaking to Kesali made her head ache, but she sucked in a deep breath and made her way to headquarters.

The Stormspeaker stood in front of a rough-hewn table, scrawling notes onto parchment with a flawless script. Shay peered over her shoulder; it was a sewer map, sketched in charcoal, of the two lowest tiers of the city.

"Good, I have a special order for you to fill. Top priority." She shoved a rough sketch across the table toward Shay. "Can you do it?"

Shay looked at the sketch, frowning. A crude drawing of a rat was depicted, with some type of metal contraption on its back. This was drawn again next to it in greater detail. It appeared to be a harness, tied snug with several delicate leather straps. "You want me to make a collar. For rats." Shay stared at Kesali, wondering if the Stormspeaker had gotten into Filipp's secret stash of ale.

Kesali waved a hand. "Speak to Peanna. She will tell you what you need to know."

Shay waited another minute, but Kesali did not look up from her parchment. "All right, then," Shay said when the dismissal became clear and left the Stormspeaker to her musings.

The stables, as people liked to call the collection of shacks and pens near the eastern edge of the cavern, was home to an entire flock of chickens, three goats, and a very disgruntled-looking falcon. Shay wondered at the logistics of transporting livestock unseen through the narrow mining tunnels, but she did not mind the fresh milk and eggs served at the mess each morning.

The stables were kept by a single woman, who currently sat on her heels, coaxing a rumpled hen off a nest.

"Come now, Sorrel, don't be like that," she said as Shay approached, clucking between every couple of words.

Peanna was a short Nomori woman with gray hair pulled back into a widow's knot. She wore a simple orange tunic, and she had a pouch belted at her waist. Her face broke into a practiced smile at Shay's approach, and she lumbered to her feet.

"Our forgemaster!"

"Blacksmith," Shay corrected automatically. "Just a blacksmith."

"No just about it. Storm's Quarry doesn't have many smiths, fewer among the Nomori. We had to bring in outsiders after the Blood Sun Solstice just to repair our city. You are valuable."

Shay felt the tips of her ears grow hot. "The Stormspeaker said you needed collars," Shay said quickly, before Peanna could ramble further.

"Ah, yes. We've tried fashioning them of string or leather, but we cannot find a way for them to stay in place and out of sight."

"Out of sight? On the rats?" Shay half hoped she had misheard Kesali on the exact nature of the assignment.

"Yes, yes!" Peanna gave a sharp whistle. After a moment, Shay jumped when two large gray rats skittered over to her and waited at the older woman's feet. Their eyes glittered black, marking them as city rats, generations of breeding apart from the blind rats of the mines. Peanna whistled again, low and throaty, and the rats stood on their hind legs.

Shay blinked. Now she really had seen everything.

"They're clever creatures," Peanna said with a fondness that Shay did not understand. "And they are helping us against Wintercress."

"They are?" Shay gave the rats a second look, wondering if their claws carried a deadly plague or if they had been trained to leap into the faces of enemy soldiers. "Are you sure?"

Peanna laughed. "They are our messengers. Wintercress knows of the carrier pigeons we use to take messages from tier to tier. It's too risky to use them, and we have secret outposts of resistance fighters all over the city. Rats are the safest way."

"But how? They're rats. How can they carry messages?"

"I train them." A note of pride cut through the older woman's voice. "My gift. I can understand animals to a limited extent, their behaviors, their needs, their strong emotions. And I can train them. I worked with the messenger pigeons in the Duke's aviary for over a decade before…" Her voice caught.

"I'm sorry," Shay said. She didn't know what else to offer. "You need collars to secure the messages."

Peanna's face went from sorrow to a bright smile in a single moment. "Oh, yes! Something simple, so as not to draw attention to them. But something that will keep the written missives secure. Can you do that?" she asked earnestly.

"I've never done armor for rats before," Shay said. "But I can definitely try." She froze as Peanna hugged her, thanked her again, and summoned more rats with a sharp whistle.

Shay watched as a veritable horde of gray fur poured out

of a nearby crack in the cavern wall, suppressing a shudder and wishing that Jeta had been a master of curtain weaving. Then Shay would never have had to forge collars for trained messenger rats.

❖

The next few days found her hammering away at the forge in order to get the first wave of Peanna's trained rats—*my stars*, she had called them—fitted with their new collars. The ingenuity of the message system did nothing to improve Shay's opinion of the assignment. Though, in truth, she would not have been so much on edge if not for Drina Gabori.

The Nomori Elder had remained in the cavern of the resistance. She supposed it made sense; with her daughter passed on and her son-in-law mired in the resistance, the former Gabori matriarch must have decided she had nothing left but to join. Unfortunately, she had taken to loitering around the edge of the forge, watching Shay with sharp, unreadable eyes.

Finally one morning, Shay could not stand it any longer. After sending Peanna off with the newest iteration of rat collars, Shay marched to where Drina lingered at the edge of the raised platform that housed the smithy. The woman's hawk-like gaze followed her to where she stopped only paces from the older woman.

"Do you have an order for the forge?" she asked, crossing her arms. "A nice new leather whip, perhaps?"

Drina narrowed her eyes, appraising Shay like she was a heifer at the market. Shay tried her best not to squirm under the Elder's gaze. "No," Drina said finally. "I seek nothing yet." She turned and slowly walked away, leaving a bad taste in Shay's mouth.

Two weeks Shay spent in the belly of Storm's Quarry, hammering away at the forge, dodging questions from friendly Nomori and Erevan alike. Two weeks she had managed to pull herself off her pallet each morning to slurp down the bland oatmeal the mess provided before lighting up the forge with a careless wave of her hand. For two weeks, she had held herself together.

Then she caught sight of her empty cot one too many times, and her heart came undone.

She made it to the cavern wall before collapsing against the cool stone, shaking. Knees to chest, head down, eyes closed— *you are stronger than this*, a voice at the back of her mind chided, but she didn't want to be strong, not now. She wanted to be home.

If any of the patrolling guardsmen saw her, they kept their distance. It had not taken long for rumors of the blacksmith's fiery temper to circulate among the shanties. No one put themselves in her way if they could avoid it.

"You are troubled."

Shay started. She looked up to see Drina Gabori leaning against the rough stone not five paces away, her gaze fixed upon the myriad of stalactites that grew from the ceiling.

"What—what are you doing here?" Shay let go of her knees and stood. "Come to make sure I'm not up to something murderous?"

Drina did not look at her as she said, "I find sleep has deserted me as of late."

Shay wasn't sure what to say to that. "So you've come to pester me, then?"

"How can we sleep, so separated from the water and the stars? Encased in this prison of rock," Drina went on, as if Shay hadn't spoken. "It's a wonder we haven't all gone mad."

"Yeah, a wonder." Shay was pretty sure the Elder had gone mad. She hated Shay, hated everything she was. Why was she here now, sharing as if they were old friends?

"I bring news of your family."

Shay's mouth went dry. "Nadya isn't here," she said, though she knew that wasn't what Drina spoke of.

Drina ignored her attempt at dissuasion. "Wintercress did

not take your sister's role in the ousting of Aster well. She was taken to the palace a week ago, she and her family. They have not been heard from since."

"Okay." Shay felt a curious emptiness in her chest at the news. She had hated her sister—the reason for her parents discovering her *nivasi* blood—for years. Ten months ago, she had faced her sister for the first time in years in order to save the city. Now she did not know what to feel. "Is that," Shay asked, finding her voice, "all you wished to speak to me about?"

"Lying does not become someone of my age." Drina sighed. Her sharp gaze met Shay's. "I am unsure of you, Shay. Unsure of what you and my granddaughter mean for the future of our people. *Nivasi* carry a great power, and if is it allowed to run unchecked—"

"What about your power?" Shay shot back. She faced the older woman. "You can pry into people's minds, read their emotions. Don't try to tell me that's not dangerous in its own way." She flung out a hand. "Or Peanna and her rat army? What if it wasn't rats, but sabercats or even worse? Who is to say she's not dangerous? My sister could tell the essence of a person or a thing with a single touch. How is that not power?"

Her breath came heavily now, as every bit of anger she had toward the Nomori poured out of her. "Look around you, *Madame* Gabori. This cavern, this city is filled with dangerous Nomori, and only two of them bear *nivasi* blood. You like to separate yourself from us, but what really separates us? When it comes down to it, the Nomori are a dangerous race, every single one."

Drina stared at her, expression hard and unreadable, until Shay began to twitch under her gaze. "You sound like one of them."

"One of who? The bad *nivasi*? The ones you tell children stories about to make them fear the dark?"

"The Erevans."

Shay shook her head. "I don't know what you mean."

"Saying the Nomori are dangerous, down to every last child…I heard the speeches of many Erevans, from politicians to crazed drunkards. There was a time, not long after Duke Isyanov took us in, that one couldn't walk more than ten paces in the upper tiers without hearing it." Drina shook her head. "They feared us. Some still do."

Shay swallowed hard against the lump in her throat. "Well, you should know what it's like, then."

"Whether *nivasi* should be welcomed, banished, or killed is a matter for more peaceful times. Our people's history with your kind is fraught with bloodshed, though I am not convinced it wasn't partially of our own making." Drina smiled grimly, her teeth yellowed and thin. "The other Elders would accuse me of heresy for saying that, no doubt." She lifted a hand. "I know my gift makes some uncomfortable. My own granddaughter avoided me whenever she could for years."

"A true mystery why," Shay muttered.

Drina ignored her. "As useful as my gift can be, or Peanna's, or your sister's or any of our women, we are not an army unto ourselves. Not like you and Nadya. Not like the Cressian creature who somehow shares your blood. Our methods are extreme and need to be rethought, yes, but do not pretend that hounds and wolves are the same."

Shay opened her mouth, but she found it hard to argue with Drina's words, much as she disliked them. No Nomori woman, or man for that matter, could defeat a *nivasi* in a fair fight; if they could, Storm's Quarry wouldn't be overrun with Cressians soldiers at the moment.

"So why did you come here?" she said finally. "Why skulk around the smithy watching me? It wasn't to tell me of my sister's death. Do you think I'm going to go off like Gedeon?"

"I watch you because it is my duty to protect the Nomori, and I came here tonight because I had news and because…your emotions resonated."

"My what?"

"You miss Nadya. I miss her as well."

Shay looked at Drina as if she had sprouted wings. "You've done a poor job of showing it. Since she left, or before."

Drina did not argue with her assessment. "I have done a poor job of many things." She sighed again, and for the first time, the elderly Nomori woman looked ancient and tired. "I have made many mistakes, and I have little time left to rectify them. I have lost my only child." Her voice hitched. "And I have pushed away my granddaughter. I hope to one day make right that wrong, if possible. And I pray to the Protectress every morning and every evening that she returns safely so I may do so."

"Good," Shay said, her voice thick with emotion. "I need her to. More than anything."

Chapter Eleven

"You've never ridden a horse before, have you, Nadezhda?"

"Not everyone in Storm's Quarry had a courtier's upbringing, you know," she snapped at the smugly grinning man beside her. Her gaze, however, remained fixed on the beast in front of her.

Horses were a rare sight in Storm's Quarry. The space and upkeep they required made them a luxury only a few in the fourth tier could afford. Not only that, but their size made them far more of a nuisance on the narrow city streets than anything, and as someone raised in the lowest tier of the city, Nadya had only ever caught glimpses of the creatures as they pulled carriages that carried the wealthiest of the city's elite.

The midnight gelding that stood before her looked nothing like the sleek mounts of the fourth tier. His coat was rough and shaggy, his mane clipped short and braided. Bits of wild grass speckled his fur. He raised his head from the sparse grass only once to blink at Nadya with liquid black eyes before returning to his meal.

She hadn't expected the size. The creature's shoulder stood at height with her head, and though she knew her strength could match the rippling muscle in front of her, her knees felt a bit weak.

The small trading outpost they had stopped at was a solitary place, its handful of thatched-roofed buildings nestled in the grasslands right beneath the foothills of the Stygian Mountains. Over the tall scraggly peaks of those mountains lay the Kingdom of Wintercress. Without a guide or knowledge of the terrain, it would be foolish to cross them alone, and so she and Levka were headed west toward the Brine of Lazuli. Or at least, they would be, once she had mounted her horse.

"You aren't frightened of a horse, are you?" Levka swung himself up into the worn leather saddle with graceful ease.

Nadya bit her lip. "Of course not. I just don't think it's necessary. I can keep pace with a horse."

She had never raced against one, but her *nivasi* blood gave her speed far greater than any normal person. The black gelding flicked his tail lazily, as if agreeing with her.

Levka laughed. "You think you can. Maybe for a few hundred paces you could keep up, but these creatures are bred for stamina." He stroked the tightly braided mane of the chestnut mare. "We would leave you behind within an hour."

The not-so-subtle taunt gave Nadya the courage she needed to spring upward, swinging her leg over the beast's back. The horse didn't flinch at all. Nadya tried not to squirm as she settled into the saddle. It was higher than she had anticipated, and her stomach lurched a bit when they started to walk, then trot. Eventually, Levka goaded his horse into a light canter, and Nadya closed her eyes and sent up a prayer. She tried to let herself be swayed into calm by the repetitive movement, but her mind was too distraught to listen. Several hours into their ride, her horse had to suddenly sidestep a sinkhole in the road, and she jerked upright, squeezing her legs against the beast's sides.

The horse did not appreciate her sudden strength, giving a stern grunt and slowing to a walk.

"Goodness, be careful. We don't want their owners to think these horses were appropriated by common thugs, do you?"

"Wait, you stole them?" Nadya yanked back on the reins, causing a sharp whinny from her mount. She patted his shoulder in apology while glaring at Levka's back. "I thought you paid for them."

Only a few thin tendrils of trust had built between them as they escaped the city together, Nadya leading the way and, as uncomfortable as it was, Levka watching her back. Now, several of those tendrils snapped, and she wondered if she had been right after all to agree to the former magistrate's plans.

"With what coin? The Guard seized my manor and assets. I have nothing to my name, and what few coins the younger Isyanov gave you need be reserved for ocean passage." Levka clicked his tongue, and the chestnut mare slowed to a stop. He looked back at Nadya. "We need to reach the coast and soon, before Wintercress gains more of a foothold in Storm's Quarry. You cannot tell me you've never stolen for a greater good."

She bit back an argument as she remembered breaking in to a physician's office to get her mother medicine last year. The medicine hadn't worked, only delaying the inevitable, but still she had done it.

"We are giving them back," she said with a grimace.

Levka smiled broadly before turning back around and goading his mount into a trot. "Of course we will, Nadezhda. We aren't common thieves, after all."

❖

Nadya had only been in Storm's Quarry briefly, and half that time she'd spent unconscious, but already she missed the city. The grasslands they rode through felt wide and empty, with only a smattering of rocks and deer herds to provide any break to the yellow-green prairie. She missed the steep marble walls, the closeness that narrow streets and tall buildings brought.

When they rode up to one of the farms on the outskirts of the fishing village of Nim, they reined in their mounts and left them in a secure paddock; amidst the small herd of horses, theirs blended in seamlessly. Nadya had initially protested once again taking advantage of innocent folk, but Levka only rolled his eyes. "We'll need the horses on the way back, Nadya. Unless you plan on dying in Wintercress. I certainly do not, and I'm not about to walk back to Storm's Quarry."

She had relented. As much as she hated to admit it, Levka was right.

The fishing town of Nim owed no allegiance to any nation. It sat nestled against the Brine of Lazuli, its collection of log houses and docks spreading out along the coastline like a flock of rock gulls. Although many nations through the world's history had tried to claim Nim as their own, somehow the fishing town had stubbornly resisted. It was a neutral port of sorts, a place for ships that traded up and down the ocean's coast to dock and their sailors to drink and rest. Nadya heard half a dozen languages during their first hour in town and saw hair that spanned the colors from honey to jet. In the bustling early evening, with the fishermen brought in their daily catch of crabs and silverfins, no one paid any mind to the Nomori and the Erevan who walked their streets.

"Hold on," Levka said, putting a hand to Nadya's arm. "Wait here."

She glanced around. They stood on a street corner near the center of town. Behind them was a bunkhouse, still empty of its nightly patrons, and across the knobbly cobblestoned road was a tavern. Its carved sign bore the name *Tiny's Alehouse*. From where she stood, Nadya heard the whistles and chattering of patrons and smelled the rich oaty liquor. Nothing suspicious, she thought, and scanned the street again. Only travelers who kept their eyes to themselves and boisterous natives who called out to one another in greeting.

"Did you see something?" she whispered.

"Nothing so dramatic. I need you to wait here. I'll be right back." Levka stepped forward, but Nadya grabbed his arm. He struggled for a moment before turning to her and glaring. "What are you doing?"

"I'm coming with you," she said, releasing him after a long moment.

"No, you're not. There could be Cressians here, and while it isn't unusual to see an Erevan outside of Storm's Quarry, your people aren't exactly common. We don't want to raise any unnecessary questions."

She heard the steady thumping of his heartbeat—he wasn't lying—and nodded. "Fine, but at least tell me where you're going."

Levka gestured to the tavern. "To get a drink, of course."

Nadya hated him so much in that moment.

While he slipped into Tiny's Alehouse to buy his drink and put his plans into action, Nadya loitered awkwardly in the street. She was grateful the folk of Nim paid a stranger so little mind; indeed, it seemed a place full of those people who would be out of place anywhere else.

Her boredom and nerves got the best of her, and Nadya's pacing took her up and down the street, following narrow alleys into dead ends and back out again. So preoccupied by her thoughts of Levka and what might await them in Wintercress was she that Nadya did not realize she had company until three men casually blocked her path out of one of the narrow alleyways.

Stars, why now? She cursed silently and glanced warily from face to face until one—scrawny with a gold ring in his ear—snarled in Erevo, "Give us your purse, lady."

"You don't want to rob me," she said slowly, listening as two more pairs of boots approached from behind. "Trust me. You should leave."

"Coin. All your coin. Now!" he barked and flashed a rusty dagger at her. Around him, the rest of the gang drew their weapons, a motley collection of knives, clubs, and one shovel.

Nadya inwardly cursed her luck. Nothing drew attention to a

traveler like a fight, and these thieves weren't about to leave her alone. She needed their coin to get to Wintercress, so giving it up to avoid trouble was not an option.

The scrawny thief seemed to think she was taking too long, so he lunged forward and grabbed her wrist. His last mistake.

Nadya grabbed ahold of his hand. Delicate finger bones snapped under her grip. He yowled, and she threw him backward, straight into the chest of one of his friends.

"Leave me alone," she warned as hesitance gleamed in the eyes of the other two thieves. "Or you'll get more of that."

The faintest crunch of leather upon gravel—Nadya whirled around in time to catch the cutlass blade that arced toward her head. Her right hand stopped it midair, and the thief who was sneaking up behind her, a woman with the tight curls of the South Marches, stared in horror.

She wrenched the cutlass from the thief's grasp. It clattered into a ditch ten paces away.

"Anyone else?" she said, turning to each of them. "Or will you leave me in peace?"

As if sharing the same thought, the gang of thieves turned and ran as one. Their footsteps faded in the direction of the docks, no doubt heading there to hole up and ready themselves for their next target.

"Damn luck," she muttered, checking her tunic for stains. No blood had been spilled; her father would have been proud. "Just what I need, stars-cursed thieves trying for my coin."

She froze as the words left her throat. It was a coincidence, wasn't it, that she was attacked as she waited for Levka to conduct his business in the tavern? It had to be…

But even as she tried to reassure herself, a cold feeling enveloped her, as if someone had poured seawater down her back.

Nadya strode out of the alley, listening and watching for any sign of Levka. The streets were as busy as before, and no one looked twice at her. At least the commotion of the fight hadn't caught anyone's attention, but had that been its purpose?

She narrowed her eyes. "Damn magistrate," she muttered, staring at the tavern door Levka had vanished through. Was he still there? Had he used the commotion to slip out and leave Nadya behind? He didn't think a handful of thieves could take her out, did he?

Anger bubbled in her chest, but she clamped it down. Making a scene might bring the wrong kind of attention, and Levka hadn't been wrong about wanting to avoid that.

She crossed the street, nearly cutting off a cart of fish and its irate handler, and entered the tavern. Tiny's Alehouse smelled like piss and dead fish, and Nadya bit back a retch. No one looked at her, as most of the patrons were currently shouting at a very short man who stood atop a table, juggling a pair of tankards. She caught one of the barmaids, who, after being given a terse description of Levka, pointed her to a private room at the back of the tavern.

The door swung open at her touch, and room's two occupants turned to look at her in surprise. Levka's companion, a young man wearing a sailor's coat with tarnished brass buttons, smiled, while Levka glared at Nadya.

"And this must be the lovely lady," the sailor drawled in thickly accented Erevan. "Pleased to—"

"Out," she growled at the young man, and something in her eyes must have betrayed her anger because his face drained of color and he walked out without another word, shutting the door behind him.

"Nadezhda, I told you to wait—"

She didn't give him the chance to finish. In half a moment, she had crossed the room and grabbed ahold of his neck.

"What in the heavens?" he gasped as she pushed him up against the wall. Despite their height difference in his favor, his boots hung above the ground. "What are you doing? We're on the same side, remember?"

"Are we?" she hissed. A nerve in her wrist throbbed. This felt eerily similar to the morning of the Blood Sun Solstice, when

Nadya had strung Levka up in anger at his role in the bloodshed, only to be witnessed by her father. She shook the memory off. "Did you try to have me killed?"

Levka's eyes flashed with surprise. "What are you talking about?"

"I just got ambushed by five armed thieves. Are you telling me you had nothing to do with it?"

"I did not." His words were calm, and despite the bruises that spread across his neck like rivulets of purple ink, he showed no fear. "Put me down, Nadya, and we can speak like civilized people."

Nadya took a deep breath. He weighed nothing in her grip, and yet she felt like stumbling backward under his composed words. She lowered him to the ground. He staggered out of her grasp and leaned against the wall.

"Have you gotten bloody stronger?" He cursed, losing his calm expression and putting one hand out in front of him, as if to fend her off. His other hand went to his throat. "Give me a moment to breathe, please."

"I'm…" She wasn't sorry, not exactly. Not until she knew for certain that he wasn't responsible for the attack.

"You're a monster." His matter-of-fact words stung hard, and Nadya opened her mouth to protest, but he cut her off. "Don't try to argue it, because it does not matter. You might be a monster, but Storm's Quarry was taken by another, more powerful one. You are needed to fight the Cressian *nivasi*, and so I don't much care about your monstrous nature. In fact, it is preferable given the current circumstances."

Levka straightened and brushed off his rumpled tunic. "Let me make it clear—I did not send a bunch of common thugs after you. I might be a lot of things, but utterly incompetent is not one of them. And I have never underestimated you. If I wanted to take you out, it wouldn't have been with a gang of thieves."

She hated the truth that rang in his words. Could it have been just a coincidence? She was a young woman traveling in an unfamiliar land, unaccompanied at the time. She would have looked an easy target. Maybe it had been a random encounter, and nothing more. "Fine," she said finally. "You didn't do it."

"That's it? A stating of the obvious and no apology?"

"I hate you," Nadya added, unwilling to apologize for a reasonable misunderstanding, but the bite had left her words.

"Then we feel the same about each other." Levka cleared his throat. "Now if you're done assaulting me for the time being, I suggest we go find some lodging before we draw more unwanted attention."

They had coin enough for a single room at the bunkhouse, and despite Nadya's vehement argument that she could sleep in the stable, Levka did not budge. "You won't find any answers without me, and if I am slain in the night by Cressian soldiers, the fall of Storm's Quarry will be on your head."

Reluctantly, she agreed.

The portly matron of the establishment gave them a toothy smile as she showed them up the rickety stairs to a line of doors. "This one's yours," she said, unlocking the nearest door. It swung open with a creak to reveal a single bed with a thin straw mattress and nothing else but dust. "Have a good'un," the matron said cheerfully as she trotted back downstairs.

Nadya and Levka stared at the bed.

"You take it," she said.

"I'll have it," he said at the same time.

She rolled her eyes but stole a scratchy blanket from the bed and made herself comfortable on the floor as close to the wall as she could. The floor was hard and cold, but Nadya didn't care much. The day's traveling and subsequent fight left her tired enough to sleep anywhere. She lay down and closed her eyes.

Sleep did not come.

"This is too strange," she whispered into the dark room.

An exasperated sigh came from the bed. "Pretend I'm not here. Or that you don't feel overwhelming fury at my presence."

"If only it were that easy," Nadya muttered. "You aren't afraid at all. After all, you called me a monster."

"You are one. I've known that for a long time. Now, stop moaning about it and go to sleep."

"Why are you even here if you think that?" Nadya argued. "You know, after what you did on the solstice, a lot of people in Storm's Quarry would call *you* a monster."

"Like I said"—his voice went soft—"you need monsters to defeat monsters."

❖

They bought passage two hours before dawn. An older woman, hair streaked gray and skin weathered from decades at sea, looked the two of them up and down with calculating eyes. A few gold coins changed hands and she stepped aside to let them board her small cargo ship. The *Seawitch* was its name, and it bore the moniker easily. A midsized vessel, its sides had taken on a grayish hue from years at sea. It would carry Levka and Nadya to Brome, where it would leave them and a dozen crates of dried silverfin and several bolts of woven blue cotton on the docks.

After climbing aboard and setting sail, it took Nadya exactly one hour at sea to realize that, Nomori or not, she hated boats. Since realizing that, she had spent nearly every moment on the starboard deck, one arm draped over the railing, ready for her next fit of retching. Her fingers gripped the railing hard enough to crack it in several places.

Her nausea roiled behind her eyes, so overwhelming that she did not notice Levka's approach until he stood over her, his shadow disrupting the high noon sun.

"How many times have you thrown up your breakfast?" he asked with raised eyebrows.

Nadya shot him an annoyed look. "Why do you care?"

"Because we need to discuss the next stage of this venture, and I have no desire to be retched upon."

"Then stand over there and talk," she mumbled. None of the ship's crew had dared come over this way, to avoid her sickness.

"Fine." Levka leaned against the rail, staring out at the Brine of Lazuli. To anyone watching, the two passengers appeared to be enjoying one another's company, gazing at the water together. In truth, the former magistrate's proximity made Nadya nearly as sick as the waves.

"Brome is a large port city, and it won't give up any secrets easily," Levka said quietly, no doubt trusting Nadya could hear him over the sound of waves lapping the *Seawitch*'s stern. "Whatever knowledge Wintercress has stored there will not be easily accessed, particularly by outsiders."

"Makes sense," she managed to say. She hadn't expected anyone to hand off the secrets of their *nivasi* to her.

"And unfortunately, we cannot simply punch our way to the answers."

She was too queasy to rise to Levka's jab. Instead, she grunted and closed her eyes, breathing in slowly.

"We will have to disguise ourselves. Merchants would be our best bet. No one would question a pair of foreign merchants coming into Brome on a trade ship, asking questions, looking to make purchases."

"They won't until they see our purses," Nadya said. They had used nearly all the coin Marko and Kesali had given them to book passage.

Levka sighed. "Just let me do the talking when we get there, and this will all go smoothly. Until then, I suggest we both try to rest up."

A few moments passed before Nadya realized he was still there. She opened her eyes. "What?" she snapped.

Levka studied her face, his own slightly amused. "You are a poor excuse for a Nomori, you know?"

Her laugh at the unexpected remark turned into retching, and Nadya leaned over the side of the vessel once again.

CHAPTER TWELVE

Three weeks had passed since Nadya left with Levka, and Shay had begun to settle into her new routine. Waking up at the unseen dawn, lighting the lantern beside her pallet, and stumbling out to the mess. Warming the coals of the forge on her way there, and then scarfing down whatever the mess served for breakfast. Grunting to Filipp as he came to sit in his favorite spot, still smelling of spirits. Filling the orders of the day, maybe getting a visit from Alla or Peanna or Peanna's rats. Shay would never enjoy Storm's Quarry, but the determination with which the people in the resistance worked to save their city gave her hope that this could be done. That Nadya would return safely, and Wintercress could be overthrown.

Of course, she kept that optimism locked up tight in fear of losing it if she shared it with anyone. She took on the grim expression of most every person in the resistance, and Shay found herself having to remember that she wasn't part of it, not really. *I am here for Nadya,* she'd tell herself, *nothing more. Once Nadya comes back with whatever Nomori secrets they find, she and I will finish this. We'll go out fighting, or we'll leave a freed Storm's Quarry behind.*

One bleary-eyed morning, after a night that she had dabbled a bit with Filipp's stash of liquor, putting up with his drunken rants in return for a bottle of ale, Shay got to the smithy to find

Marko standing in front of the forge, his forehead creased in thought.

"Need something?" she asked, rubbing her eyes.

If he was offended by the lack of decorum, he didn't show it. "We've got an assignment for you," he said, turning toward her. If possible, Marko looked worse than her, with large dark circles under his eyes. His fingers tapped against the hilt of his rapier.

"More rat collars?" Shay gestured to the forge. "Or it is lizard leashes this time? I am your ever humble servant, here to carry out any order."

Marko didn't smile, and Shay let the grin drop from her mouth. "Something wrong? Have you heard from Nadya?"

"No, nothing like that. We can only hope she and that—" He couldn't even bring himself to call Levka a name. "We can only hope they are successful in finding a weakness in the Cressian *nivasi*. That's not why I'm here." Marko drew in a breath. "We need you."

"Figured." Shay crossed her arms. "Neither us of is getting younger, so…?"

"We need the Shadow Dragon."

Marko didn't meet her gaze as he said it. Shay sighed; she had expected this to happen at some point. She was a decent smith, to be sure, but her real talent lay in fire and blade.

"Stars, I hate that name," she muttered.

The Duke raised his eyebrow, but he remained silent.

Shay sighed. "I knew it was only a matter of time before you called on me. I might be the only smith in the resistance, but I'm also your only—"

"Yes, you are," Marko said hurriedly. "I had hoped to avoid using you like this, but it was foolish to think we could overthrow Wintercress without the help of someone like you."

Someone I don't know I can trust hung in the air between them, unsaid.

"What do you need me to do?" she asked finally, careful to keep her voice down. Not many stirred in the cavern this time of morning, but she did not want to advertise her *nivasi* nature. Suddenly, the thought of being hated and feared by the people she worked with day after day turned Shay's stomach in a way she hadn't expected. She wasn't supposed to care, and yet she did, in a most vulnerable way.

Marko began walking toward the Bulwark, and Shay followed him. "Our spies gave us word in the night that the Prince is getting in a shipment from Wintercress this afternoon," he said as they walked. "Mostly mundane supplies, but—"

"Weapons," she finished for him.

He nodded, opening the door of the Bulwark. Kesali, standing at the war table, gave a nod to her husband and looked at Shay. The Stormspeaker's eyes were unreadable as she asked, "How much do you know?"

"Just that Wintercress is getting some weapons in today, and I assume you want them. With the materials I'm getting at the forge being little more than scrap, a load of new weapons is sorely needed," Shay said. "Is there anything else to know?"

Marko and Kesali shared a quick glance. "No, that is the heart of it," he said. He took his place next to his wife. "Our spies will follow the shipment as it comes it, tracking its progress throughout the city as best that they can. We should get a rat message before dark."

Shay choked back a snort with the seriousness that he referred to their unconventional communication system. "Which will tell me where to go," she said, composing herself. "I go in as the Dragon, take out any soldiers guarding the shipment, and what? Carry crate loads of weapons back by myself? I'm not Nadya."

Marko flinched at her mention of Nadya, but Kesali's face was carefully blank.

"You will have help at the time," Marko said.

"Trust us, and do your part," Kesali added. "Everything should go according to plan."

Shay did laugh this time, a sharp sardonic chuckle that

echoed throughout the small room. "Let's be honest with one another. There is no trust here." She raised a hand as Marko opened his mouth in protest. "I am fine with that. But we shouldn't fool ourselves. You do not trust *nivasi*," she said, pointing to Marko. "You do not trust me." Shay pointed to Kesali, and then gestured to herself. "And I do not trust anyone within the walls of this city. There, now that we aren't trying to lie to ourselves, we can move on. You'll have someone there to back me up and help transport the weapons home. Got it."

It was all she needed to know.

❖

The city of Storm's Quarry stood silent.

Shay couldn't help the cold feeling that crept up her spine as she darted through the streets of the third tier. Winds brought in salty air off the Kyanite Sea, mixing with the odors of decay that clung to the city streets. The night air rustled the refuse and pulled at the signs of long-deserted shops. She felt as if she ran through a city of ghosts. Hollow eyes peered out of barred windows, the Sirens of the dying city.

Her hatred for Storm's Quarry usually burned so hot, but the stillness ate at it, gnawing away at the edges until Shay felt only numbness as she surveyed the wreckage of the city from atop a roof.

Her target was in sight.

A regiment of fourteen Cressian soldiers surrounded the crates of weapons. One of them, wearing the silver stripes of a sergeant, lifted a lid and examined the contents. Shay caught a glimpse of rows of gleaming saber blades before the lid snapped shut. He uttered some orders in Cressian, and his men got to work moving the crates to their final destination: the palace.

Not tonight, Shay thought, and she leapt down.

Unlike Nadya, she didn't land hard on the cobblestones,

cracking the ground. Shay let her momentum carry her into a roll when she hit the ground. She rose, and her blades ignited in a spray of white light.

For a moment, none of the soldiers moved, their faces falling and mouths opening in surprise and terror at the sudden appearance of a *nivasi*. Shay didn't give them time to collect themselves. Her blades flashed out, and the nearest soldier dropped, his uniform sizzling and smoking.

That broke the regiment's paralysis. Soldiers surrounded her. Their sabers lunged for her throat, and Shay dodged and parried, melting off any blade that dared to get too close.

One soldier staggered back. His blue eyes shone with fear at the *nivasi* before him before he turned and sprinted down the alley.

"Damn it," Shay swore. Another soldier swung his saber down at her head. She blocked it, slicing through the iron like melted butter with her sword of light. He cursed in Cressian and aimed a kick to her chest.

His boot connected with a shield of fire. He fell back, howling. Shay silenced him with a single slash of her blade.

If anyone escaped to raise an alarm, Prince Trillium would send reinforcements. More soldiers or, worse, the Cressian *nivasi*. Shay didn't like the odds of her escaping another fight with that woman alive.

Fire bloomed at her feet, incinerating the bits of wood and paper that littered the street. She gathered brilliant orange flames into her hands. They turned blue, then white, becoming pure light as she concentrated on strengthening and controlling the power that raged within her.

The running figure had nearly reached the end of the alley, and Shay, desperate, drew back her arm to sling her blade of light and any other fire she could muster. Damn it all if the neighborhood burned down. But before she could let her power loose, the Cressian soldier came to an abrupt halt. He let out a single gurgle and slumped to the ground, revealing a man standing there, rapier gleaming with blood in the moonlight. He moved into the light of the fight, and Shay could have whistled for joy.

The Guardmaster had come.

Out of alleyways and leaping down from rooftops, fighters of the resistance swarmed upon the scene. Their rapiers and bayonets glinted in the light of her fires as they got to work, cutting down the Cressian soldiers who remained. Some tried to flee, realizing the hopelessness of the battle they now faced. None made it far.

With the addition of two dozen warriors on her side, Erevan and Nomori men alike, the resistance made short work of the remaining Cressian soldiers. Shay sent a bolt of fire into the back of the last retreating man, and he fell to the ground with a shriek before being consumed by flame and turned to ash.

She wiped her brow. Her sleeve came away grimy with soot and smeared war paint.

"Secure the crates." Shadar Gabori barked out orders behind her. "You have two minutes. We need to get these out of sight before anyone comes to see what the commotion was."

"Good fight." He greeted her when he approached the northern side of the street that Shay kept a wary watch over. He had not, she noted, sheathed his rapier.

Shay moistened her cracked lips and nodded. "You as well. Marko mentioned I'd have backup, but I did not expect the Guardmaster himself."

Shadar's mouth tightened at her informality with his new Duke, but he did not remark upon it. "The Duke did not know I'd be here. He wishes that I would stay holed up in a safe house, sending others out with orders to save our city. I like to let him think that I do." Shadar drew a deep breath. "I believe he is worried that I'll be reckless in the aftermath of my wife's death. That I have nothing left but to die for this city."

"You have Nadya," Shay said automatically.

He nodded and cracked a brief smile. "I do. And, fortunate for our city, Storm's Quarry does as well."

Shay did not have a reply, so she nodded and stood back as the Guardmaster finished ordering his troops about. Like a well-built engine, the resistance fighters split up in groups of five and six, carrying the crates of Cressian weapons.

"What about them?" an Erevan man asked, nudging one of the soldiers' bodies with his boot. "Should we hide the evidence of the fight?"

"No." Shadar shook his head. "We leave them. There isn't time to hide all traces of our fight, and we do not have the men to spare them a burial. Their own commanders should take care of it."

The air that hung over the street grew heavier. Shay tugged at her chestplate, avoiding the gaze of any of the resistance fighters. The Guardmaster's words were a bitter reminder that those they killed were not innocent, but neither were they criminals. Jeta's voice rang through her head. *It is easy when the lives you take, the people you catch, are hardened souls, their lives burned dark with sin. War is different. War has no villains, no heroes, only victims.* She shook herself to rid her mind of the words.

The Cressian Prince is guilty, as was Councillor Aster, Shay reminded herself. *Anyone who falls under their command...we can't afford to separate them. Not if we are going to win.*

"Leave everything but the weapons," Shadar was saying. "Let Wintercress know that there are still those in Storm's Quarry who have the strength to fight back. And let our people know that we are still fighting for them."

In less than an hour, the resistance had deserted the street, vanishing back to the various safe houses around the city and to the cavern underneath it. Shay kept her distance from the Guardmaster as their small group navigated the dark mining tunnels. He headed straight for the Bulwark when they reached the cavern, and Shay straight for her bunk.

The next morning found her at the smithy as usual, this time wrangling with the newest design of collars for Peanna's rats. Lighter and better fitting, Shay was proud to say. The thought elicited a chuckle out of her. If only her forgemaster could see her now.

"Shay."

She turned to see Shadar Gabori standing at the edge of the smith's platform. Cursing silently, Shay dipped her newly shaped collar in the bucket of acrid water that had been brought fresh this morning. Steam curled into the still cavern air. Once the piece was cooled, she set it carefully on the table and dropped her tongs onto their hook.

"Guardmaster," she greeted, maintaining her best passive face. She wasn't surprised that he had chosen to stay the night in the cavern after reporting the events of the fight to Marko and Kesali. She had, however, hoped to avoid his notice as much as possible.

Shadar surveyed her workspace with a critical eye. Shay found herself straightening defensively. True, it wasn't much, and none of the equipment was up to par with what Jeta usually insisted upon for their work, but she was proud of what she had made of it.

Finally, he nodded and said, "I've heard you are doing good work here. Not just going after Cressian shipments after dark."

"Trying to. Not much to work with, but your men will have more than sharpened sticks for the fight. Especially with the new Cressian materials." *Please, please, go away.* Her fingers rapped against her leg nervously.

"Glad to hear it. Do you have a moment to speak privately?" he asked, and Shay's stomach sank down to her knees.

She actually wished Kesali had summoned her for an early morning meeting, or that Filipp hadn't been so hungover that he didn't even make it to his favorite rock to sit and berate Shay on her smithing technique. "Of course," she said through gritted teeth. "Can we speak here? That way I can keep an eye on things." *And have the advantage of familiar territory.*

He inclined his head. "Very well."

This was going to be fun.

The Guardmaster approached the smelter as if it was an enemy entrenchment. He waved off Shay's offering of a seat, instead opting to pace back and forth in front of the smoldering coals. Shay stood off to one side, waiting for him to speak. She latched on to the calm energy of the furnace's low flame, soothing her inner fire. The last thing she needed was to set the smithy ablaze in front of Nadya's father.

"You traveled with Nadya these past months, yes?"

Shay nodded. "We did travel together, along with my forgemaster. We followed a caravan down to the northern edge of the South Marches. Kipperwell was the last place we stopped. Your message found us there." She tried to hide the bitter edge in her voice.

"You've been an apprentice long?" Shadar asked.

She frowned, unsure of the point of this line of questioning. "Yes, nearly a dozen years now. Ever since..." Shay paused. How much did he know of her origins? The Guardmaster was no fool, she knew that much, so she plunged onward. "Ever since I left Storm's Quarry."

Shadar didn't even flinch. She had guessed correctly that he surmised her past long beforehand. "That is an innocuous way of putting it."

"The past is the past. Can't change what happened," Shay muttered. She fiddled with the edge of her tunic. "Is that what you wanted to speak about?"

"In part. I wanted to ask you about my daughter and what your intentions are toward her."

Shay could have melted into the floor right there. She swallowed hard and glanced around, but there was no sign of Kesali or Marko to rescue her; at this point, she'd take Peanna and her trained rats for a distraction.

"Nadya and I are—" She couldn't bring herself to say *friends*. Nomori frowned upon same-gender relationships, another thing Shay was grateful to have left behind. Still, she was not ashamed of her relationship with Nadya, and she did not want to lie about it. "We are close," she said finally. "Shouldn't you have asked Nadya about this? Before she left, I mean."

"She had just lost her mother. The last thing she needed was…well…" Shadar cleared his throat. "I am asking you. She is my daughter, and I am concerned for her…choices." He paused in his pacing, drummed his fingers against his leg, and looked at the wooden shelf to the left of Shay's head.

Thank the stars he's an uncomfortable as I am, but the thought did not untie the knot of nerves in her chest. "Because I'm a wandering apprentice, not a good Nomori who lives inside this city's walls? Or is it because I'm *nivasi*? Or"—she did not hold back the anger that edged her tongue—"is it because I'm a woman?"

Shadar sucked in an audible breath. He looked directly at Shay for the first time. "So you are…involved."

She groaned. "I'll say it plainly—we are together. Romantically. Is that what you wanted to know?"

Shay would apologize to Nadya when she returned for the graceless way her father had been told about their relationship. Right now, she just wanted the Guardmaster to be anywhere but the smithy.

"Did you persuade her into such a thing?" he asked, after apparently recovering from Shay's frank answer.

"Did I what?" Shay shook her head. Her temples pounded; she needed a long drink of water, and then a longer drink of spirits. "No, I did not. I didn't lure her into a relationship or into my bed." Shadar flinched at her bluntness. Before she lost the nerve, Shay continued, "You are unbelievable, you know that?"

The edge of the Guardmaster's mouth twitched.

"Your daughter is a *nivasi*, one who dresses up every night like a carnival performer to protect the city against criminals. She has fought a mind controller, broken into a Cressian stronghold, threatened a Cressian dignitary, and now she's off on a dangerous mission into Wintercress itself, and this is the choice that upsets you? You were all right with her leaving Storm's Quarry to find herself. Why does me being with her change that?" Shay let out a caustic laugh. "Stars, you were all right with her being *nivasi*? No one else in your family was, and yet that didn't stop you. Now you find out that she has a preference for women, and that's the final straw?"

"I—" Whatever Shadar had been about to say deserted him, and he did not meet Shay's eyes.

"I know the Nomori disapprove of what Nadya and I have." Shay pressed on, knowing that if she did not say it now, she'd never work up the nerve to do it again. "I think it's ludicrous, but that is the way things are with your—our—people. But they also disapprove of what we are. You were strong enough to leave that hatred and fear behind. Why not this?"

The Guardmaster swallowed visibly. "You do not understand. We have lost so much over the centuries. This city has been a haven for us in many ways, it has been our *Natsia*, and still it takes from us. We cling to whatever we can. You are too young to know what it is to be a leader to our people."

"And it was *our* people who declared that I never see past my sixth birthday." Shay turned around. The dull orange glow of the coals seared blue then white as Shay's anger fueled the forge. She took several breaths, gaining control of herself. "If you'll excuse me, Guardmaster," she said, but it was not a request.

Shadar did not argue. Shay heard his retreating footsteps leave the smithy, and she slumped against her workbench. It was too much, she thought, Nadya's absence, the resistance, her sister's death, and now the Gabori family demanding answers about their relationship. How foolish she had been, Shay thought with a grim smile, to believe that she and Nadya had found their happily ever after on the road together, no secrets, no old-fashioned Nomori traditions, and no Storm's Quarry.

Happy endings were for heroes. Not creatures that parents warned their children of, that fueled the nightmares of young and old alike. Not creatures like her.

CHAPTER THIRTEEN

One far too early morning, just over three weeks since Nadya left, Shay yawned and walked out of the mess, nearly slamming into the chest of Shadar Gabori. The Guardmaster, though out of the traditional crimson uniform of his order, looked as polished as ever in gray Nomori trousers and a lightly embroidered tunic.

Shay staggered back, swallowing the last bit of biscuit she had been chewing. She sighed and glanced around. "I don't want another argument. Not this soon after breakfast, at least."

"I am not here to argue." He gestured away, past the smithy and to the makeshift barracks where the warriors of the resistance slept and trained when they weren't engaged in other duties. "Come, practice with me."

"What?" Shay was sure she hadn't heard correctly.

"I've seen you fight. You know how to use a blade. I'd like to observe you close-up."

"To gauge my weaknesses?" Shay was only half kidding as she said it.

He chuckled. "Out of curiosity, more than anything. And I find sparring relaxes the mind."

She agreed with him there. Shay followed him through the cavern. She waved to Alla, who gave her a small smile as she folded up clean laundry. At least, Shay thought wryly, someone knew where she had gone if the Guardmaster decided to do away with her.

The Guardmaster's skill with a blade was well known throughout the resistance. He had been the trainer, then confidant, of the young Duke, after all. Two minutes after picking up a pair of practice rapiers—neither was keen to use their true weapons—Shay held no doubt about Shadar's ability.

Nomori men were fast and strong, their preternatural fighting skills a supposed gift from the Protectress that mirrored the psychic gifts of Nomori women. Shadar Gabori was stronger and faster than any guardsman Shay had fought before, and it was only her experience sparring with Nadya that had kept her from being knocked to the ground so far.

It was still quite early, she reminded herself as the Guardmaster's blade sliced downward a hairsbreadth from her nose. Shay spun out of his reach and brought her own rapier up in a defensive stance, wincing as iron clanged upon iron. They parted once more, circling one another.

Shay still wasn't convinced that Nadya's father wasn't trying to kill her while making it seem like a training accident. Shadar raised his blade until it was perfectly parallel to the ground and pointed at Shay.

"I must apologize," he said suddenly, and Shay nearly dropped her practice rapier.

He did not take advantage of the obvious opening her stuttered movements provided and continued to circle her. "For my words last week, the morning of our raid on the Cressian shipment."

She remembered them well. "Why?" Shay asked, her blade flashing toward him.

He parried it with ease and followed up with a crescent-shaped attack that nearly knocked Shay off her feet. "Because I was wrong. About you."

"Really?" Shay cleared her throat. "I mean, what made you realize it?"

"You did. You spoke the truth, if a bit bluntly." He smiled and lunged. Shay barely had enough time to block his blow before it landed on her shoulder. She twirled around his blade, drawing it up and releasing it, then dashing away to the far edge of the practice circle.

"My forgemaster always says the truth needs no softness," she said, breathing hard.

"Your forgemaster sounds like a wise woman."

"The wisest I know." Shay struck quickly, aiming for his unguarded side. Shadar swiped her blade aside with his own as if it was an annoying insect.

"I was reeling from the death of my wife. I still am," Shadar said suddenly, and the sorrow that dripped from his words brought a cold chill to the base of Shay's neck. "I lost my city, my Duke, and now my beloved Mirela. When I saw you with Nadya as her mother lay dying, the way you held one another...I knew that you were together. And it pained my heart, because it felt as if I was losing my daughter as well."

"Nadya loves you," Shay said. She brought her rapier up in a defensive stance. "Not even your disapproval of her blood or her choice in partners could change that."

"Protectress help me, I am not deserving of that love." An instant after he spoke, Shadar struck. Too distracted by what he had said, Shay misread his movements. She blocked too late, and before she could draw a breath, her back slammed into the hard ground.

Shay lay there a moment, wondering what assortment of bruises she'd wake up with the next morning.

Shadar leaned over and offered his hand, and Shay took it, still reeling from the speed with which he had taken her down. "Good fight. You've more than raw talent, and you don't rely on your weapons to carry you through the fight. Something my daughter is still learning."

"Thanks." Shay held the practice rapier awkwardly at her side.

"I hope I get a chance to meet your forgemaster one day. I would like to speak with the woman who trained and raised you."

The thought of the two masters meeting—one the commander of the Duke's Guard, the other of the art of the smith—made Shay's temples ache. She didn't know if she would survive such an encounter, and she was sure Nadya would feel the same way. Yet she could not help but be grateful that Shadar was taking such an interest in her life. Perhaps it did truly mean that he had left behind the Nomori distaste for their relationship.

"Well," Shadar said after Shay couldn't find any words, "thank you for humoring an old man with a bout of sparring. But now, we are needed in the Bulwark."

"We?"

The Guardmaster nodded. "Come. There is a special assignment for you." He sheathed his rapier and began walking out of the barracks area.

Shay bit back a barrage of questions. She hung up her practice weapon, hoping no one would notice the scorch marks on the hilt, and followed him.

❖

"You want me to what?" Shay blurted out, unable to keep her silence any longer. "Forgive me, but I could have sworn you just laid out a suicide mission in which you send me to up to the palace, which happens to house the Crown Prince of Wintercress, his weaponized *nivasi*, and nearly the entire Cressian regiment." Shay shook her head. "But I couldn't have heard that right."

She stood in the Bulwark. Shadar had positioned himself behind her, his back to the door, a casual hand on the hilt of his rapier. Marko and Kesali leaned over the room's only table, as covered in parchments and maps as always. In the far corner, Drina Gabori sat in a rickety chair that squeaked every time she shifted her weight. Shay had wondered at her presence at what seemed to be a war council, but she wouldn't put it past the

Nomori Elder to have invited herself, with no one being brave enough to tell her otherwise.

Kesali sighed. "We are not trying to throw you to the wolves, Shay."

"Really, because it feels like just that." Shay immediately regretted her words when the Stormspeaker's face hardened. She didn't like Kesali, and doubted she ever would, but the Stormspeaker had earned her grudging respect in the past weeks with the way she worked tirelessly for her people. Such jabs felt petty and left Shay with a sour taste in her mouth.

Behind her, Shadar spoke. "This evening, the Prince will greet a new regiment of soldiers sent by his father. He and his *nivasi* will be at what remains of the front gate. It's the best time to infiltrate the palace."

"Am I getting backup again?" Shay asked to buy herself time to think through what they were asking of her. It sounded suicidal; even with the Prince and the *nivasi* away from the palace, it was a fortress unto itself.

Marko shook his head. "You will be on your own. Will you accept the assignment?"

His question carried far more behind it than whether or not Shay would break into the palace. *Will you be part of the resistance? Will you fight for us? Will you die for us?*

"Fine," Shay said. "But I expect to be present during the interrogation."

"That will be fine," Kesali agreed, surprising Shay will her lack of argument.

"Great. Should be a ball, then," Shay muttered.

She was completely wrong.

For every Cressian soldier patrolling the lower tiers there seemed to be three in the palace, and they all enjoyed loitering in Shay's path. As soon as she crested the staircase and slunk along the wall of the palace's courtyard, Shay had to slow to a crawl to look around every corner and listen for any sound of a guard. One alarm, and she'd have to blast her way in.

And, as the Guardmaster had told her sternly, if she got caught on the way in, there was little chance of getting out unnoticed. So she took no chances.

Shay suffered no delusions that this separated her from Nadya, a stark difference that somehow they'd managed to overcome. Nadya, in all her goodness, abhorred taking a life and avoided it at all costs. Gedeon's death, however necessary, still haunted her, Shay knew. But she had no such qualms about taking a life that had brought pain to others. Looters, thieves, rapists— they had all found death under her blade. Cressian soldiers were no different. She had killed before, and she would kill again, and so when the only way to clear a tricky corridor in the upper wings of the palace was to draw a glowing dagger across the throat of an unsuspecting recruit, Shay did so without hesitating.

She paused as she passed by the entrance to the throne room. The last time she had been there, she had risked her life to save the city she despised from a poison in its water supply. For Nadya, she had told herself at the time.

Always for you, Nadya, she thought as she snuck up behind an unsuspecting soldier who guarded the hall to the palace's living quarters. Her fist smashed down upon his head, and he crumpled instantly. She might not have Nadya's strength, but she certainly could apply some force when necessary.

"Should have worn a helm," she whispered to the unconscious soldier as she stepped over him and continued down the hall.

Fire shot from her hands, an extension of her own body, and melted the lock on an ornately carved door, just down the hall. The wood charred and smoked, and the door swung inward.

Shay ignored the lavish quarters and their finery, protected from the city's damp by a suffocating amount of cleaning ointment, and walked into the room. She was not alone.

A figure in white turned away from the window. Councillor Aster smiled at Shay. "I assume you have come for me."

❖

A shanty at the far edge of the cavern had been evacuated, stripped of all furnishings but for two wooden chairs; one sat in the center of the room, and one in the corner. Several guardsmen were posted in a circle surrounding the building, but far enough away that they could not hear the interrogation within.

When their prisoner had been secured and the door latched tightly, Marko stepped forward and tore the blindfold off Aster's face.

Despite being dressed only in a disheveled nightgown and tied to a chair, Councillor Aster carried a commanding presence, and she looked down her nose at her captors as if she was evaluating some hogs for sale. She certainly didn't seem like someone who had been smuggled between buildings and through mining tunnels for the better part of the night, hot blades of light a hairsbreadth from her vulnerable back.

"Well, I cannot say this is unexpected," she said in drawled Nomori. Shay's eyebrows shot up; she didn't know the councillor spoke the Nomori language, and the sharp breath from Drina's corner indicated that the Nomori Elder had not expected it either.

"Nice to see you again, Lord Marko. Or is it Duke Isyanov now?" Aster asked with a slight smile, and Marko's white-knuckled hand closed in upon the hilt of his rapier. "And you as well, Lady Stormspeaker. Commander of your own small army, I see. Everything your mother trained you for, no doubt."

Kesali's mouth drew into a tight line, her lips nearly disappearing. "Your smugness does you no credit, Aster. There will be no escape for you."

"Right. Here comes the part where you threaten me." Aster nodded to Shadar and Shay. "With your guardsman and *nivasi* here for physical force, if necessary. Have you thought through your torture methods? Do you know the best ways to extract knowledge from an unwilling source?"

She continued when no one spoke. "I do, you see. Did you honestly think to intimidate me? I was born and raised in the imperial court of Wintercress. I have been trained in every type of political intrigue. I have been tortured to test my resolve, and I have never been broken. You are all fools if you think to get anything from me."

Shay bit back a wave of reluctant respect for Aster.

"We do not wish to torture you, child." Drina rose unsteadily to her feet. Shadar was instantly at her side, offering an arm for her to lean on. "We wish only to speak with you."

Aster laughed. "And a wizened old Nomori woman will be my undoing?"

"That depends," Drina said, her voice suddenly edged like a knife, "if your training included resisting the power of a Nomori psychic."

Nearly imperceptibly, Aster swallowed hard. Shay could not help but grin. Such a little loss of control by the councillor was tantamount to begging from another, less powerful mind. This was going to be fun.

Kesali stepped in front of Aster. "We don't care for knowledge of Cressian troop movements or the secrets of your cousin's *nivasi*."

"Or," Shay couldn't help but add, "the schedule of the High King's bowel movements."

The Stormspeaker glared at her, but her eyes carried a hint of amusement.

"Well, you certainly didn't bring me here to discuss the weather." Aster leaned back in the chair. "Apparently I have all night, so take your time, by all means."

"Do you like your cousin?" Kesali asked suddenly.

The innocuous question seemed to suck the heat right out of the room, and Shay shifted her stance, watching Aster. The councillor did not flinch, but the slightest hesitation marked her words.

"Of course. The Crown Prince is the heir to the throne of Wintercress. He is loyal to the crown, a powerful leader, and ruthless in the name of the High King in all he does. There is nothing to dislike."

"Personally, though," Kesali pressed, "do you enjoy his company? Do you like to stand behind him as he leads your nation from conquest to conquest?"

Councillor Aster raised her eyebrows. "Are you actually trying to convince me to your side by manipulating my supposed jealousy of my cousin? Come now, Lady Kesali, you are better than that."

"Your high opinion flatters me." Kesali gave the councillor a venomous smile. "I do hope you hold on to it as we proceed."

Proceed she did, as an hour passed. Aster dodged each of questions that Kesali, Marko, and Drina threw at her with graceful ease. As time wore on, however, not even the councillor could hide her weariness. Her answers grew shorter and sharper, but still incredibly useless.

The interrogation seemed to be getting absolutely nowhere, and Shay's back had started to hurt from standing still for so long. How much would Nadya's father look down on her for walking out?

"Has he always been so...regal?" the Stormspeaker asked suddenly. Kesali's voice brought Shay's attention back to the proceedings at hand.

Aster had paled somewhat as the hour grew later, but her tongue had lost none of its bite. "He is the Crown Prince. I'm sure you can figure the rest from there."

"But you knew him as a child. Grew up together, if I'm not mistaken. You've seen him at his best and at his worst. Or have you always eaten up his shadow like the good soldier you are?"

"My loyalty is not in question!" Aster's voice rose and cracked. "I have stood behind him, and I have taken his edict out into foreign lands. My devotion to the throne of Wintercress is known throughout the imperial court. I have worked for my kingdom through danger, risking my life. Over and over."

Kesali shrugged. "I'm sure the Prince has done the same."

"Ha! He has served his father graciously, but it was I who volunteered to come to this disgusting city to prepare it for annexation. It was I who worked through fire and storm. When plague took root in the imperial court, my Prince didn't dare leave his chambers, but I was there, holding court in his and his father's stead." She paused, breathing heavily. "Prince Trillium is a great man, and he recognizes all I have done for our nation."

A brief knowing look passed between Drina and Kesali in the aftermath of Aster's rant. The Stormspeaker turned back to the councillor. "If he holds you in as high esteem as you seem to think, then I am sure you will be rescued in no time. Until then, you will be our guest."

Shadar stepped outside to signal a few guardsmen. Shay stood to one side as they led Aster out of the makeshift interrogation chamber. She was not sure what just happened, but she wasn't about to let that Cressian woman observe any weakness.

"So," Shay asked when Councillor Aster had been escorted out by two guardsmen, "what is the plan? Why all the questions about Prince Trillium's past? Doesn't seem like much to use, honestly."

Her question had been casual curiosity, laced with a bit of bite; she'd risked her neck to bring in the councillor, and yet they did not seem to be any closer to regaining the city. It wasn't that Shay did not want to put herself in danger. She'd known when Nadya first received the message from her father that danger was all that awaited them. But if she was going to break in to the most secure part of the enemy-controlled city again, it had better be worth it.

A quick, indiscernible look passed between the two young royals before Marko quickly said, "General questioning, nothing more." Behind Shay, the Guardmaster shifted his stance but remained silent.

What were they hiding? she wondered, and the fire in her core began to spark. *Give them a chance to tell you the truth. They owe it to you, after all.*

Shay shook her head. "Seemed like there was something else going on."

"We wanted to get a better sense of what was happening in the palace, between the Prince and his advisors," Kesali added. "Anything that might give us an edge."

The lamps that hung on iron hooks flared suddenly as Shay's temper roared within her. She kept it on a leash, but it swirled and bubbled in her chest. "Don't lie to me."

"Shay, perhaps you should calm down," Shadar began, but Shay whirled around to face him.

"I am calm! I risked my neck to bring you the councillor. Now, I know you all are not stupid enough to waste the first opportunity to interrogate her, with the time you have before Trillium realizes she's missing, by taking the temperature of the drama in the palace. So tell me what is going on."

"We can't," Kesali said, crossing her arms. "The situation is too delicate, and you—"

"I what?" Shay snapped. "I'm a dangerous *nivasi* who can't be trusted?"

"She can be trusted." Drina's unexpected words came from the corner of the room where the old Nomori sat, hands folded neatly upon her lap. Shay stared at her, the fires in her chest dying down at the sudden vote of confidence from a Nomori Elder, of all people.

"You're reading me?" she asked.

"I read everyone, Shay. It is only a choice for me whether to dive deeply into someone's emotions or not. I do not need to do that with yours to know that you may be *nivasi*, may harbor some prejudice toward Storm's Quarry, but you do not have a traitorous thought in you. To betray those you fight beside is as alien to you as breathing water." Drina spoke with an even tone, her words confident and sure. She looked to the royal couple. "Do you doubt my word?"

Marko's face flushed as red as his hair, and Kesali could not meet Drina's eyes. "Of course not, Madame Gabori," she said. "We are just being cautious."

"And you, husband of my lost daughter?" Drina turned to

Shadar without acknowledging Kesali's words. "Can you accept the words of a Nomori Elder? Or does your instinct to protect Nadezhda from everything, even love, cloud your gaze?"

The Guardmaster bowed his head. "Forgive me. I know better than to question your word."

"Good." Drina gestured to the table that had been brought into the room. "Now, please explain your plan to us."

Kesali and Marko shared a look before he nodded.

"We are going to take back the Nomori tier," Marko said, rolling out a map. Fine-lined ink outlined each successive tier of the city, and the detail brought neighborhoods and tiny streets to life. Shay's gaze skimmed over it, noting the marked safe houses that dotted the first three tiers of the city.

She frowned. "Why? Prince Trillium is in the palace. So is his *nivasi*. We won't retake the city while the two of them still stand within its walls."

"You're right," Kesali said with matter-of-fact certainty. "But we do not have the strength nor the numbers to defeat the Prince within the palace."

"But when Nadya comes back…" Shay's words faded as she realized what they were saying. "You are planning for her failure. For her never returning." Her stomach twisted.

Shadar stepped up to the table. "No, of course not. She will come back. My daughter would die before abandoning her city, and I wouldn't bet against her in any fight that finds her in Wintercress."

His surety eased the roiling in Shay's chest. She swallowed and nodded. "Good. Because she's coming back." *She's coming back to Storm's Quarry, and she's coming back to me.*

"We will need her," Marko continued, "if our plan is to succeed. Without the Cressian *nivasi* out of the way, we'll have no hope of holding the Nomori tier."

"And you want to do that because…?" Shay asked, still unsure of why they'd favor the lowest tier in the city, far away from where Prince Trillium sat on his ill-gotten throne, over storming the palace.

"Even with the Cressian *nivasi* incapacitated and you and Nadya on our side, any fight with the bulk of Trillium's forces would be a foolish waste of life. If we can control the Nomori tier, we will hold the supply houses that Marko's father, Protectress grant him peace, set up in the weeks before the invasion." Kesali pointed to several marked squares on the map as she spoke. "And, most importantly—"

"We will control the only way into the city," Marko finished, and the royal couple looked at each other, sharing a small smile.

Shay resisted the urge to roll her eyes, because as she thought it out, it was a good plan. A very good plan. "You force Trillium to withdraw his forces to the upper tiers. The Nomori tier becomes easy pickings, and Nadya deals with the Cressian *nivasi*. Suddenly, Wintercress has to negotiate for the return of its Prince."

"Precisely," Shadar said. "It will not be easy, by any means, but it is possible, if all the pieces fall into place."

"It is ironic to think that the Nomori tier is now the battleground for the future of Storm's Quarry." Drina's voice carried no animosity, much to Shay's surprise, but rather a wistfulness she did not think the older woman capable of. Every pair of eyes turned to focus upon the Nomori Elder. Her fingers brushed the metal seal of the Protectress that wrapped around her throat on a leather band. "When your father brought us into the city, we were relegated to the lowest tier. The poorest Erevans once lived there, but they moved themselves to the second tier to avoid being neighbors with the witch people, as they called us." The corner of Drina's mouth upturned in a slight smile. "They called it the sea scum tier. We called it home, close to the waters of the Kyanite where our blood, borne upon the waterways of this world, felt closest to the Protectress. No place in this city has felt so much hate, has been deemed so insignificant, and now…"

Shay heard her own heartbeat in her eyes as Drina paused, finally looking up to the faces that hung onto her every word.

"And now," Drina finished, "now our *Natsia*, our long road home, has become the only path forward for Storm's Quarry."

Chapter Fourteen

The port city of Brome, marking the far eastern edge of Wintercress's sovereignty, was built into the side of the Stygian Mountains. As the *Seawitch* rounded a steep cliff face, the spindly guard towers of Brome came into view. Nadya's breath caught in her throat. The city's buildings rose up the mountainside in a mosaic of browns, grays, and whites.

On the far corner of the starboard side of the ship, the one Nadya had become intimately familiar with during their weeklong voyage as her seasickness never let up, she and Levka made last-minute preparations before their arrival. She thanked the Protectress that her nausea had abated to a slight twinge in her stomach; she truly didn't think there was anything left in her to retch up.

"We will pose as merchants," Levka said. He straightened his vest and rubbed at a speck of dust that had settled on his collar. "Husband and wife, both interested in acquiring rare artifacts. We've heard of an ancient temple in the area, and we will pay good coin to gain access."

Nadya groaned at *husband and wife*, but it was a good plan. It would give them the excuse they needed to ask around the city for information on access to the temple. "I pray this works," she said. "Surely a Nomori and an Erevan will be conspicuous, though."

"Not as much as you would think." Levka pulled on a velvet overcoat of deep jade that he had…reappropriated from one of the crewmen. "Most people this far north can barely tell the difference between a bear and a squirrel. With the number of travelers coming up from the South Marches, we'll blend right in."

She hated that there was nothing to do but trust him.

The port master, a tall man with silver hair and gnarled hands, stopped them before they could leave the dock after disembarking from the *Seawitch*. He looked them over with sharp, appraising eyes, and Nadya swallowed hard.

He barked out a few words in flowing Cressian, and her stomach twisted. They would be caught before they even entered. She shifted her feet, readying herself to block if the port master lunged with the saber belted at his waist.

But beside her, Levka smiled at them and replied in fluent Cressian. He gestured to himself and to Nadya, and she tried her best to hide her surprise. What other skills, she wondered as he slipped the port master a coin and steered her off the dock, was the former magistrate hiding?

The city of Brome suddenly extended up before them. Stained windows glinted in the sun, and a myriad of people wandered about, carrying food and other goods that Nadya didn't recognize. It was as if she had stepped into another world.

"Unfortunately, we don't have any time for sightseeing. I suggest you close your mouth, Nadezhda, or risk having a seabird nest in it."

She jerked back to Levka, who wore a patronizing smile. "Fine. What are we going to do?"

"I have a plan."

"A plan? The same one that you refuse to share me with?" she hissed as they made their way through the crowded streets.

"Ah yes, well, you cannot fault me for that. There are aspects of it that are beyond your comprehension."

"If we weren't in a hostile city surrounded by people I would hit you with such force that you flew out into the ocean," Nadya said, forcing a smile.

"I have no doubt." Levka's jovial tone sounded equally fake. "But if we're going to find a way into the temple, I will need to get going. To the Cressian scholastic society, to be precise. Does that satisfy your annoying urge to be privy to everything?"

"It's a start," she muttered.

After pointing out that she would stick out in any house of scholarship like a pigeon among gulls, Levka left Nadya in the shopping district with some infuriating line about buying something nice. She watched him vanish into the crowds, heading toward an outpost of the Wintercress Society of the Noble Scholar. Its brick building bore a stained glass window of an owl devouring a snake while holding a candle in its opposite talon. It was just as well Levka insisted she didn't accompany him; she would have probably choked on the insufferable air the place gave off.

Levka returned within the hour as Nadya wandered between stalls and the open doors of shops. She understood little of what was said around her but admired the intricate rope art and painted starfish proudly displayed all the same.

Levka stormed up to her, his erratic heartbeat drowning out the calls of sellers and distant crash of the waves. "Damn this city!" he swore.

Nadya had never seen him so disheveled, not even on the morning of the Blood Sun Solstice when she had confronted him in the throne room. "What happened?"

"It's completely locked down," Levka said, running a hand through his hair. "There is a veritable army between the road and the entrance to the temple. Not to mention the second army that is no doubt waiting inside."

Nadya shrugged. "I've dealt with Cressian soldiers before."

"Yes, I am very familiar with your hack and slash manner.

The thing is, Nadezhda, we need to not only get in but have time to study the temple." Levka had assumed a mocking tone, as if he spoke to a child. "That won't be possible if the entire nation of Wintercress knows of our presence, will it?"

"All right, I get it." Nadya crossed her arms. "We can't fight our way in. But what are our other options? They aren't exactly going to open the temple up to a couple of travelers, and I don't know that our disguises would hold if they did."

Levka turned away from her and said, his tone abruptly changing, "Don't worry, I have a secondary plan. I suggest you find a place to get some sleep. We will be quite busy tonight."

Nadya didn't even bother asking what he had planned for them. He wouldn't reveal anything he didn't want to, and he got a perverted pleasure from keeping her in the dark. She had a feeling she'd need to bail them both out of whatever situation he got them into, but if it gave them the knowledge they sought about the Cressian *nivasi*, all this would be worth it.

❖

"To access a secure site, you need someone who specializes in getting people where they aren't supposed to be," Levka said as they left the inn several hours after dusk. "Lucky for us, a port city is rife with smugglers and pirates."

"And you will barter with what coin exactly?" she asked, only to receive a smug smile in return.

Protectress, save us. She went along only because, so far, Levka's schemes had proven to be brilliant. Unstable and dangerous, but brilliant.

He led them away from the inn, down narrow, twisting city streets. Despite the late hour, Brome was alive with sound: the bubbling of a wood flute, laugher of sailors enjoying their first ale ashore, shrieks of children chasing one another through lines of drying linen. The life of the city, however, soon gave way to eerie alleys and an oppressive atmosphere that warned off any who fell on the right side of the law.

Nadya averted her eyes from the stares that followed the two of them. She pulled her cloak tightly against her chest. "We really shouldn't be here," she whispered.

Levka did not even glance at her. He walked with squared shoulders, meeting the gaze of every person they passed. "One doesn't find smugglers in the posher parts of any city. Or rather, those kind of smugglers are far more difficult to find, and harder to impress. These cretins will do for our purposes."

She winced. "It won't do any good to get ambushed before we meet with anyone."

Levka simply shrugged and continued onward.

Nadya followed him, shaking her head. He either had no sense of danger, was completely suicidal, or believed so thoroughly in his own superiority that he couldn't possibly imagine anyone attempting to cross him.

He came to a stop at the corner of a dark alley. A pile of refuse occupied the adjoining lot, running into the warehouse that he pointed out. It was a squat gray building with a squat gray man standing in front of the door.

"Who are we talking to in there?" she whispered.

He gave her a look, and Nadya glared at him. "You cannot be serious." She shook her head. "You're not leaving me outside again while you go in and make deals."

"You do not speak Cressian. Neither do you have any sense of tact or persuasion. You're a liability in there, Nadezhda." Levka held up his hand when Nadya opened her mouth. "You don't trust me. Fine, I don't trust you. But there is a reason you agreed to do this with me. You need me for this part, and you know I will do anything to see my city freed." His eyes burned into hers.

Nadya looked away first. He would do anything, including betray her. She couldn't help but recall his soft words from the week before, when they'd first shared a room at Nim's inn: *You need monsters to defeat monsters.* If there was anything she could trust about him, it was his devotion to Storm's Quarry.

"Go ahead," she said, backing away. "I'll wait out here. Try not to get yourself killed."

Levka flashed her a smug smile and approached the lookout at the door of the warehouse. After a hushed conversation in Cressian, he disappeared inside.

Night grew darker in the lower parts of Brome. Nadya kept out of sight as best she could, loitering across the street from the warehouse. She drummed her fingers against her leg nervously. She couldn't quite hear was what being said inside the stone building, and the heavyset man who stood in front of the door, arms crossed, dissuaded her from trying to move closer.

They would either emerge together with the information they needed, she thought, shrinking in the shadows, or she would emerge, short one former magistrate. Either way, a win.

A girl's yell broke through Nadya's thoughts.

Down the street, three grown men cursed and sprinted after a smaller girl. She wore a thin dress and a scarf around her head, blond hair streaming out as she ran. In her arms, she clutched a large sack.

Nadya bit her lip. She knew exactly what Levka would think of her interfering and drawing attention to herself, and that made up her mind.

She waited, timing it so she did not move until the girl's pursuers were nearly on top of her. Then Nadya leapt forward, slamming one of them to the ground. She twisted and thrust her shoulder into the chest of another. He went down without a sound.

The girl screamed and backed away from her. Ignoring the queasiness that rose in her throat, Naya turned away from the Cressian girl and grabbed the arm of the remaining man.

"Run," she said in Nomori. Whether he understood or not, her message was clear. As soon as she let him go, he dashed down the road, tripping in his haste to get away.

A deep shout echoed down the street. Nadya turned, and her chest constricted. A uniformed Cressian soldier stood there, his saber out and pointed at her throat. Was this man here for the girl as well? How far was she willing to go to protect her?

The girl, however, cried out in Cressian and ran toward the soldier. Nadya moved out of her way. She dropped the sack when she reached him and threw her arms around him. The soldier returned the embrace one-handed, never dropping his weapon.

Nadya couldn't understand her distraught words, but the similarity of their features—the green eyes and broad nose—was unmistakable. This girl must be his daughter, and he glared daggers at Nadya as if she might attack at any moment. Another hurried exchange, and the girl took off running toward a row of buildings on the opposite block.

The Cressian soldier kept himself between Nadya and his daughter until her figure had disappeared into a nearby building. His blade never wavered as it pointed at Nadya's throat.

This was an enemy soldier, but this was also a father protecting his daughter. Nadya felt a pang of homesickness and grief, and she lowered her arms. Hands out in front, as if approaching a wary animal, she backed up until she stood ten paces from the soldier. Her stance didn't change, in case he decided to lunge for her.

Idiot, she could hear Levka chastise in her mind. *If we are found out, we will have to leave Brome without getting the information we came for. And without that, Storm's Quarry is lost. Is the future of your city worth one man?*

The Cressian soldier did not lower his saber. "You are the Iron Phoenix," he said in heavily accented Erevo, and Nadya's stomach sank. Whatever cover they had, this man could blow it at any moment.

"You escaped Storm's Quarry?" His voice carried an undertone of contempt, and the flash of derision in his eyes came not from her title, Nadya was sure, but from her actions.

Defensive words rose up in Nadya's throat. She wanted to

explain to this stranger, to this enemy soldier, that she hadn't left Storm's Quarry to its fate. That she was here, in Brome, seeking knowledge to expel Wintercress from her home.

"I am going back," she said finally, and the Cressian soldier straightened, eyes sharp and searching as he stared at her.

Silence stretched between them. He did not lower his saber, and she did not back down from her offensive stance, hands balled into fists and at the ready.

"You saved my child. A debt is owed."

Of all the things she expected him to say, that was not it. "She needed help," Nadya said. "You owe me nothing."

"You didn't have to." His stare intensified, and Nadya found herself struggling to hold his gaze.

What did he expect her to say? That she would have let a teenage girl get hurt in order to keep herself hidden? *Maybe that's exactly what they've been told of me here.* The thought turned her stomach as much as an ocean wave.

"I am not a monster," she said quietly, wondering why she needed this man, a stranger and an enemy, to believe it.

The tip of his saber bobbed up and down, as if in agreement, and then, in one fluid movement, he sheathed the blade. "Perhaps not." He crossed his arms. "What does the Phoenix seek in Brome so far from Storm's Quarry?"

Nadya glanced back at the warehouse, where Levka negotiated for the help of pirates to break in to the Nomori temple. He would be furious if she shared anything with anyone, let alone a citizen of Wintercress. She found herself fingering the outline of the metal band around her upper arm. Her seal of the Protectress warmed to her touch, and Nadya drew a deep breath. "The ancient temple of the Nomori."

The soldier raised his eyebrows, but he nodded slowly. "Very well guarded."

"I noticed."

A small smile cracked his face. "Yes. I spent a rotation there just after the excavations stopped. Very cramped and musty. We slept on the ground."

She winced in sympathy.

"There is a back entrance to the temple."

Her expression gave way to disbelief. "What?" Her heartbeat thudded in her ears as Nadya tried to calm down. "How do you know that?" *Why are you telling me?*

"Because we caved it in. Gunpowder and some sparks. Captain decided it required too many men to guard both, and the back entrance is small, hardly noticeable. We filled it with rock and left it alone." He studied her for a long moment. "Rocks that are too big for a person to move."

But not for the Iron Phoenix. Nadya caught herself before she squealed. She met the soldier's pointed gaze and bowed deeply. His eyes widened in surprise as she said, "Thank you, sir. Any debt between us is repaid in full."

He nodded once and turned to walk away.

Nadya belatedly wondered his name as she watched him go, and her elation faded a bit as she realized she'd likely never know it.

"Excuse me," she muttered as she, gently as possible, shoved the lookout away from the door enough to slip inside the warehouse. Her nerves got the best of her, and his head slammed into the door. He slumped to the ground, unconscious. She paused a moment to ensure he was still breathing, and then entered the door.

Levka stood within a ring of five pirates, all armed to the teeth. Their leader sat on a wooden crate, leg dangling off its edge lazily. He had a golden stud in his ear and a saber on his belt. It was drawn the instant he realized Nadya had entered the warehouse.

She swore she saw a blood vessel pop in Levka's forehead, but she ignored him and put on her best vapid smile.

"Pardon my husband," Nadya said in her best imitation of an

Erevan courtier accent. "He is often lost and forgetful. A simple fellow, really, one with delusions of adventure." She slung an arm around Levka, whose eyes crinkled with anger. He was, at least, smart enough to keep silent.

"I just put him to bed with a glass of warm milk a couple of hours ago," she continued, enjoying herself perhaps a bit too much. All the while she spoke, she edged herself and Levka toward the door. "I go to check on him, and he's gone. The innkeeper said he left muttering about ancient treasures."

"Is that so?" one of the men said in stuttered Erevo. He looked from Levka to Nadya, his fingers stroking the sword at his belt. "Should keep better watch over such a fool. He could've been killed wandering around here."

"What about the coin he promised?" a slim woman piped from the corner. She had a triangle tattooed over one eye, and she twirled a dagger around her fingers without glancing at it. "He said he knew someone who could break into the treasury house in return for our help. We can't let that walk out the door."

Nadya shot Levka an acidic glare. So he had bartered her strength in return for being smuggled into the temple. She would need to have a friendly discussion with him about that once they were out of here.

"He knows all of three people, one of whom is his mother. I apologize, gentlemen, madam," she said and inclined her head. "But you've been misled. I will take him away before he causes you any more lost time." She bit the inside of her mouth, waiting. Nadya knew she could take on the half dozen pirates in the room, but she doubted she could do it without calling attention to them.

After a long moment of silence, the man with the gold earring laughed. "Take your husband, madam, and see that he keeps himself out of trouble."

Nadya ducked her head in thanks and nearly shoved Levka out the door.

"What in the name of the forgotten gods are you doing?" Levka exploded as soon as they were out of earshot. "You ruined everything! Didn't you learn after Nim? I had nearly cinched us a deal, and you barge in with your petty insults and—"

"I found us a way into the temple," Nadya said calmly, knowing it would infuriate him even more. "While you were playing merchant with a bunch of pirates, using my skills as barter, I might add, I found out about a secret entrance in the back of the temple. No guards, only a couple of large stones in place to prevent entrance." She couldn't help the triumphant grin that spread across her face at Levka's disbelieving look. "Don't worry," she added, "I'm sure you will still be useful for something."

CHAPTER FIFTEEN

It did not come as a surprise to Shay when, one morning not long after Aster's interrogation, she walked up to the smithy to find the messenger boy with the missing front teeth waiting for her.

"The Duke and Lady Stormspeaker want to see you."

She tossed him the last bite of her breakfast and made her way to the Bulwark.

Marko and Kesali barely looked up as she entered.

"Once we have word from Nadya that she is returning with the tools to deal with the Cressian *nivasi*, we can put the second phase of the plan into action. Until then, we must make Prince Trillium as nervous and frightened as possible." Kesali finally glanced at Shay. "That's where you come in."

"I guessed as much." Shay glanced between the two royals. "Well, what am I to do to the dear Prince?"

"He fears sickness, according to what his cousin revealed. We will use that. After all," Kesali said with the wicked smile that was beginning to unnerve Shay in its ruthlessness, "a city at war is ripe for plague."

There were several signs of plague, the Stormspeaker had informed her. Rats, for one. In ancient stories that spanned races and nations, rats were always depicted as the demons that carried sickness upon their breath. Peanna had already sent her rats out into the lower tiers. Instead of delivering messages, they followed Cressian troops, skittering and squeaking enough to gather the attention of the soldiers.

Next, quarantine. Kesali and Marko had sent unassuming Erevans and Nomori out into the first two tiers of the city to begin a gossip campaign. Word traveled among those still living there, and families began painting different symbols upon their curtains and doors in black ink. A single line dotted at each end: *there is sickness here*. Two lines crossed over one another: *there is death here*.

And finally, victims. This, as Kesali had instructed, was where Shay would come in. Those who had already perished in the Cressian invasion would give their deaths for the future of the city. Erevan and Nomori families alike had donated their dead for the greater good of the city, forsaking the death rites that each held so dear. The fallen of Storm's Quarry had discreetly been piled up around the Nomori tier.

Shay halted in front of one such pile of dead, the third she had visited that night. Gray limbs stuck out underneath a layer of rubble, wriggling with maggots. She gagged at the smell, a mixture of sulfur and vomit that twisted her insides until she couldn't breathe.

It's just like lighting the coals of the forge, she tried to tell herself, but her words were less than convincing.

Blue fire bloomed at her fingertips and soared into the pile of dead flesh. Insects gave one last rustle before they were turned to ash. The scent of smoked flesh overwhelmed that of decay, but it made Shay even sicker, if that was possible. She struggled to contain the ferocity of her flames. Wintercress needed to recognize the burned corpses for what they were in order for this plan to work. After a minute that felt like it had stretched for hours, the pile of bodies before her lay charred, but unmistakably human.

Her gruesome task done, Shay called fire into her hand. It formed a small blade, and she crouched on the cobblestones in front of the burnt bodies. Carefully, she carved two crossed lines into the ground, melting the stone until its message became clear: *beware of the plague dead.*

If this was not enough to force Prince Trillium to withdraw his troops, then Shay did not know if anything would be.

She rose to her feet and felt it—a slight tremor in the ground. Shay had only time to throw her arms up over her face before a barrage of stone slammed into her.

Pain. It ripped through her core like lightning. She did not even have time to draw breath before fire burst from her chest. Strong flames bathed the street corner in dazzling orange and white light. It burned through the haze of pain that clouded her mind, and Shay snapped her eyes open. Two long blades of white fire, distilled into the purest light, extended from her hands.

Fifteen paces away, a slim woman in a simple white uniform stood. Her hands rested at her sides.

"You," Shay hissed. She brought her blades up in front of her, crossed and ready.

The Cressian *nivasi* looked as she had the day of the Duke's execution, not a glimmer of sweat or a hair out of place. Her sharp blue eyes watched Shay like a peregrine falcon assessing a field mouse.

But Shay was no mouse.

"I'm no common guardsman, if that is who you were expecting. It'll take more than a bit of rock to take me down."

The blond woman tilted her head. "I remember you." Her words carried an eerie, flat tone, and Shay instinctively backed up.

"Yes, and I remember you. You got lucky last time. That ends tonight." She spoke with reckless confidence that she did not feel. Shay knew that without Nadya and the knowledge she sought in the ancient Nomori temple, she stood little chance against this creature, this woman with the blood of Wintercress, the power of the *nivasi*, and the ability to move mountains.

The Cressian *nivasi* did not answer. Instead, two chunks of stone ripped themselves from the ground with a terrible grinding noise. They floated in the air on either side of her like twin cannonballs, and Shay swallowed hard.

Her back ached with the memory of the last fight she and Nadya had with this impossible woman. Only dumb luck had saved them, and Shay had a horrible feeling that she had run out of luck.

Shay shifted her weight from foot to foot. If she took off running, the Cressian *nivasi* would no doubt pursue. Half the city might be destroyed in the process.

Offhandedly, she wondered when she started caring about whether or not Storm's Quarry was destroyed.

Her blades of light flared, and she charged toward the *nivasi*.

Shay dodged the first barrage of stone, weaving her way around the oncoming boulders. She kept her stance light and mobile, pausing on the ground gave the *nivasi* a chance to trap her in its embrace.

Three steps. Three steps before her blades could pierce the thin leather armor the *nivasi* wore and burn her to cinders. Three steps from victory against Wintercress, Shay failed.

A shield of stone sprang up in front of the *nivasi*. Shay's blades carved it like hot butter, but she lost her momentum. In the few moments it took her to reduce the shield to smoldering gravel, the *nivasi* got her chance.

The earth rose up on either side of her. Shay jumped back to avoid being crushed between the two slabs. Another stone slammed into her legs, knocking her to the ground and extinguishing her blades. Shay tried to get her feet underneath her when she saw the largest rock yet floating over her. It landed with a sickening crunch.

Less than a minute after the battle had begun, she was trapped beneath a boulder. Its weight pressed down upon her lungs until Shay saw stars.

Nadya...

A thousand thoughts flashed through her mind of the future they would never have together, here in Storm's Quarry or out on the road, and suddenly it didn't matter if Nadya insisted upon staying in this city, because she was enough for Shay. She would always be enough.

Forgive me for leaving you.

The edges of her vision began to blur. Shay kept her gaze steady despite the tears that began leaking from the corners of her eyes. No one was going to say that Shay Rissalo died with her eyes closed.

"Well, what are you waiting for?" she said through gritted teeth. "I can feel the stars calling me. Can't you hear them singing? Does whatever twisted abomination you are give you Nomori blood too?"

A pause, and Shay's vision swam with darkness, fading away as the pain in her chest receded and she embraced the void.

Except she wasn't dead. Again. Jeta's rare and deep laugh echoed in her mind as Shay's breath came back to her. Once, twice. Her chest throbbed in pain as it rose to fill her lungs, but she clamped on to that pain. It meant she still lived.

The rock that had been crushing her hovered above the ground, less than a pace from the bridge of her nose.

Shay stared at the death that hung over her. The *nivasi* fire in her chest, as burned-out as it was, raged against her inevitable fate, a tiny dragon against the darkness of the night sky.

Slowly, the boulder rose.

Hardly daring to believe it, Shay took her chance. She rolled to the side, screaming as her ribs cracked and threatened to suffocate her once more. But she was out from under the shadow of earth.

She scrambled to her feet. Gravel and dust fell from her armor. She glanced down, and saw a perfect silhouette of herself, sprawled out, seared black into the cobblestoned street. The tired and low flame within her sputtered out into her hands, and she turned toward the *nivasi* with the barest outline of daggers grasped in each palm.

"Come on, then!" Shay shouted, voice hoarse. "Fight me!"

The Cressian *nivasi* raised a hand, and a tremor ran through the ground. Shay steadied herself, praying to any of the gods that might listen for some kind of miracle.

The large chunk of stone that had nearly crushed Shay levitated and, as if carried on a gust of wind, settled into the large pit whence it had come. It scraped against the ragged edges of the indentation in the street. All of a sudden the grinding noise stopped and there was only silence.

The Cressian *nivasi* nodded once and turned away.

Shay wondered if she really had died and was currently drifting through some impossible future.

"You're just going to walk away? Leave me here?" Shay couldn't hide the incredulity in her voice. Even as her better sense screamed at her to seize the opportunity and run away, she couldn't bring herself to move.

"They did not tell me to kill you." The Cressian *nivasi*'s Erevo was accented with the familiar lilt of the northerner race. She stared at Shay, her face devoid of any emotion.

Shay swallowed against the dryness in her throat. "That's it, then? You will let me walk away because Trillium didn't give you an explicit order to kill me?"

"Yes."

Her matter-of-fact tone staggered Shay. "How can you do that? You don't even know why I'm here."

"I was told to patrol this area and halt any insurgent activity. I have done that. My Prince asked nothing more of me, and so I will do nothing more." Something sparked in her searing blue eyes, but it faded back to placid obedience so quickly that Shay doubted she had even seen it.

The Cressian *nivasi* turned and began walking away. Debris drifted out of her way, and the street knitted itself back together as she passed. When she turned the far corner of the block, the scene looked as if nothing had taken place, except for the blood that trickled down Shay's forehead and her silhouette seared into the cobblestones.

CHAPTER SIXTEEN

The ancient Nomori landing site was located on the coast, north of Brome. It took several hours to reach, as Nadya and Levka had to travel on foot. Despite his grumblings, Levka agreed that stealing horses again was too risky. It meant that Nadya had to drag him up and over some of the rougher coastal terrain, but soon enough they reached their destination.

It was entirely nondescript. The rocky beach disappeared, and the gentle blue-black waves of the Brine of Lazuli drifted inward, vanishing in the darkness of the overhanging cave. Vines draped its edge, and moss, from dark forest-green to brilliant emerald, covered the rocky face of the cave. If not for the regiment of Wintercress soldiers that patrolled along each side of the cave carrying lanterns, and the small wooden boats tethered to rocks near its entrance, it would have been completely unremarkable, just another natural feature of this part of the world.

Nadya was sure her ancestors had intended it that way.

She and Levka stood several hundred paces from the entrance, hidden from view by the large, jagged rocks.

"Aren't you glad I insisted we find another way in?" Levka asked, his face smug as ever in the night's darkness.

"Forgetting that I'm the one who found us the secondary way in." Nadya scanned the coast. "There," she said, pointing.

"See those upright rocks? The moss has been scraped off them. They were moved. Probably to seal up the back entrance to the temple."

Levka didn't argue as she led him through the maze of boulders, sand, and gravel, out of sight of the Cressian troops who guarded whatever lay within the temple.

The boulders at the hidden entrance stood higher than her shoulder, and their surfaces bore the gouges of a lever and rope, no doubt what the Cressian forces had used to maneuver them into place.

"Keep a lookout," Nadya told her companion. She stretched her arms around the first rock, barely encircling half. She lifted and staggered backward.

A dark tunnel emerged from behind the stone. Beside her, Levka muttered, "Gods, it's true."

Without another word, they headed inside. Nadya pulled one of the large rocks back to cover their tracks lest a Cressian patrol come to investigate.

The tunnel's height grew as they ventured farther in, and Nadya went from brushing her head against the rough stone to barely reaching it with her fingertips. They trudged through mud. Tiny rivulets of water ran past them, escaping to the coast behind. Intertwined with the scents of salt water and crisp aquatic plants, a cloying tinge of decay colored the air. Nadya hoped it came from long ago, but her nose twitched.

"What do you suppose these tunnels were for?" Nadya asked.

"Runoff." Levka traced the smooth tunnel floor with a boot. "See how worn away it is compared to the walls? My guess is this place was once, centuries ago, an inlet of the Brine of Lazuli. The Nomori took their rafts in through the main entrance. These tunnels provided an outlet for the water to run off, to avoid flooding the temple."

It was, perhaps, the most civil exchange they had ever had,

but Nadya did not stop to dwell upon it. Ahead, the tunnels opened up, and as she approached, Nadya's chest tightened.

It was as if she was walking into the counterpart of the cavern beneath Storm's Quarry. The ragged tunnel walls gave way to a cave. It rivaled the size of the Nomori square back home. Its center held a deep pool of salt water, so black that Nadya could not see into its depths. Surrounding the pool, an immense stone wall rose up, covered in etchings. Several openings led to mysteries farther inside the temple. Above them, stalactites hung with pointed grace just as they did in the cavern of the resistance back home. The night sky just barely came through the arched opening, and in the distance, Nadya heard the low chatter of the Cressian regiment stationed outside the entrance to the temple.

The etchings, upon a closer look, were deep grooves carved into the natural dark stone of the cave's walls. They started just beyond where Nadya and Levka entered and continued on around the full circumference of the cave. Nearest to her, she picked out illustrations of people and boats, of lightning in the flat gray skies, and of blades and death.

"Fascinating," Levka muttered behind her. He ran his hand over one of the wall's intricate carvings.

She felt as if she had walked back into another time, before muskets and rapiers, steam pumps and printing presses, back to an age where stories were told by voice and inscribed in stone. Where her people spent their lives on bamboo rafts, following the stars and the currents, chanting in their ancient tongue.

"These tell the story of how the Nomori came to be." Levka traced a spiral carved into the dark stone of the cave walls. "A great gust of wind parted the waters of the World River, and from the silt, people emerged."

"You can read it?" Nadya couldn't hold the awe from her voice.

"Of course. Why do you think I let you drag me across the land?" His voice lacked its usual smugness, and his gaze was fixated upon the carvings. "I studied ancient texts under the Head Cleric. I have enough knowledge to interpret it generally."

"Go on," Nadya said, eager to hear more. "I know the story from Nomori gatherings. The Elders sing it, but I want to hear what my ancestors wrote."

"The people of the river," Levka continued, walking slowly along the wall as he pointed to each subsequent carving, "wandered aimlessly for many generations. They knew not where they traveled, or why. Only that the river sang in their blood."

He stopped in front of a large, intricate scene. Nadya stood only a pace behind him. The weathered gouges in the walls took the shape of a great sky dragon. Swirls of flame billowed out of its mouth onto the crouching figures below. Next to it, the same dragon flapped its wings and breathed flame, but a woman stood between the Nomori and its destruction. She stood as tall as the mountains and carried a five-petaled flower.

Levka's voice grew quieter. "A great beast came down from the sky and threatened to destroy the world. Wherever its fiery breath touched, water burned away and became land. The Nomori could not escape its hunger and found themselves trapped before the terrible creature."

Nadya held her breath even though she knew what was coming.

"A lady of the stars took pity on the Nomori and came down from the sky upon a trailing comet. She fought the dragon, overcoming its flame, and saved the Nomori from certain death. Then she offered them a path, guidance by the stars as they wandered the waterways of the world. In return for following her stars, she bestowed upon them gifts, gifts of the mind for Nomori women and gifts of the flesh for Nomori men. The nomadic people accepted her offer. Thus, the Nomori found their Protectress."

Her seal burned hot as Nadya reached out and gently trailed her fingers over the flower that the carved Protectress held. "A pact we still honor," she whispered.

Levka stepped back. "Yes, well, those stories won't give us any way to deal with the Cressian *nivasi*. We should keep moving. Dawn will come all too soon, and we cannot be here when the scientists return."

After walking a few more paces along the wall, he stopped and pointed to the multitude of footprints on the muddy cave floor. "This is where Wintercress's studies began, do you see? They weren't concerned with fairy stories of a Protectress."

As they moved forward into the temple, its serenity was displaced by clear evidence of Cressian presence. Fresh boot prints covered the muddy ground, along with tools that had been left behind: compasses and scrapers, measuring sticks and charcoal pens. A table was erected in one area, and Levka bent over it and studied the cramped Cressian handwriting that covered the notes that lay there.

"From what I can tell," he said after several minutes, "Wintercress has been researching the origin of the *nivasi*."

"Great," Nadya muttered. "Why are they so interested in us?"

Levka sighed dramatically. "Other than having two *nivasi* uncover their plot to poison the city's water and throw their councillor out on her hindquarters? I can't imagine." He peered closer at the instruments. "This is a thorough and vast operation. It is hard to believe that it's only been up and running for the past ten months."

Nadya swallowed hard. "You think it started when I started going out as the Phoenix?"

He leveled an even stare at her. "Could have been. It's likely, at least, that they already had their sights set on Storm's Quarry. The Blood Sun Solstice simply provided them an opening. If that's the case, then it stands to reason they would seek to understand, and copy, the power that ran loose in the city."

Silence stretched between them as Levka cleared his throat and looked away, as if realizing what he had just said.

"Do you regret it?" Nadya asked quietly.

Levka was still for a long moment. "Would it comfort you more to hear that I do, or that I do not?"

She considered for a moment. Of course, she wanted him to regret it; it was the least he could do after the devastation he had caused. But, she thought as her gaze traveled along the temple's carvings, would his regret be for the Nomori that had died? Would it be because he had realized that not all *nivasi* were monsters? Or simply because of the ill-timing of the massacre he had enabled?

In the end, she didn't have an answer, so she moved past him and continued to follow the carvings on the cave wall. After a moment, he joined her.

Ahead, another collection of Cressian instrumentation was strewn about. Tools and charts, books of notes, charcoal rubbings of the carvings: the clutter covered the wooden pallets laid out against the wall. Nadya resisted a strong urge to kick them away. This was a sacred place, and Wintercress had defiled it with their studies.

"Here. You should find something familiar."

She looked to where Levka pointed, and the awe that bubbled up in her chest at the majesty of the temple began to fizzle and shrink as she examined the wall. It depicted two groups of figures separated by a river. On the left, the Nomori stood in a close-knit group, rapiers drawn. And the other side…

The figures carved into the wall emerged out of a circle and bore grotesque expressions, with wild eyes and serrated teeth. Some had large curved horns sprouting from their heads. Others were wreathed in flames, or had talons for fingers.

Levka gestured to the monstrous figures. "*Nivasi*," he said. "The first, I would guess."

Nadya shifted uncomfortably beside him. She gazed at the carving and her stomach turned sour. Finally she tore her gaze away and looked at the tools and notes underneath. "Why would Wintercress care how *nivasi* come to be?"

Levka raised an eyebrow. "To recreate them?"

"But…" The words faded in her throat. The former magistrate wouldn't understand. Couldn't understand. *Nivasi* weren't an alchemical formula to be unlocked. They were…more than that. Nadya fingered her seal. The Protectress gave her these powers so she could in turn protect Storm's Quarry. Her family. Shay. Kesali.

Wintercress could not replicate that, not if they had a hundred years and all the knowledge of this world.

Levka frowned. "This is strange. See this circle here? It looks like it might be an impact crater."

"Like where the Kyanite Sea is now?" Nadya asked, thinking of the perfectly round inland sea and the city that sat at its center.

"Exactly." Levka pointed to the horned figures that arose out of the carved crater. "This seems to be saying that the origin of the *nivasi* is connected somehow to falling stars."

"Could it be another myth? The Nomori revere the power of the stars," Nadya said, uneasy.

"Could be anything. Your ancestors weren't exactly being articulate when they created this temple." He looked away from the wall and nodded. "We should keep moving. There's another station set up there. Maybe the scientists left something a bit more indicative about their purposes."

Ahead, a boxy white tent took up the entirety of an overhanging ledge that looked out over the still waters of the inlet. Nadya's fingers tingled with anger as she saw the broken shards of what might have been pots in a pile near the carved stairs that ascended to the ledge, as if the Cressians had just dumped them off without thinking of the history they destroyed in the process.

As she climbed the natural steps up the overhang, she heard an even breath coming from within the tent. They were not alone. With a swift wave of her hand, Nadya signaled to Levka to wait behind her as she approached the tent's open flap.

A single Cressian soldier, no doubt a night guard left behind to protect what lay in the ornate wooden case that stood within the tent, leaned back against one of the tent poles. He stiffened as Nadya's shadow fell across his field of vision.

Before he had a chance to draw his saber, Nadya struck. Her hand shot out, slamming downward into his chest and knocking the breath from his lungs. He slumped to the ground, unconscious.

Levka nudged the soldier with his boot. "Out like a lamp. You are efficient, if nothing else."

She couldn't decide whether that was a compliment or an insult, so she opted not to respond. Instead, Nadya peered into the cabinet he had been guarding. Its polished maple surface looked so out of place against the rocks and moss that made up the temple's walls. Inside, sat a single glass vial, no bigger than her forefinger.

It reminded her of the vials that physicians distributed their medicines in, but she doubted this had any medicinal properties. Nadya picked up the glass vial and sniffed it. It smelled like water, with a faint metallic tinge to it. She frowned. Did they collect it from somewhere in the temple? she wondered. Why put a guard on something like this?

"Could it be important?" she asked. "It cannot be just ground water, can it?"

"The scientific and alchemical achievements of Wintercress far outstrip any other nation in the known world," Levka said without looking up. "You could be holding a corrosive acid. Or the means to an explosion without gunpowder." He flipped open a notebook and began reading, muttering under his breath in Cressian. His eyes slowly widened. In the quiet of the temple, with only the soft lapping of the Brine of Lazuli in the distance, Nadya heard the thump of his heart quicken.

He had found something.

Levka began reading more intently. "The scientists interpreted those carvings of *nivasi* as we did, with some connection to craters and falling stars. But they pulled out the myth. There's quite a bit in here about the Protectress mythology being a foolish children's tale."

Nadya hadn't expected anything else of Wintercress. They disliked her people even more than Erevans, if that was possible. "But what does it say they found?"

"I am getting to that," Levka snapped. Instead of annoyance, however, excitement laced his tone. "They did experiments, some right here. Apparently, something about this place was conducive to their studies. Many of the subjects died. It took months to get the correct proportions in the serum."

That explained the scent of death that hung underneath the salt-tinge in the air. She did not want to consider how many bodies had been carelessly dumped around this place.

"The *nivasi* aberration is physical," Levka read slowly. "Whether it takes the form of changes to the body to allow incredible strength or to be immune to flame, these mutations manifest themselves physically. Even the mind manipulator had physical changes to his body."

Nadya shuddered at the memory of Gedeon's void-like eyes. Where once the memory would have overtaken her, however, now it remained only an unpleasant, bitter-tasting image in her mind. She had the strength to resist falling back into the darkness.

"Furthermore," Levka continued, ignoring or unaware of her discomfort, "*Nivasi* are only found among the Nomori people, and rarely. The Nomori themselves are anomalies among the other known races in the world. Their so-called psychic gifts and physical prowess, segregated by gender, still defy scientific explanation, but a thorough study is ongoing in the imperial court."

Nadya wondered how many of her kin were taken from Storm's Quarry after the initial invasion in the name of such scientific study. She would have to tell Kesali; once they expelled Wintercress, they needed to get their people back.

"It goes on for several pages to describe the peculiarities of the Nomori," Levka said, flipping through the manuscript. "But this, this is where it gets…interesting. They hypothesize that the physical remains of meteoroids—stardust, if you will—is the origin of *nivasi* power. If ingested at a young age, it combines with the natural Nomori gifts, augmenting them in such a way to produce something entirely different and far more dangerous."

He pointed to the glass that she held. "That vial contains stardust dissolved in water, concentrated to a point that it would affect even a non-Nomori. What you are holding is the essence of the *nivasi*."

Levka's words echoed around in her mind, and yet Nadya could not grasp them.

"It makes quite a bit of sense, actually." Levka continued to speak, but his words sounded faded and as if from far away to Nadya. "*Nivasi* are supposed to be incredibly rare among the Nomori. Once every century, perhaps. That's what the old writings indicate."

The old writings. The ones that warned the Nomori of her kind, calling her monster, creature, beast. Tears sprang to the corners of Nadya's eyes. She had overcome that hate by believing that the Protectress had chosen her. Had bestowed this strength upon her.

Levka's voice droned on. Each word was a nail into her heart. "Despite their recorded rarity, three known *nivasi* have come out of Storm's Quarry in the last twenty years. An extraordinary, and very dangerous, surge. If exposure as an infant is what turns Nomori into *nivasi*, then Storm's Quarry could be a factory of these monsters. The Kyanite Sea is thick with stardust, as it now sits where a fallen star once did. Even the fresh water within the city's walls must be tainted. That is where your *nivasi* blood comes from, if Wintercress is right. And I believe they are, considering they recreated the process to turn one of their own into a weapon. Your Nomori blood is saturated with stardust.

Sheer bad luck. It could have been any of the Nomori children born in Storm's Quarry."

As he spoke, Nadya's breath grew ragged. The vial slipped suddenly from her hands. Levka swore and dove forward, catching it. He struggled back up to his feet.

"Get ahold of yourself, Nadezhda," he said, but she hardly heard him.

Levka grabbed her arm. In the distance, she heard him yelling into her ear. "Calm down! Do you hear me? The *nivasi* come from stardust, nothing more. This, this is as much *nivasi* as you are." He waved the clear vial in front of her face, but Nadya barely saw it.

"This is our answer, Nadezhda." The vial's contents sparkled in the flickering lantern light as Levka tilted it back and forth.

"It's a lie," Nadya snapped. "It's another Cressian trick, a trap they laid with their alchemy. Poison!"

"Just because the truth isn't what you want to hear"—anger rose in Levka's tone—"because it means you aren't different from Gedeon or Durriken the Butcher. No gift of your Protectress separates you from the monstrous *nivasi* that have plagued this world for generations. Your abilities are not divinely given. It was the random chance of fate that you ingested enough stardust to be twisted into one of the *nivasi*. Nothing more."

Nadya did not respond. Her arm shot out before she could think better of it, and Levka shouted, "No! This is our answer! Can't you see that?"

She pulled the blow just in time. Levka staggered backward, but the vial in his hands was safe.

"Never," she whispered, "never compare me to him again."

Levka's eyes were wide and his fingers that held the glass trembled. For days, he had needled her, only now pushing far enough to see what he might unleash. Nadya sucked in a harsh breath. She didn't want to hurt him, but his words dug deep into her skin like barbs, and her first instinct was to tear them out.

"Nadezhda." He began speaking again quietly. "You don't have the power to overcome the Cressian *nivasi*, and we don't have time to study all of these notes to see if she has a weakness we could exploit. We have to use this."

"So?" Nadya asked, but her voice was low and hoarse as Levka's inevitable plan hurdled toward her, unstoppable.

"So," he said slowly, holding up the vial to her, "you consume this. Let its stardust mix with what's already in your blood. If you take this, you will be strong enough to move buildings, I'd guess. You could crush a man's chest with a single brush of your fingertips. Think of it. Take the power like Wintercress did, and become strong enough to defeat them."

"No." The whisper turned into a shout, clawing its way out of her raw throat. "No!" She backed away from Levka and the vial of evil he carried. "I won't."

Levka's words were drowned out by the sound of blood pumping through her ears. Nadya turned and ran. She leapt off the ledge and landed in the soft mud, slipping. Her trousers were covered in grime when she struggled to her feet, but Nadya couldn't care less. She ran, following the wall of ancient carvings that seemed to mock her. *It's lies, lies you've believed*, they chanted as she sprinted past.

A small opening in the mosaic wall of the temple appeared in front of her, and Nadya took it. She plunged into darkness. As her eyes adjusted to the dimness, she skidded to a halt.

Before her stood a shrine to the Protectress.

It could be nothing else. The small space was lined with a thin shelf of soil that held the remnants of flowers long rotted. At the center, a pool, dried up, was carved into the cave floor. Above the pool, the Protectress stood.

Carved of the same dark stone as the temple, the statue towered over her. Deep green moss clung to the carved folds of the robe she wore. In her hands, the statue held a five-petaled flower. Underneath the hood, she had no face.

Nadya fell to her knees before the statue.

Hear me if you're there, she pleaded silently, but the words begged to be spoken aloud. "If you truly are our Protectress..."

The statue before her looked solemnly on, the featureless face eternally serene. Nadya felt none of the tranquility of the shrine.

"Tell me there's another way. That I do not have to become a monstrosity in order to save my home. My family." Nadya's voice choked, and her eyes welled with tears. "Tell me there is more to *nivasi* nature than stardust and bloodlust. Tell me..." She couldn't force the words out.

Tell me I am different from Gedeon.

No response came from the faceless statue. Nadya grasped her seal and slowly tugged it off. The metal, smooth and warm from years of wear, felt alien under her fingertips for the first time. She ran her fingers over the etching of a five-petaled flower, a smaller version of the carving before her, and prayed.

Hear me if you're there.

It could have been mere minutes passing, or it could have been hours that went by as Nadya knelt at the shrine of the Protectress, silently praying for answers different than the one they had uncovered here. She was given no response.

Footsteps on gravel broke through the silence of her plea, and Nadya turned.

Levka stood at the entrance of the shrine. He shifted from foot to foot, no doubt ready to bolt if she made an aggressive move toward him. "Have you finished?" he asked. Instead of the usual smug bite, his voice carried only fatigue.

Nadya wiped her face. She sniffed and stood. Turning her back on the cracked statue of the Protectress, she nodded. "Yes."

"And?" A note of fear echoed underneath his words. Nadya ran her gaze over him. Dark circles hung under his eyes, and he clutched that Cressian vial with white knuckles.

His city is dying, and his only hope rests on the decision of his greatest enemy, she realized. Levka was a great many terrible things, but he was loyal to Storm's Quarry to a fault, and now...

Now, it rested on her. The fate of Storm's Quarry always had, it seemed.

"I will take it."

The tension ran out of Levka's body as his shoulders slumped forward. She heard his heartbeat calm. "Good. Here," he said, holding out the vial.

Nadya shook her head. "No."

"What? But you said—"

"I will take it," she repeated, her own heartbeat thudding against her chest. "But not now. I want to wait until we get back to Storm's Quarry."

Levka frowned. "We don't know how long it will take for the effects to take root. You should do it now. Why wait?"

Nadya took a deep breath. "Because once I take that, I will be dangerous. If it increases my strength as much as you say…" *I will be a danger to everyone near me. Including Shay.* "Please," she said finally. "Please, I need a chance to say good-bye."

He stared at her for a long moment before nodding. "You've earned that much. I will send a message to the resistance, letting them know we are returning with a way to combat the Cressian *nivasi*. Are you ready to depart?"

No! her mind screamed, and the statue behind her seemed to echo the word. But Nadya swallowed and nodded stiffly. "I am."

With a soft *clink*, she dropped her metal seal at the base of the statue and left the shrine without looking back.

Chapter Seventeen

It began slowly. Fewer patrols along the battlements and in the Nomori tier after sundown. A lack of response when a scuffle broke out among the drunkards on the second tier. Deserted outposts along the lower parts of the great staircase.

Then, one day, a barricade sprang up between the second and third tiers. White Cressian uniforms blazed in the hot afternoon sun as they patrolled along the staircase and the interior battlements. Those who tried to cross between tiers were denied entry.

A new decree from the Crown Prince came out: the lowest tiers of the city were to be quarantined to stop the spread of plague.

Hope strengthened each swing of Shay's forge hammer. Against all odds, and her own pessimism, the resistance's plan was working. Prince Trillium had withdrawn all but a skeleton guard on the lower tiers. All that remained before the final assault could occur was for Nadya to succeed in her mission to find a way to defeat the ultimate weapon that Wintercress had.

At dawn, a week after Shay's perplexing encounter with the Cressian *nivasi*, a young Nomori boy came hurtling through the camp. "Message for the Duke! Message for the Duke!"

Marko no longer flinched, Shay noted from where she stood at the smithy, when someone referred to him by his father's title.

He had been sparring nearby with several of the new recruits, but now dropped his practice rapier off and waved the messenger forward.

The young Duke scanned the message for only a brief moment before looking up and finding Shay's gaze across the raised platform of the smithy. He nodded once.

Her stomach began buzzing with a sickening sensation as she followed him through the cavern's paths.

In the Bulwark, Shay finally got her hands on the note. She ignored the others in the room—Kesali, Marko, and Shadar—and her fingers shook as she unfolded the parchment.

Today is the twenty-fifth of the dry season, the message read. *Tonight, we will leave and begin traveling back home. We have found what we sought, and we should arrive on the final day of this season.*

Today, Shay thought, and her chest tightened. She would see Nadya soon, and if the message was to be believed, she and Levka had been successful in their mission.

Below the neat script of the former magistrate, a familiar hand had scrawled a brief note: *You are the price I pay to save my city. Forgive me.*

Shay dropped the note. It floated down to the floor with barely a sound, and yet to Shay it sounded like the very walls of the cavern shook. *Forgive me*, Nadya had written, and yet Shay couldn't help the anger that roiled in her chest.

Damn this city! Damn this city and all it has taken from me.

Face burning, she turned and left the Bulwark. The Guardmaster shouted after her, but Shay was past listening. Cursing under her breath, she stormed through the center of the cavern. People took one look and dodged out of her way. Before long, she reached the far edge of the tunnel that she and Nadya had originally been brought through. A lifetime ago, it seemed.

She stopped, and it was only then that Shay realized she had been followed.

"No one will stop you." Kesali stepped up beside her and

gestured at the tunnel's entrance. "If you try to leave. No one would pursue you."

Bitterness welled in her throat. "So, I'm a coward, then? A scared little girl who runs from a fight? Or am I a selfish bastard who only fights when they have something to gain? It's hard to remember."

"That's not what I meant." The Stormspeaker stepped closer to her, extending a hand. Shay didn't move as Kesali grasped her shoulder. "I do not know you well, Shay, but I know you would die to defend Nadya. To defend your forgemaster. That makes you a hero, not a coward. But I cannot ask you to die defending a city that has done nothing but spurn you." Her hand fell away. "Or a resistance that never trusted you as it should have."

Forgive me. Nadya's haunting note echoed in the silence of Shay's thoughts. She could only imagine what had been found in that ancient Nomori temple for Nadya to write those words. What solution to the Cressian *nivasi* could possibly demand such a price from them both? Hadn't this damned city taken enough from them? Shay's hands curled into fists. Whatever it was, it couldn't be worth it.

You promised! she screamed at only herself. *You promised when all this began that nothing would separate us.*

That thought faded, and Shay turned to look back at the cavern of the resistance. It buzzed with more activity than usual, each person wearing an expression of grim determination. By the smithy, Alla handed out armor to a line of waiting fighters. Shadar stood ten paces away. Every newly armed person that passed him got a nod and a handshake. Rats scurried along the edges of the cavern, carrying the message out to those stationed around the city. Peanna's handiwork, Shay knew. Even old drunk Filipp had gotten up off his rock. He shuffled around, carrying boxes and parcels to and from different areas of the cavern.

She wasn't fighting for Storm's Quarry. Or those who had thrown her out so many years ago. She was fighting for the people that scurried about before her. For Alla and Filipp and

Peanna. For the Gaboris and their devotion to Nadya. For Marko and Kesali, who, despite everything, had taken in an unknown *nivasi* like her.

For the place she had found here.

If Nadya's note held the truth, and their relationship was the price to be paid for the salvation of Storm's Quarry... Shay swallowed against the thickness in her throat. Then these people were worth it.

"You aren't going to be rid of me that easily."

Kesali smiled. "I am glad to hear that, Shay."

Without another word, they turned and headed back to the Bulwark. When they arrived, no one commented on Shay's sudden exit. Shadar only gave her a deep nod, respect shining in his eyes.

"It has to be tonight," Marko was saying. "We don't have a choice. We cannot postpone the assault any longer."

"We should wait for Nadya," Shay said, crossing her arms. "We do not have a way to deal with the Cressian *nivasi* until she comes. I barely survived a fight with her. Your army will not stand a chance."

"We know." Shadar sighed. "But we have very little choice. Our spies got word in from the northern roads. Those troops Prince Trillium called in to deal with the so-called plague? They will be here in two days' time, maybe less. With the addition of a thousand or more Cressian soldiers, we stand very little chance of winning, *nivasi* or no."

Kesali nodded, her expression solemn. "Nadya and Levka should beat the incoming troops by several hours, if the message was correct. We can only hope they make it before..."

A long silence reigned before Shay swore loudly. "Before we are buried up to our necks in rubble. Stars, it was never going to be easy, was it?"

Across from her, the Guardmaster mirrored her sardonic smile. "It never is."

❖

The resistance would strike at dusk.

Scouts throughout the city reported that Cressian soldiers changed shifts at dusk, and so the few that remained in the lowest two tiers would be in flux, and therefore vulnerable. Despite Prince Trillium withdrawing the bulk of his troops to the upper tiers of the city in order to avoid what he thought was its plague-riddled underbelly, several hundred soldiers remained in the lower tiers. It would be no easy fight to take back the gate.

Marko led one force of resistance fighters, Kesali another. Shay had never seen her fight, but she held a long battle staff with such confidence that she had no doubt the Stormspeaker could defend herself and knock a few Cressian heads at the same time. Shadar led a third force, where Shay was to be placed. Those among the resistance who were stationed throughout the city had their own orders, and they would join the fight once it commenced.

"You know why we fight," Marko said, standing on top of one of the cavern's makeshift buildings. The resistance, fighters and support alike, flooded the paths around him. "We fight for our home." He pointed to Kesali, who stood in the front of the crowd. "Twenty years ago, my father dared to save this city. To protect us from the Great Storms, he brought in a Stormspeaker and her people. Nomori and Erevans have not always gotten along. At best, we have become cautious allies. But now, we must come together once more, to dare to save Storm's Quarry from the grip of Wintercress. What say you?"

Shay thought she might go deaf from the thundering reply.

An hour later, the cavern lay nearly empty. A pair of scouts led the forty-odd fighters of the Guardmaster's force through one of the mining tunnels. Shay found herself marching up front, next to Shadar.

"Nervous?" the Guardmaster asked without dropping his gaze from the tunnel ahead.

"Not a bit," Shay lied. "You?"

He gave a small smile. "Not in the slightest."

As they crested the lip of the tunnel and spilled out into the streets, Shay was struck by the sudden realization that she needed to ensure Shadar's safety. Nadya deserved to see her father one last time, at least, before her plans for the Cressian *nivasi* had begun.

The Guardmaster's force split off into groups of three and four fighters. Shay stubbornly clung to him as he led the way down one of the deserted streets of the southern corridor of the Nomori tier.

We need to hold on to the element of surprise for as long as possible, Marko had said before the resistance's force had left the cavern. *Wintercress has superior numbers, not to mention their weapon. We need to remain undiscovered until the last moment before our three forces rendezvous at the gate.*

And so they did.

Shay's blades of light danced in the shadows of narrow alleys and abandoned streets. Each flash took another Cressian soldier out of the fight. It became mechanical; every patrol they stumbled upon was dealt with swiftly and quietly. Like hunting rabbits in the South Marches.

Ten Cressian soldiers surprised the force, launching themselves off a low-slung roof and into the middle of the alley. One large man, wielding a saber that looked more like a broadsword, kicked the Guardmaster in the back while he took out two other fighters. Shadar hit the ground hard, and a shout tore from Shay's throat as the Cressian brought his monstrous saber down.

Shay lunged forward. Her blade cut through the Cressian soldier's flesh, severing his arm. His saber fell to the ground, useless. Before he could scream, Shadar's rapier darted upward and neatly cut his throat.

"Thanks," he said to Shay, wiping the blood from the corner of his mouth.

She nodded. "Right place, right time."

Without another word, they went back to back as their blades made short work of the remaining Cressian patrol.

Street by street, they retook the Nomori tier. When a warehouse or safe house had been reclaimed, a few of the resistance fighters—mostly those too injured to go on—stayed behind to guard the precious acquisitions.

The Nomori square and the outer gate of Storm's Quarry were in sight, but Shay couldn't help the twinge of worry that squirmed down her neck. Despite their stealth, lives had been lost. Too many to keep track of. Shay could only hope that the other two forces had fared better, or they would be overwhelmed trying to take the gate.

She ran a fiery blade through the neck of a Cressian soldier to ease her tension.

Out of nowhere, a horn split the air. Her blades faltered, fingers growing cold. She met the gaze of Shadar down the street, whose eyes held grim resignation. Wintercress was now warned of the attack.

"Forward!" the Guardmaster shouted, holding his rapier aloft. "To the gates! To your Duke! Forward!"

The resistance swarmed the streets, sprinting for the gate. Shay led the charge. Fire bloomed in her hands, chipping away at the few Cressian soldiers who had formed a half-hearted defense before the gate.

On the other side of the Nomori square, another yell carried through the air, and Kesali's force spilled out onto the open ground. Marko's followed not a minute afterward, and while their numbers had been reduced, hope swelled in Shay's chest.

We might actually do this.

More Cressian soldiers arrived at the square, but the resistance had its own reinforcements. Erevans and Nomori poured out of the surrounding buildings. Old and young, brandishing kitchen knives, hammers, and other assorted tools, crashed into the line of Cressian soldiers with the fury of a Great Storm. Immediately the Cressians were pushed back. Their weapons flashed wildly as they struggled to hold any sort of ground.

"For Storm's Quarry!" The cry resounded from the battlements across the square and beyond.

Shay let out a whoop. Her blood pounded in her ears, hot and fast, giving her an energy the belied the fatigue of her limbs. She held up a flame-drenched hand. "Rout the Cressians!"

For an instant, they were winning.

Then the ground split open to swallow the cheering resistance fighters.

Shay leapt back. She slammed against one of the jutting stones that remained of the city's gate. Her back throbbed at the impact, but her reflexes had saved her life. She knew the screams of those who fell down into the ravine as it closed once again would haunt her nightmares for years to come.

If she lived that long, that was.

In the middle of the fallen Cressian soldiers, a short blond woman walked toward her with purpose. The Cressian *nivasi* had arrived.

Anger exploded in her chest. These were her people, and she had promised to do her best to protect them. They had taken her in, temper and all, and Shay was not about to let the resistance be obliterated by this *nivasi*.

Not while she had breath.

"Leave them be," Shay shouted. "Fight someone who can hit back." Fire sprang into her hand and soared across the square, aimed at the Cressian *nivasi*'s chest.

Moments before the fireball struck, a stone rose up out of nowhere, blocking it. The blonde stepped forward. Her expression was as blank as ever as she considered Shay. "Then I will kill you first."

Shay's blades of fiery light flared. "You couldn't do it last time."

"Last time, I was not told to." The Cressian *nivasi* glanced back to the gates that led to the higher tiers. "I have now been told to destroy you and the rest of the resistance."

Shay did not bother replying.

A pillar of earth shot out of the ground, catching her flames before they made contact. Shay didn't wait for retaliation. She sprinted toward the Cressian *nivasi*, blades aloft.

Musket fire cracked through the air. Pain exploded in Shay's shoulder, and she staggered to a halt. Her armor had caught the worst of it, but blood still oozed out of the bullet wound. Shay cursed and cauterized it with a quick burst of fire. Her vision went white with pain for a moment and then returned.

The *nivasi* no longer stood alone.

Cressian troops rallied around her. With each tremor of the earth, their soldiers ate up the morale that seeped from the resistance fighters. Fatigue and fear battled on the faces of those who had been whooping in victory just moments before. And then, from between the rank and file of common fighters, a tall figure in brilliant white-gold armor emerged. The saber in his hand dripped with blood.

Trillium, Crown Prince of Wintercress, raised his blade, pulling down the mask that covered his face. "Men of Wintercress! We will drive these scum back to the plague-infested water from which they came. For the glory of the High King!"

Shay didn't hesitate. Her blades pulsed with fire that shot across the battlefield, straight at the smug face of Trillium.

Instantly, rocks gathered up from the ground and formed a protective shield. Once more, her flames fizzled out against stone. Shay caught another curse in her throat when the stones that guarded the Prince broke apart and shot straight toward her.

Nothing stood between her and oncoming death. Shay's fire couldn't protect her. She had less than a moment to contemplate the end, and only one thought rose above her fear: Nadya.

Looks like you're not the only one who broke our promise.

A bloodcurdling yell broke through the clamor of the

battlefield as a shadow launched itself off the battlements and into the fray. Something hit the *nivasi* square in the chest, and the Cressian weapon went down.

The rocks collided with Shay, but the supernatural force that had been propelling them forward was gone. She struck the ground. Her armor protected her from being gashed by the sharp-edged stones, but it did little against the bruises that were slowly rising up and down her arms. Shay barely paid attention to her injuries. She struggled to her feet.

Across the square, the Cressian *nivasi* had been slammed into the side of a two-story building. Where she had been standing, the Iron Phoenix now stood. Her gray cloak rippled around her like water, and her hands were curled into fists. Underneath the hood, familiar eyes shone strong in the burning battlefield. Nadya had returned.

Chapter Eighteen

Tonight the Kyanite Sea stood eerily still. Its waves moved with subdued grace, perhaps in lamentation for the war that haunted its core. A slight breeze stirred Nadya's braid as she leapt off her horse and pulled the hood of the Iron Phoenix over her head. The bridge over the Kyanite stretched out in front of her.

Was it her imagination, or could she already hear screams from the city?

"Were they mad enough to begin the assault before we arrived?" Levka slowed his horse but did not dismount.

"Doesn't matter." Nadya checked to ensure that her hood was secured, and then she took off sprinting down the bridge, Levka cantering beside her.

The sounds of battle grew louder as they approached: the clanging of iron upon steel, the crack of musket fire, and the screams of the injured and the dying. Without giving it a single thought, Nadya started scaling the crumbled wall, jumping from one sharp-edged stone to another. She had gotten halfway up when she heard Levka's shout.

"Wait, damn you!"

She turned back to see Levka struggling to ascend the ruins of the former great wall. His foot slipped, and he started to fall backward. Nadya reached out with breathless speed and caught his hand. She swung him back to the pile of stone.

"There must be an easier way in," he muttered while reaching inside his coat pocket. He brought out the glass vial. "Take it." He tried to shove the vial into her hand, but Nadya caught his wrist once more.

She froze. *More time*, she screamed in her mind. *I need more time.* She had imagined returning to the cavern of the resistance. Speaking to her father, to Kesali and Marko. Spending one last night with Shay in which she said everything that she would never have the chance to again. If even a fraction of Levka's predictions about the effects of the serum came true, then she would truly be too dangerous to be around, and suddenly, Nadya couldn't breathe. It was now. Not sometime in the nebulous future, but right this instant that she had to give up everything to save her city.

She couldn't do it. Not yet.

"I need to say good-bye."

Levka swore in a language she didn't recognize. "Nadezhda, your foolishness could cost us the city. I know I agreed back in Wintercress, but that was before the final assault had started." He gestured up to the top of the marble ruins. "My people. Your people, they are dying right now. You need to do this."

"I need to try on my own first," she said quickly, ignoring his angry grunt. "Find me in there." With those words, she leapt upward and landed on the top of the slanted, crumbling battlement. The marble beneath her feet cracked. She straightened, but the scene below nearly knocked her down once more.

Storm's Quarry had become a war zone.

The higher tiers of the city still glistened in the dying sunlight, perfect and serene. That spell broke, however, as a flash of fire drew Nadya's eye down to the scene below. The Nomori tier had become a battleground.

Smoke curled up from smoldering piles of rubble that littered the streets that she had once played in as a child. The buildings that bordered the square had been demolished. Skirmishes turned around corner, every outcropping of stone into a desirable territory for which the motley forces of the resistance battled against the pristine white uniforms of Wintercress. The ground had been ripped up, a gash that cut deep across the square, and Nadya's stomach turned at the thought of facing the Cressian *nivasi* once more.

In the midst of it all, a dark-clad figure wielding brilliant blades of light stood alone before a regiment of Cressian soldiers. Fire flared once more from her hands. It shot straight and true, streaking toward a tall, ornately armored figure that could only be Prince Trillium.

Nadya held her breath as she watched the ground itself rise up to defend the Crown Prince of Wintercress. Bedside him, a nondescript woman in the white of a Cressian uniform stood, commanding the very ground that the battle raged upon.

The Cressian *nivasi* raised her hands, and the stone that had protected Prince Trillium shattered. Large chunks of earth and cobblestone levitated in the air like primitive spears, aimed at the resistance fighters. Aimed at Shay.

A shout tore from Nadya's throat as she launched herself off the battlement. Cold air whipped around her, tugging at her hood, but it remained firmly in place. She reached out with white-knuckled fists, and slammed into the Cressian *nivasi*.

Instantly, the chunks of earth lost their momentum and crashed into the ground.

Nadya didn't stop to see if the *nivasi* was truly unconscious. She turned and sprinted toward Shay, who staggered to her feet.

"Nadya?" Shay whispered. "You're here?"

Nadya's throat swelled, thick with emotion. "I am, Shay, I am." She gently touched Shay's face. The filth of battle covered her features, but Nadya thought she had never look more beautiful. A cold realization swept over her. This would be the last time she touched Shay like this. "I am so sorry," she choked out.

"You found a way to win, Nadya." Shay's smile was tired, but genuine.

Nadya shook her head. "If I go through with it, it will be the end of us. We won't—we won't be able to be together." Tears sprang into her eyes as the truth tumbled out of her lips. "I—I have to become a monster to save this city."

Shay responded, "I love you."

How could I ever have been so fortunate as to find you again. Nadya gazed up into Shay's dusky eyes. Instead of trying to voice all the thoughts that whirled around in her mind, she leaned up and kissed Shay, savoring the taste and sensations that she had grown to know so well over the past year.

The ground began to tremble once more. Their kiss ended abruptly, and Shay staggered against her as a shout ripped through the battlefield.

"To me, Storm's Quarry!" Marko stood atop the crumbling battlements, rapier aloft. His simple leather jerkin and thin blade provided a sharp contrast to Trillium's finery. Around him, resistance fighters joined in the cry. Brandishing their motley assortment of weapons, Erevans and Nomori alike roared in unison at the soldiers who had taken their home.

"For Storm's Quarry!" Nadya looked to Shay. This was good-bye, she realized, and her chest went cold. "You have your fight," she said quietly, "and I have mine. Stars go with you."

She barely heard Shay's whisper over the sounds of battle as she dashed forward. "And with you."

She had gotten her good-bye. Nadya swallowed against a dry throat and glanced around for Levka, but he was nowhere to be seen on the battlefield. She couldn't help the relief that flared in her chest at getting to put off consuming the serum.

Perhaps, just maybe, she might not need it after all.

A large chunk of rock smashed into her side, and Nadya hit the far wall of the Nomori tier with a sickening thud. She heard a few snaps, but she could still stagger to her feet.

She needed to draw the *nivasi*'s attention to her, no matter how painful that might be. After all, even without the Cressian serum, she could withstand the blows. Or at least, Nadya hoped she could.

The white-clad figure across the square raised her hands, and the stone that Nadya leaned against threw her forward. She skidded across the ground, disturbing the bodies of fallen Cressian, Erevan, and Nomori alike. Before she could stand, stone flew at her chest, battering her until she dodged out of the way. Slowly. Painfully.

The Cressian *nivasi* had yet to break a sweat as her blank gaze and deadly aim followed Nadya across the square. The battle raged on around her in the streets and alleys of the Nomori tier and the ground itself fought against her. She had to face what had become apparent even to her. She could not, in fact, withstand the onslaught of the Cressian *nivasi* without the serum.

A large boulder hit Nadya square in the chest as she fended off several Cressian soldiers. She screamed and dropped to the ground. It roiled and trembled underneath her. *Up*, she willed herself, *get up!* Her limbs shook as she struggled to her feet, bits of gravel falling off her armor.

Suddenly a familiar shout broke the air, and a large form slammed into her. A spike of rock was hurtling toward her, and she staggered out of the way of the missile before it crashed into a nearby pile of rubble, exploding with force upon impact.

Shadar Gabori fell to his knees, clutching his right shoulder. His leather armor was torn and bloody, and his rapier hung limply in his right hand. He looked up at her with a pained smile. "You made it home," he rasped.

This time, Nadya heard the whistling of sharp rock cutting through the air. "Papa!" she yelled, launching herself forward. A barrage of rock and earth hit her back as she shielded her father.

"I—" Words failed her. If—when—she took the serum, it would be too late to tell her father good-bye.

The Guardmaster of Storm's Quarry rose. He transferred his rapier to his left hand, and then popped his shoulder back into place with a sickening crack. "Fight well, daughter," he said, "and we will see one another again."

Before Nadya could respond, he charged a group of Cressian

soldiers who had cornered two resistance fighters. Three perfect slashes of his blade, and the soldiers dropped to the ground.

All around her, the fight for the freedom of Storm's Quarry raged on. The streets that she once ran down as a child now became tactical avenues in which small groups of the two forces hammered at one another. Musket men crouched behind large chunks of rubble, reloading with frantic fingers as their comrades brandished rapiers above them. The fighting spanned as far as she could see in the Nomori tier, and it had spilled over into the higher tiers of the city. Although the bulk of the resistance's forces were concentrated down here, gunshots and screams echoed from all levels of Storm's Quarry.

A pillar of earth shot up from the ground in front of her. It collided with her chest, pushing her up into the air. She flew across the Nomori square, landing with a thunk on a solid rooftop.

Everything hurt. Blood dripped down her face, stinging her eyes. Underneath every breath, she heard the soft cracking of her ribs. She rolled over onto her side and retched against the pain. Only blood escaped her mouth to pool on the rooftop next to her head. She tasted nothing but copper, smelled nothing but blood.

"Nadezhda!"

The fuzzy voice continued to pester her ears as she blinked slowly, trying to regain her senses. *Get up, Nadya*, she screamed at herself. *Get up and fight! You cannot give up this easily.*

A hand grasped her shoulder, pulling her to a seated position. Nadya sat atop the Nomori bathhouse, its low roof filled with debris both familiar and alien to her. Levka Puyatin crouched next to her. His tunic had been torn down the side, and it seeped blood. He was pale faced and shaking, and Nadya couldn't ever recall a time she had seen the former magistrate look more vulnerable.

She supposed she didn't look too well at the moment either.

"You are being destroyed out there. If you keep going like this, that *nivasi* will kill you. I'm sorry, but you cannot win without this." Levka held the vial of concentrated stardust out to her. "Storm's Quarry needs you. It needs the Iron Phoenix, with power to stop all this destruction."

Blood bubbled out of her mouth as Nadya laughed harshly, unable to hold back the tidal wave of emotion that swept over her. Sharp pain shot through her rib cage, and she winced. "Never thought you'd say that, did you?"

Levka raised his eyebrows. "No, I did not. Especially in the midst of a fight."

"Right." She struggled to her feet. To her surprise, Levka rose with her, steadying her arm. "Thank you," she said quietly.

He nodded. After a long pause, in which the screams and rumblings of the fight faded until Nadya heard only his heartbeat, Levka said, "I do regret it. No matter how much I've tried to do so, my ends never justified the means." It was his turn to laugh. "I tried to rid my city of *nivasi* only to prepare it for invasion by the most powerful of your kind."

"You still see us as the same."

"You are the same. Dangerous creatures, possessing power no mortal ever should." He looked at the vial in his hand. "But we mortals have found a terrible way to use it." He placed it in her bloodied hand, closing her fingers around it. His eyes found hers, and Nadya could not look away. "There is no redemption for what we have done—what I have done. I—"

The stone rooftop of the bathhouse crumbled beneath them without any warning. Nadya had only a moment to shove Levka out of the way before she fell through, hitting the ground with a sickening crack. Stone poured down on top of her. It cut off the light from the stars as the earth bored into her, flattening her against the ground, the vial of stardust protected by her arm. Her stomach screamed with pain as the stone forced itself down farther and farther. Underneath, the cobblestones cracked. She couldn't draw a breath. Her vision swam until she saw stars, and darkness began to creep around the edges. A darkness like the suffocating void Gedeon had forced down her throat.

Hear me if you're there. She prayed to the stars above that she could not see with the last bit of consciousness she had. She received no answer. The empty place on her arm where her seal had always been ached. How could she expect an answer here, in the midst of a city, when she found only silence in a shrine steeped in the presence of the Protectress? Tears welled at the corners of her eyes. How could she think she was destined to be the Iron Phoenix, to save Storm's Quarry, when she held everything special about her in a glass bottle?

I choose to believe otherwise.

Her mother's words, spoken when she was within sight of the Protectress, echoed in her mind, drawing Nadya out of the fog that had enveloped her.

Pain laced every part of her body. She struggled against the weight of the stone above her, but it did not move. Grunting, Nadya managed to move her hand to the small space in front of her face. In the dimness, the glass vial glinted. If she took it now, trapped as she was, she'd have the strength to break free. To fight the Cressian *nivasi*. To free her city from the hand of Wintercress.

Nadya knew Levka was right. Storm's Quarry depended on her taking the Cressian alchemical power for herself, becoming a *nivasi* powerful enough to defeat the one that commanded the very earth. Strong enough to tear away the stone that now crushed her.

Monstrous enough to hurt everyone she loved with a single touch.

It could have been the pain, the strain on her body to keep functioning as a building's worth of stone pressed down upon her, but Nadya felt vomit rise in her throat at the thought of turning herself into a creature like the Cressian *nivasi*. Into…

Kin.

The word echoed so strongly in her mind that she wasn't sure it was her own.

Kin. The Cressian *nivasi* might not have been born of Nomori blood, but the stardust that infused her body was the same that thrummed through Nadya now, barely holding off the mountains of stone from crushing her.

She had spent so long separating herself from Gedeon, from the tales of Durriken the Butcher. Believing that she was special and chosen, and somehow set apart on a different path from the vicious *nivasi* that littered Nomori legends. Meeting Shay had chipped the first cracks into that facade, and the discovery at Brome had shattered it.

Perhaps, she thought as her lungs struggled to rise, this was the gift given to her—a life that was not dictated by carvings of stone in an ancient temple.

Could she risk her city and the woman she loved on such a belief?

A roar tore loose from her throat and Nadya heaved upward with all her might. The stone above her barely moved, and she pushed again. Blood trickled out of her mouth and down her chin as she pushed, lungs bursting, at the rock above her.

A grind. A crack. A whiff of fresh air, and Nadya summoned the rest of her strength.

It was barely enough. She rolled out from underneath just as the pile of stone crashed back down. Nadya knelt, catching her breath. In her fist, she still held the glass vial.

Make a choice, Nadya. Shay's voice echoed in her mind. *Make a choice that there is no backing away from.*

But the choice had been made. Pocketing the vial, Nadya emerged from the ruins of the bathhouse. She imagined she looked a sight, limping, blood gushing down from the cuts on her head. But her gaze was steady and she made her way with purpose toward the weapon that had nearly destroyed her home.

The Cressian *nivasi* stood in the center of the square, where the fountain once stood. Where Nadya and Kesali had shared their first dance and first kiss. Anger thrummed beneath her skin at the loss. Wintercress had taken so much from Storm's Quarry, from her people. She only hoped she had the strength to take it back.

Around the square, the fighting between the resistance of Storm's Quarry and the Cressian army had ceased, as Nadya sensed all eyes turned toward her and the Cressian *nivasi*. In the distance, near the warehouse district of the Nomori tier, white flames rose in the air. Nadya sent a silent prayer for Shay, that she would make it out of this fight in one piece.

"I have been told that I may accept your surrender, if you offer it," the Cressian *nivasi* said in her uncanny monotone. "That you will make an interesting specimen."

Nadya suppressed a shiver. "I would die before surrendering. Before becoming an experiment for Wintercress." *Before becoming like you* hung in the air between them, unsaid.

"Then you will die." She held up a hand, and the ground beneath Nadya opened so quickly she did not have a chance to leap away.

The earth swallowed her legs, then her waist. It squeezed her on all sides, and Nadya fought back the panic that rose in her throat. "I do not want to fight you!" she shouted.

The ground stopped moving.

"Why not?" The Cressian *nivasi*'s voice held a bit of emotion—confusion—for the first time.

"Because you and I are the same," Nadya said, struggling to free herself. The earth held tight. Her bones creaked like she was being sucked through one of the lower tier's steam pumps. "Because we are kin!"

Her final word echoed across the battlefield.

For a terrible moment, Nadya was sure the darkness that flickered across the *nivasi*'s face would lead to her being buried alive in the square that she'd once played and danced in. But instead, the earth opened slightly, and Nadya wrenched herself free.

"No!" Prince Trillium stumbled through the debris, pushing

his royal guards aside. He shook his blade at the Cressian *nivasi*. "You are no kin of this woman, this Iron Phoenix. You are mine. Because of me, you were made. You fight for me, for Wintercress. And for Wintercress, you will destroy the Phoenix."

Nadya swallowed against her dry throat. Whatever hold the Prince had over his *nivasi* was powerful, and she didn't know if she could break it. The glass vial in her pocket felt as if it weighed ten stones, a reassuring, yet terrible last resort. "I only want to speak to you. I know what you are. How you came to be." She withdrew the glass vial of stardust serum and held it aloft.

"This woman wants your power for herself," Trillium cut in. "See the vial she carries? It is filled with the same miraculous chemistry that created you." The Prince spat at Nadya. "Lies and only lies spew from her mouth."

The Cressian *nivasi* slowly turned her eyes upon Nadya. "You found the cave? Where I was made?"

"Yes, I did. I was seeking answers, not power," Nadya explained.

"And yet it is power that she now holds. Destroy the vial and the one who carries it, my lodestone. It is what you were made for."

Nadya felt the earth stir as the *nivasi*'s powerfully blank gaze fixed upon her, the intensity of her icy eyes growing with each rumble of the ground. *I choose to believe.* Mirela's words became her own thoughts as she clutched the vial of her own essence. *I choose to believe that you are listening from the stars. I choose to wear this cloak and fight for my people, my city.*

I choose to be more than stardust.

Nadya held out the vial. Prince Trillium started forward, crying, "Do not let her drink it!" Around him, the remaining Cressian soldiers moved in on Nadya. The eyes of the Cressian *nivasi* never wavered. Rocks lifted up all around her, but Nadya just took a slow breath, and then shattered the vial upon the cobblestones. Its contents sprayed everywhere, mixing with the mud and blood and seawater that covered the ground, eventually to disappear back into the waters of Storm's Quarry.

"I never sought this power."

Both Prince Trillium and the Cressian *nivasi* stared at her, before the Prince ordered, "Now destroy her."

But the woman did not move.

"Neither of us chose to be this way. Maybe it was fate. Maybe the stars or the storm gods. Maybe it was pure bad luck that our blood was mixed with the essence of the night sky, giving us a life we never asked for."

The words poured out of her with a fury that took away her breath. "But our lives are not built on that circumstance. We have choices. I am the Iron Phoenix of Storm's Quarry."

She drew a deep breath and grasped her hood. "And I am Nadya Gabori of the Nomori," she said, pulling her hood back. The cool salt-tinged air stung the cuts on her face. She resisted the urge to look down, all too aware of the resistance fighters and Cressian soldiers watching their exchange. Seeing her without the comforting anonymity of the guise of the Phoenix. Crown Prince Trillium stared at her, surprise written across his features. But the Cressian *nivasi* only regarded her with blank eyes.

"I have no name, but I call myself Lode." The *nivasi* paused. "I am the lodestone of Wintercress's future. Is that what you mean?"

Beneath the bruises and cracked ribs, Nadya's chest ached for her. Unmade from her old life and remade into a weapon, this woman—Lode—seemed to have defined her entire life around the machinations of Wintercress and its Crown Prince.

Just as Nadya had seen herself first as only a monster, and then as only the Iron Phoenix.

"No, it isn't." Throwing caution to the wind, Nadya stepped toward Lode. "You can be more than his weapon."

"Do not listen to her lies," Trillium said.

Lode asked at the same time, "How do you know?"

"Our blood," Nadya said slowly, reaching out to touch Lode's hand. "Our blood is the same. You can make a choice, just as I have. Choose to be more than the weapon that he intends you to be. Choose your own path."

"I—" Lode hesitated. She held up her hands. Bits of rock debris swirled around them, reminding Nadya of Shay's fire. "I do not know who I am."

"I do. We are the same. We are kin, connected by stars. Can you feel it?" Nadya asked and grasped her hand. The words she had needed to hear years ago when her *nivasi* powers surfaced, when she was a scared little girl who didn't know why she had become a monster, rose in her throat. "You are not alone."

The ground stopped its trembling, and the city of Storm's Quarry seemed to hold its breath. Not even a breeze off the Kyanite Sea disturbed the stillness as the Cressian *nivasi*, a woman called Lode, considered Nadya's words.

"I would not choose to be this way. I want—I want to feel again."

"Cease this at once!" Prince Trillium's eyes flashed with anger. Blood splattered his once immaculate armor, and the ceremonial saber he carried shook with unrestrained fury. "You are mine. I made you. Do not forget that."

Lode seemed to consider this for a moment, before she glanced at Nadya. "I have not forgotten. I have chosen."

"Then you have chosen treason." He lunged forward suddenly. His saber sang through the air. Before Nadya could react or Lode could summon another shield of stone, a streak of flame shot through the air. It ripped through Trillium's blade, melting the hilt, and struck him square in the chest. Fire consumed his armor and then his screams, and Trillium, heir to the throne of Wintercress, was no more.

Shay, standing fifteen paces away, lowered her flame-wreathed hands. "Better than you deserve, bastard," she muttered under her breath.

Nadya's heart felt like it would beat out of her chest as she passed her gaze over Shay's frame, searching for injuries but finding none beyond the cuts and bruises of battle.

Was it over now? Nadya wondered. She glanced around. Lode stood still, looking at Trillium's body with detached interest. The Cressian soldiers in the square did not move. Their eyes flicked between the body of their Prince and the weapon that no longer fought for them, uncertain of what to do.

"Storm's Quarry!" The voice of Marko Isyanov rang out across the square. He emerged from a group of resistance fighters, Kesali at his side. They looked battered and worn, but uninjured, to Nadya's relief. "Storm's Quarry," he bellowed again, "the day is yours!"

A cheer rose up among the resistance fighters, growing steadily in volume as disbelief faded to relief, then to joy.

"Wintercress," Kesali shouted at the soldiers who stood uncertain, "what say you?"

"The Kingdom of Wintercress surrenders." A clear voice split the air. Nadya's mouth fell open to see Councillor Aster picking her way carefully through the carnage of the battlefield. "As the highest ranking official here, I am authorized to cede the city of Storm's Quarry back to you." She stopped in front of Kesali and Marko. Aster wore a white dress, somehow still spotless, unsullied by the death and grime that surrounded her. Her graceful silhouette and perfectly knotted golden hair provided such a contrast to the blood-spattered leather armor of Marko and Kesali. And yet, it was Aster who knelt before the rulers of Storm's Quarry amidst the filth of the battle.

"I was released by Drina Gabori so that I might come here and beg you for the lives of our soldiers. Call off the fighting, and let us retreat in peace."

"You were given a chance at peace," Marko said, putting his rapier to Aster's throat. "My father gave you that chance, and your Prince cut off his head. Why should we not do the same?"

Kesali put her hand upon his, forcing her husband to lower his blade. "Because we are better than them. Your father died for peace. We must honor his sacrifice."

Silent tears left trails in the grime of battle that coated his face as Marko nodded. "You're right. Lady Aster, we accept your surrender."

Guardsmen that Nadya recognized from years of delivering lunch to her father at the Guardhouse pulled themselves away from the resistance fighters. They rounded up the remaining Cressian soldiers with thinly concealed anger. Shay glared at any who protested, her flaming blades flickering at her sides. Those protests instantly died down. The councillor herself was escorted from the square by two guardsmen, and Nadya felt a bit of reluctant respect for the woman.

"What happens now?" Marko asked, glancing warily at Lode, who seemed unaware of the fear she inspired in the resistance.

"I will go," Lode said simply.

Nadya stepped forward. "You don't have to." She heard Marko swallow back a protest, and Kesali take in a sharp breath. She ignored their wariness. "You could find a place here."

"No." Lode gazed out through the ruined gate, out to the edge of the Kyanite Sea and beyond. "I must go." She looked back at Nadya. "I followed him because he was all I knew. But I have been given a choice. I feel the earth, and it calls me away. Somewhere, it holds the answers I seek."

"I understand," Nadya said. She had done the same thing, after all. It took following Shay to the South Marches and then following Levka to Wintercress for her to realize that Storm's Quarry truly was where she belonged.

Without another word, the Cressian *nivasi* walked away from the remains of the battle. The rubble of the fallen gate gathered itself up and moved out of her way as she passed. Before long, she had disappeared from sight.

Silence fell over the Nomori tier as resistance fighters and yielding Cressian soldiers alike watched the mysterious woman leave as abruptly as she had appeared two months beforehand, paving the way for the destruction of their city.

What now, indeed? Nadya wondered, gazing at the incredulous faces around her, illuminated by the smoldering flames of the battlefield. Her eyes lingered on Kesali and Marko, their movements strained with fatigue. Then her father, who kept a wary eye on the Cressian soldiers, positioning himself between them and his new charges. Finally, Shay.

Shay wore a smile that lit up the darkness of the battlefield. Her blades of light had extinguished, leaving her hands in shadow. War paint and blood stained her face, and her steps came slowly, lurching. Despite the fatigue of battle, she carried herself tall and nodded to all who greeted her.

"Long live the Duke!" The cry started softly, as a few resistance fighters raised their voices and their weapons. "Long live the Stormspeaker!"

Slowly, the chant was taken up throughout the square, and then into the tier as those who fought for the resistance added their voices to the cries. Even those who had hidden away from the battle—the elderly, the young—came out of their barricaded houses and joined in. Erevans poured in from the second tier, mingling with the Nomori, cheering and weeping together. In the higher tiers, Nadya saw people gathering all along the staircase. The entire city celebrated the victory as their shouts echoed off its marble walls.

Kesali and Marko were soon surrounded by cheering Nomori and Erevans alike. At a sharp whistle from Shadar, a few more members of the Guard, even out of uniform, held back the masses from their leaders, but the faces of the guardsmen shone with the same unbelieving joy. There would be much mourning and rebuilding in the days ahead and many more years of distrust within the walls of Storm's Quarry, but for now, they smiled and shouted together.

"Long live the Duke! Long live the Stormspeaker! Long live Storm's Quarry!"

Nadya pulled her hood up once more, falling back through the crowds. She noticed Shay doing the same, and she turned to follow her partner, when a voice called out, "Phoenix!"

The crowds parted like water for the Stormspeaker as she strode toward Nadya, who checked to ensure that her hood was fastened down, its mask tight across her face. She might have revealed herself to Lode earlier, but she didn't wish to do the same to everyone in Storm's Quarry. To the people of the city, the Iron Phoenix was a force, not a person, and she wished to remain that way, a masked guardian protecting her home.

Gasps echoed around the crowd as Kesali embraced Nadya without hesitation. Nadya wrapped one arm around her, trying not to wince as her ribs were jostled.

Kesali released her with a worried look. "You're hurt."

"I'll be fine," Nadya said truthfully.

They stared at one another for a long moment. Under the light of the stars, Kesali glowed. Despite the dirt and blood that smeared her face, and the bruises that marred her bare arms, she was gorgeous. A true Stormspeaker of Storm's Quarry, Nadya thought, and her heart filled with pride for her oldest friend.

"Thank you," was all Kesali said, but it was all Nadya needed. A thousand things passed between them unvoiced. Promises of loyalty and friendship that no distance nor enemy force could hope to deter.

Marko strode up beside them. He threaded his fingers through Kesali's, giving Nadya a grateful nod. Then he raised their arms and shouted, "For the Iron Phoenix! For the Shadow Dragon!"

Heat rose in her face as the people of Storm's Quarry took up his chant. Their voices surrounded her, overwhelming any words she might have said. Where once Storm's Quarry had called for the head of the Phoenix, now they cheered her name in celebration.

Beyond the cacophony of the crowds and the frantic racing of her heart, Nadya heard the waves of the Kyanite Sea. Underneath their gentle sound, she felt the tug of the waters, the pull of the stars. And a single voice: *Well done, child.*

The crowds of citizens parted enough so that Nadya could see Shay. She was equally surrounded by celebration, her stiff-backed posture oozing discomfort. But her eyes lit up as they met Nadya's across the square.

Nadya barely had time to register her movement before Shay slammed into her and wrapped her arms around her, uncaring of the crowds that surrounded them.

"By the stars, we did it," she whispered, breathless. "Nadya, we did it."

Nadya returned Shay's embrace, holding her close in the familiar way that she had feared never doing again. But here she was, pressing her face into Shay's shoulder, breathing in her metallic scent. Not as a monstrous *nivasi* of Cressian alchemy. Perhaps not as a protector of Storm's Quarry chosen by the stars. But she was Nadya Gabori and the Iron Phoenix, and here, in the midst of celebration, she had at long last arrived at the end of her long road home.

"We did, *Natsia*," Nadya said quietly, then pulled Shay down for a kiss that tasted of sweat and blood and was altogether perfect.

The battle for Storm's Quarry had been won.

EPILOGUE

It began with a loaf of bread.

Six weeks had passed since Storm's Quarry had been set free by the resistance, and slowly, the city had begun the slow process of healing. On the night of the full moon, the late Duke Isyanov was sent off in a great pyre that could be seen from every corner of the city. The next morning, Marko and Kesali were coronated by the Head Cleric as the new leaders of Storm's Quarry in a ceremony that brought out every citizen of the city. Nadya and Shay stood near the elevated dais, and Nadya's heart nearly burst with happiness for her friends.

The next night, Mirela's ashes were returned to the sea and sky, and a wave of peace washed over Nadya as she watched the ashes float away on the soft current of the Kyanite.

On the morning of the sixth week, Nadya awoke to find a loaf of bread on her doorstep. It was still strange to think of the Gabori house as hers, but her father hadn't wanted to stay there—"It pains me to stand where your mother once stood, but I know you will make something out of that old place"—and so she had begun to call her childhood dwelling home once more. Her mother's jewelry workshop remained untouched still.

The bread was simple, a brown loaf studded with nuts, burned at the edges. It had been wrapped in paper, which bore the creases of many failed attempts. Nadya cradled it in her hands as if she held the crown jewels of Storm's Quarry.

Shay wanted to marry her.

A Nomori proposal entailed the man bringing bread to the home of his intended, a way to symbolize how he would provide for a family. Her throat grew tight with emotion. Nadya never thought she would get such a proposal, and certainly not want it.

Nadya waited for two hours before she sought Shay out in her favorite alehouse on the second tier. Even as supplies and free time were scarce in the aftermath of the war, the tavern was full to bursting with patrons. Nadya didn't care as she pushed her way through the crowds to where Shay sat, pale and sweating, clutching a full glass.

Their eyes met, and Nadya said, "Yes."

Shay lunged forward to embrace her, and in the crowded tavern, they kissed.

In between kisses, Nadya whispered, "I cannot believe you did this. It's perfect, love."

"I can't believe it either, to be truthful. I had to ask Drina's permission. While your father was in the room, I might add." Shay shuddered. "You were worth it. Barely, though."

"I'll take it," Nadya said with a smile.

Word spread fast through the Nomori tier that the strange Gabori girl and the even stranger newcomer were to be wed. Walking the markets together or volunteering in the cleanup crews had earned the two of them plenty of disgusted looks. Nadya had expected no less.

What she hadn't expected, however, was a royal guest just a week after Shay's proposal. Duke Isyanov the Younger, as he was now being called, stood outside her door. Down the street, several guardsmen tried to blend in with the early morning crowds.

Marko gave Nadya a small smile when she answered his knock. "This feels familiar," he remarked.

"It was a year ago that you came down here to ask me how to propose to Kesali," Nadya said. "I doubt that's what you're here for now, though." Her words carried a note of uncertainty.

He had, after all, told her the Phoenix would face the justice of Storm's Quarry.

When she dared to look up, Marko met her gaze squarely. "You've earned your pardon, Nadya. I won't barge in and destroy the life you've built. Kesali trusts you, and I—I would like to call you friend once more."

She nodded, throat suddenly dry. "I'd like that, Marko."

The Duke was not the only visitor the Gabori house saw in the weeks after Shay's proposal. Marriages like theirs were not done in the Nomori culture, and Nadya had been at a loss as to how she and Shay might be wed in the Nomori way. Until her grandmother showed up one afternoon to speak about planning the wedding. Drina had simply waved her hand. "Your mother should rightfully be doing the ceremony. As your closest female relative, it is my duty to do so."

The next time they met up, while Nadya visited her father in the Guardhouse, Drina pressed a small wrapped package into her hand. "This was always meant for you. She would have wanted to be there."

The parcel contained Mirela's seal of the Protectress. Nadya had no words in the torrent of emotions that overwhelmed her. She embraced her grandmother, and Drina did not stiffen or flinch away.

More caravans and journeymen of all trades poured into the city each day. Marko continued the work of his father, opening the coffers of Storm's Quarry in an effort to rebuild what war had destroyed. Nadya had taken to wandering around the city's front gate, holding hands with Shay as they watched the caravans arrive. Their offers to carry supplies and direct the newcomers were always met with grateful smiles from the guardsmen on duty.

One morning, two weeks after Shay's proposal, a caravan arriving from the South Marches brought a familiar silhouette with it. Nadya caught a glimpse of the tall, brawny woman, forge hammer hanging at her side. She nearly dropped the crate she was carrying in surprise. Beside her, Shay looked up, following her gaze.

Before Nadya could say a word, Shay dashed forward, parting the crowds like prairie grass. She stopped a few paces in front of the forgemaster. They stared at one another as Nadya joined them.

Jeta said, "I heard about your work with the resistance forces." The forgemaster paused before adding softly, "You will be a great smith one day, Shay."

Shay opened her mouth several times, but nothing more than a hitched breath came out. Finally, she just launched herself at Jeta, wrapping her arms around the forgemaster and burying her head in her shoulder.

Nadya stood back as they embraced, and she focused her senses on the loud chatter of the caravaneers to avoid hearing what the forgemaster whispered to her apprentice. When they broke apart, Jeta's eyes shone in the midday sun. She looked to Nadya now, as well as Shay.

"You're good for each other," she said simply, and Nadya's throat tightened with unspoken emotion.

Shay took Nadya's hand and squeezed gently. "You didn't come all this way just to say that, did you?" she asked the forgemaster.

Jeta shook her head, a ghost of a smile on her lips. "I intend to see you married, Shay."

"And after?"

The forgemaster's gaze swept across the tiers that towered above them. "The road isn't as kind as it once was. Perhaps it's time I settle down and build my own forge."

Shay's brilliant smile warmed Nadya to the core.

❖

A month seemed an eternity, and yet it passed in a blur of rebuilding the city, keeping a watch over the streets at night, and planning the ceremony. A week before she was to be wed, Nadya went looking for Shay to steady her nerves and found her partner wandering the third-tier market, accompanied by the Stormspeaker.

Nadya's confusion must have been written on her face, because Shay smiled and teased, "Rat got your tongue, love? We're doing a bit of shopping. You could use a decent outfit, you know." She gestured to a bundle that Kesali held. "No one knows your tastes like the Stormspeaker. Duchess or not, she's a shrewd bargainer."

"And if that doesn't work, you can always glare at the shopkeepers," Kesali replied and held out the fine fabric to Nadya. "A gift for your marriage. Congratulations and much happiness to the both of you."

The silken gray tunic was stitched with silver embroidery that took the shape of a great bird. Tears pricked the corners of Nadya's eyes.

"Thank you," she whispered.

And suddenly, the eve of the wedding arrived.

In the now barren space of the Nomori square, a small crowd gathered to witness the ceremony. The Duke and Stormspeaker wore heavy cloaks with hoods to avoid attention, though Nadya picked out their beaming smiles from across the square. Others came from the resistance, companions Shay had made. Still more had known Nadya's parents, and despite the break in tradition, they gave her respectful nods as she approached the ceremonial dais.

One figure broke apart from the crowd as she made her way forward. Shadar Gabori's eyes glistened, and he wrapped her in a tight hug, whispering, "I am so proud of you." Her sensitive hearing revealed that Shay was receiving similar treatment from Jeta Forgemaster.

Finally, she and Shay both reached Drina, who stood at the dais. With the fountain long destroyed, a makeshift pool of water had been placed in front of the Nomori Elder. Nadya and Shay, both barefoot, stepped into the lukewarm salt water. They turned to one another, holding hands, as Drina began to speak. Nadya looked at Shay, and the rest of the world fell away. Shay wore a tunic of deep red that fit her like her leather armor. Tiny orange flames had been embroidered along its hem. Shay's eyes shone with excitement. She wore light face paint, and her hair had been intricately braided and put up. She radiated with a glow that took Nadya's breath away.

In the distance, she heard her grandmother's voice. "Under the stars and by the current, do you, Shay Rissalo, consent to this union?"

Shay smiled at Nadya. A tiny flame sprang into Nadya's palm as Shay said, "I consent."

Drina turned to Nadya. Her voice, normally so steady during ritual, cracked with emotion as she repeated, "Under the stars and by the current, do you, Nadezhda Gabori, consent to this union?"

Nadya looked into Shay's dark eyes and whispered, "I do consent."

It began with a loaf of bread, and it ended with a kiss.

About the Author

Rebecca Harwell grew up in Minnesota and has since lived around the Midwest, which has given her a love of winter and the prairie. She holds a BA in creative writing from Knox College and an MS in library science from Indiana University.

Her writing reflects the comic books, space operas, and high fantasy epics she loves to read. When not writing, Rebecca can be found watching *Star Trek* reruns, playing with her rabbit, and staging imaginary battles in her head. She remains unconvinced that unicorns aren't real. Visit her website at www.rebeccaharwell.com.

Books Available From Bold Strokes Books

Exposed by MJ Williamz. The closet is no place to live if you want to find true love. (978-1-62639-989-1)

Force of Fire: Toujours a Vous by Ali Vali. Immortals Kendal and Piper welcome their new child and celebrate the defeat of an old enemy, but another ancient evil is about to awaken deep in the jungles of Costa Rica. (978-1-63555-047-4)

Landing Zone by Erin Dutton. Can a career veteran finally discover a love stronger than even her pride? (978-1-63555-199-0)

Love at Last Call by M. Ullrich. Is balancing business, friendship, and love more than any willing woman can handle? (978-1-63555-197-6)

Pleasure Cruise by Yolanda Wallace. Spencer Collins and Amy Donovan have few things in common, but a Caribbean cruise offers both women an unexpected chance to face one of their greatest fears: falling in love. (978-1-63555-219-5)

Running Off Radar by MB Austin. Maji's plans to win Rose back are interrupted when work intrudes, and duty calls her to help a SEAL team stop a Russian mobster from harvesting gold from the bottom of Sitka Sound. (978-1-63555-152-5)

Shadow of the Phoenix by Rebecca Harwell. In the final battle for the fate of Storm's Quarry, even Nadya's and Shay's powers may not be enough. (978-1-63555-181-5)

Take a Chance by D. Jackson Leigh. There's hardly a woman within fifty miles of Pine Cone that veterinarian Trip Beaumont can't charm, except for the irritating new cop, Jamie Grant, who keeps leaving parking tickets on her truck. (978-1-63555-118-1)

The Outcasts by Alexa Black. Spacebus driver Sue Jones is running from her past. When she crash-lands on a faraway world, the Outcast Kara might be her chance for redemption. (978-1-63555-242-3)

Alias by Cari Hunter. A car crash leaves a woman with no memory and no identity. Together with Detective Bronwen Pryce, she fights to uncover a truth that might just kill them both. (978-1-63555-221-8)

Death in Time by Robyn Nyx. Working in the past is hell on your future. (978-1-63555-053-5)

Hers to Protect by Nicole Disney. Ex–high school sweethearts Kaia and Adrienne will have to see past their differences and survive the vengeance of a brutal gang if they want to be together. (978-1-63555-229-4)

Perfect Little Worlds by Clifford Mae Henderson. Lucy can't hold the secret any longer. Twenty-six years ago, her sister did the unthinkable. (978-1-63555-164-8)

Room Service by Fiona Riley. Interior designer Olivia likes stability, but when work brings footloose Savannah into her world and into a new city every month, Olivia must decide if what makes her comfortable is what makes her happy. (978-1-63555-120-4)

Sparks Like Ours by Melissa Brayden. Professional surfers Gia Malone and Elle Britton can't deny their chemistry on and off the beach. But only one can win… (978-1-63555-016-0)

Take My Hand by Missouri Vaun. River Hemsworth arrives in Georgia intent on escaping quickly, but when she crashes her Mercedes into the Clip 'n Curl, sexy Clay Cahill ends up rescuing more than her car. (978-1-63555-104-4)

The Last Time I Saw Her by Kathleen Knowles. Lane Hudson only has twelve days to win back Alison's heart. That is, if she can gather the courage to try. (978-1-63555-067-2)

Wayworn Lovers by Gun Brooke. Will agoraphobic composer Giselle Bonnaire and Tierney Edwards, a wandering soul who can't remain in one place for long, trust in the passionate love destiny hands them? (978-1-62639-995-2)

Breakthrough by Kris Bryant. Falling for a sexy ranger is one thing, but is the possibility of love worth giving up the career Kennedy Wells has always dreamed of? (978-1-63555-179-2)

Certain Requirements by Elinor Zimmerman. Phoenix has always kept her love of kinky submission strictly behind the bedroom door and inside the bounds of romantic relationships, until she meets Kris Andersen. (978-1-63555-195-2)

Dark Euphoria by Ronica Black. When a high-profile case drops in Detective Maria Diaz's lap, she forges ahead only to discover this case, and her main suspect, aren't like any other. (978-1-63555-141-9)

Fore Play by Julie Cannon. Executive Leigh Marshall falls hard for Peyton Broader, her golf pro…and an ex-con. Will she risk sabotaging her career for love? (978-1-63555-102-0)

Love Came Calling by C. A. Popovich. Can a romantic looking for a long-term, committed relationship and a jaded cynic too busy for love conquer life's struggles and find their way to what matters most? (978-1-63555-205-8)

Outside the Law by Carsen Taite. Former sweethearts Tanner Cohen and Sydney Braswell must work together on a federal task force to see justice served, but will they choose to embrace their second chance at love? (978-1-63555-039-9)

The Princess Deception by Nell Stark. When journalist Missy Duke realizes Prince Sebastian is really his twin sister Viola in disguise, she plays along, but when sparks flare between them, will the double deception doom their fairy-tale romance? (978-1-62639-979-2)

The Smell of Rain by Cameron MacElvee. Reyha Arslan, a wise and elegant woman with a tragic past, shows Chrys that there's still beauty to embrace and reason to hope despite the world's cruelty. (978-1-63555-166-2)